Veronica is a musician, teacher and writer whose career spans composing, writing, theatre direction and teaching. Studying music, English literature and education at Cambridge, she also holds a master of education degree from Liverpool University. One of her main loves is teaching young people of all ages and abilities, using in particular the power of the story as a tool to aid creativity. She was the director of education and in-house writer for Stagecoach Theatre Arts and music co-ordinator of the Chester Mystery Plays. She is deeply interested in young people who have been damaged or who struggle with the impact of early life events. Whilst training as a volunteer for the N.S.P.C.C. she learnt more about the tenacity and courage that characterise so many young victims. These insights have influenced her writing of *Twisted Threads, Unravellings* and *Rogue Strands*. Veronica has written and compiled many performing arts works (music, story and lyrics), and now devotes her time to her passion for writing, her work on a hospital pastoral team, her four grown-up children, her many grandchildren, and — of course — her two golden retriever dogs. Her late husband was the Bishop of Coventry.

Love's Tangled Tapestry

A Trilogy

No.2

UNRAVELLINGS

Veronica Bennetts

Love's Tangled Tapestry

A Trilogy

No.2

UNRAVELLINGS

Vanguard Press

A CIP catalogue record for this title is
available from the British Library.

ISBN 978-1-80016-588-5

Vanguard Press is an imprint of
Pegasus Elliot Mackenzie Publishers Ltd.
www.pegasuspublishers.com

First Published in 2023

Vanguard Press
Sheraton House Castle Park
Cambridge England

Printed & Bound in Great Britain

For my four children and their families

Thank you to several members of my family and one or two close friends who have read this second book of the trilogy 'Love's Tangled Tapestry' and made encouraging sounds.

Unravellings

Backstory of main characters in order of introduction in the novel.

SADIE CONNORS
Sadie Connors is the mother of Jack Connors, a severely disabled boy. Sadie was raped by her father. She ran away from home, bringing Jack up on her own, returning only after her father's death. She subsequently moved into the top flat of the Vicarage.

OLIVER LOCKWOOD
Oliver Lockwood married Connie, Sadie's sister. Oliver was a curate then became a theatre chaplain and had a brief, passionate encounter with actress Clara, believing the child she conceived to be his. He eventually married his soulmate Connie. Together they nursed her father, as he lay dying. Oliver later became a vicar in Southwark and proved to be the rock of the family.

CONNIE LOCKWOOD
Connie Lockwood was abused, at the age six by her father. The devastating effect of this was softened by her deep faith. She became a nanny and fell in love with Oliver, whose love helped to heal her. She worked hard to persuade her brother, Bruce, to see his father as he lay dying. Oliver and Connie married and had three children.

HOPE O'NEILL

Hope O'Neill was an illegitimate orphan brought up in a children's home in Ireland. Her mother died in childbirth and her father abandoned both mother and child, returning to his family in London. Hope became a nun and eventually started on a journey to London to find her father.

BRUCE CONNORS

Bruce Connors is the brother of Sadie and Connie. He married actress Clara but was impotent as a result of witnessing his father's incest with his sisters. However, after in-depth counselling and the death of his father, the problem resolved itself. He regarded Kitty as his 'miracle' daughter. By the end of 'Twisted Threads'(Book 1) Kitty's true paternity has been revealed.

CLARA CONNORS

Clara Connors is the self-centred actress wife of Bruce and mother of Kitty. Generally lacking in maternal instincts and taken up by her career, she leaves much of the upbringing of her daughter to her husband. She is a temptress to men and has not forgotten her physical encounter with Oliver the priest.

ROBBIE TAYLOR

Robbie Taylor had a violent past and had two spells in prison as a result. He formed a deep bond with Jack,

Sadie's son. Robbie came from uncaring parents and found a new life when Oliver and Connie befriended him, showing him unconditional love and offering him a home and supervised work in the youth club.

GARY JOHNSON

Gary Johnson had no chance in life, his parents having used him mercilessly in their crimes of bestiality for which they were imprisoned several times. They were indifferent to the plight of their son Gary, who joined a gang of rapists

Healing doesn't mean the damage never existed.
It means the damage no longer controls your life
(Ashkay Dubay)

PART ONE
1988

CHAPTER 1

A primal scream penetrated the air as a wheelchair careered out of control down the steep slope of the front garden and through the open gate towards the road. It tipped itself onto two wheels as it hurtled off the kerb and straight into the path of an oncoming lorry. The lorry's shrieking brakes matched the sound of the primal scream in intensity as the chair became crushed and half-hidden under the lorry's huge front wheels.

The driver collapsed forward onto the steering wheel. Out of the house rushed Sadie Connors, ghostly pale and frantically shouting,

'Jack! Jack!'

Then, as she caught sight of one crumpled wheel of her son's wheelchair poking out from under the lorry's chassis she screamed.

'Oh *No, no! No* — it's my boy!'

'It's Jack — Jack Connors,,' gasped one of the crowd of onlookers which was gathering as if from nowhere around the accident.

'The one in the wheelchair?'

'The disabled one?'

'You know, the boy who lives in the vicarage,' replied another.

'What, that sad little crippled lad?'

Their faces were pale from the shock of the drama, but still they managed to continue to speculate incessantly on the situation. Sadie knelt down and stroked what little she could see of Jack, oblivious to the pool of blood that was already daubing the road bright red and beginning to seep into her jeans.

'Jack, Jack my darling. Hang on beautiful boy, Hang on in there. Everything's going to be all right. You'll see. You'll soon be freed.'

Out of the vicarage ran Oliver Lockwood the vicar, tall, dark, slender, a large mobile phone clasped to his ear.

'Which service, please?'

'Ambulance, police, fire — all of them — to Southwark — outside the Vicarage.'

'Slowly please, sir. Where are we coming to? We need the full address.'

Oliver quickly gave the complete address and the requested details, then swiftly joined Sadie as she kept talking to Jack. Somehow she was managing to speak in soft, soothing tones even though her body was trembling violently.

'They'll soon have him in hospital,' whispered Oliver to his sister-in-law.

'I think he's dying,' Sadie whimpered, looking up. 'He's only little. He's my baby,' she sobbed.

Jack was in fact fourteen-years-old, but his twisted body and stunted growth suggested he might be half that age, although his intellect was razor sharp.

Oliver stayed kneeling beside Sadie until the police, two ambulances and a doctor's car arrived, followed almost immediately by a fire engine, its deafening two-tone siren only switched off at the last minute as it drew alongside the lorry. Still, the driver of the lorry remained slumped over his steering wheel.

Firemen with huge cutting equipment and cranes, paramedics with medical kits and a stretcher, and a doctor with skills in rapid patient assessment worked urgently at the scene.

Members of the crowd kept up their whispered running commentary.

'He was badly crippled as it was.'

'I always felt for his poor mother.'

'Never a father to be seen, was there?'

'The poor little lad must have been a burden to his mum.'

'It might be a blessing if — if, well, I don't like to say it, but... if he...'

'Maybe this is God's way.'

With movements the speed of lightning, Sadie was on her feet and rushing like a tigress towards the group. She grabbed the woman who had described Jack as "crippled" by her scarf and pulled it ferociously around her neck. The woman turned puce, spluttering and coughing as Sadie pulled it tighter and tighter.

'How dare you? How *dare* you? You stupid cow! You don't know anything, do you? My boy is worth more than all of you put together. You're nothing but rubbish for saying things like that.'

Oliver pulled her back.

'Sadie, Sadie, Jack needs you, never mind them..'

Sadie quickly returned, breaking through the medics and kneeling once again by her boy. She kissed his bloodied face, at the same time daubing her own with streaks and patches of blood, which looked to all the world like badly applied stage makeup.

Oliver went back to the group of women.

'I suggest you keep your comments to yourself and move away from this scene. Now!' Oliver was icy calm until the last word, which he shouted loudly.

'You have no idea what you are talking about. Sadie is right. Keep your uninformed views to yourself.'

The women, stunned by the ferocity of the vicar's tone, backed away and left. One of them turned and spoke violently to Oliver.

'Call yourself a man of the cloth? You should be ashamed of yourself, talking to your parishioners like that!'

Oliver ignored the remark. He'd heard it all before.

Eventually, the boy was freed enough for the ambulance crew to lift him onto the stretcher. It was clear that he stood little chance of survival, he was so mutilated. The wheelchair, recently brand new and Jack's pride and joy was now a crumpled heap of ugly, twisted metal.

'I'm sorry, love. We've done the best we can, but four axles and seven tons were rather a lot of competition for the little lad,' said one of the firemen.

Sadie pushed violently through the restraining arm of the police officer, clambered up the steps of the ambulance and pulled the sheet down from under Jack's chin. It was soaked in scarlet blood.

'My poor darling. I love you so, Jack.'

'Sorry, but you can't be in here for a few minutes,' said the doctor in attendance who was helping to set up intravenous drips. 'We need to work on him.'

Sadie started screaming hysterically and hurling abuse at no one in particular.

'Can you bring her on in your car, sir? She's not helpful here in this state.'

'Of course,' replied Oliver.

He put his arm around Sadie and steered her gently but firmly back into the house

'I will take you down to the hospital, Sadie, but first you need to come inside for a minute or two. Jack needs you strong.'

Suddenly losing her fighting spirit, Sadie meekly complied and found her sister Connie, Oliver's wife, with the teapot in one hand and a packet of glucose in the other.

'Have this first, Sadie. I'll put lots of glucose in it like our mum used to, for shock. As soon as you've drunk it, Oli will take you to the hospital.'

They all sat in frozen silence as the enormity of events took hold of each one of them. Quite suddenly, Connie got up and ran to the door.

'The driver! Who's looking after him? Are the police?'

She ran outside and found the driver, ashen-faced, answering a policeman's questions. Connie hung back, and when the interview was over she tapped the driver gently on the arm.

'Come in the warm and have a cup of tea, sir.'

'I couldn't do anything. I couldn't do anything,' the driver kept repeating, dazed.

'We know,' said Connie.

The driver came face-to-face indoors with Sadie.

'I couldn't do anything, Ma'am,' he repeated softly. 'He just came out of nowhere.'

He broke down and sobbed, wiping his tears on his greasy sleeve.

Distraught as she was, Sadie managed to put her hand on the driver's shoulder. It was the smallest of gestures, but the generosity of spirit in conveyed meant the world to the broken man.

Oliver set off with Sadie, and Connie stayed comforting the driver, not knowing how on earth he would come to terms with such a terrible accident. No one had noticed that Peter, Oliver and Connie's autistic and challenging second son, had rushed upstairs immediately after witnessing the wheelchair careering towards the road, had clamped his hands over his ears and was hiding under the duvet on his bed trembling violently and rocking incessantly.

CHAPTER 2

A woman wearing a Nun's habit alighted onto the crowded platform and watched the train as it gathered speed, gliding into the underground tunnel for its onward journey. Sister Hope O'Neill had never been out of Ireland before, so to find herself in central London had taken an immense amount of courage backed up by lots of prayers. She had saved her minimum living wage awarded by the diocese for nearly three years, had mapped out her journey in as much detail as possible, and was now on her way to search for the paternal family she had never known.

Hope's mother, Erin O'Neill, had been the victim of a late wartime encounter with a sergeant major in the army who was at first charming and considerate, but with every visit and inevitable sexual encounter became more demanding, increasingly violent and finally left her with three cracked ribs and an unwanted pregnancy. Erin had read in his service papers, which he always left casually sprawled on the bedside cabinet before he clambered onto her (wearing only his dirty army socks), that he was a sergeant major, his name was Albert Connors and he lived in London.

Albert Connors disappeared back to England shortly after the end of the war, although he visited Erin from time to time for his selfish purposes for a while afterwards. Erin

O'Neill knew that as soon as she told him she was pregnant he would turn his back on her. She was right. What she did not know was that he had a wife and small son back home in England whom he treated with about the same disregard as he did his wartime mistress. His wife was pregnant with her second child.

Erin came from a staunch Roman Catholic family whose Christianity did not run to support their daughter in her predicament. In their holy eyes, she had sinned most grievously and was in danger of heaping shame on her entire family. Erin was duly deposited to Saint Brigid's Hostel for Fallen Girls. She went into labour early, had a post-partum haemorrhage, received precious little medical assistance and apparently died a needless death at the age of nineteen, leaving her tiny daughter Hope at the mercy of the nuns at St. Brigid's. Hope (named by her mother immediately after she had given birth), officially entered the category of "War Children."

Against all the odds, the strong little golden-haired baby, the image of her ill-fated mother, survived and grew to be healthy and determined. It was this determination that led her, after three years of research, investigations and savings, to Euston station in London in search of her unknown father. She intended to give him a piece of her mind in no uncertain terms if she ever found him. She was not by nature a vindictive person, but her father's abandonment of both her mother and herself Hope had always found far too wicked an act simply to turn the other cheek, despite the high demands her faith made on her in the area of forgiveness.

Sister Hope now poured over the huge underground map on the station wall while impatiently tucking one tiny stray gold curl back into hiding under the white coif of her veil. The map's myriad of coloured lines seemed to her to criss-cross each other at random, which led to her decision to go by underground train only as far as Waterloo, and then walk along the Embankment of the Thames as far as she could towards Southwark. It looked simpler to her than negotiating more complicated station changes.

She was transfixed by what she later described in her journal as "the paralysing shock of travelling on an underground train", followed by an "intoxicating sense of celebration" as she walked from Waterloo station onto the wide paved area of the Embankment. The Thames looked spectacular in the sunshine and pavement artists, balloon sellers, and candy floss makers deftly twirling sticks around a spinning dome of pink sticky sugar added to the impression that it was "party-time" on the South Bank. In fact, it was another normal day. It was just how it always was there.

Sister Hope passed the Royal Festival Hall, which she knew had been built as part of a five-month recovery plan after the war, and further on past the National Theatre, bestowed to London for the re-growth of theatre arts. She felt almost giddy with delight at the sheer beauty of her walk as she gazed at the landmarks that she had only read about in books and had longed to see.

It was providential that, as Sister Hope O'Neill eventually arrived outside Southwark Cathedral, her head was full of images of London at its most beautiful. After asking directions, she came to the far corner of her destination — East End Street As she approached she was greeted by a desperate cacophony of sounds of tri-tone screeches of ambulance, police and fire engine, all playing a wildly discordant symphony in different keys, but every one as urgent and alarming as the other. Sister Hope glimpsed at a woman kneeling by a huge lorry and scrabbling underneath to try to reach whoever it was that was trapped. A wheelchair was just visible under the lorry, with its wheels crushed and distorted.

She was mesmerised by the scene and despite herself, watched on as the victim (was it a boy? — it was hard to tell with such a sea of scarlet on and around him), was eventually lifted onto a stretcher and carefully, carefully into the ambulance. She then saw the woman, presumably the victim's mother, being led slowly back into the house by a man who clearly cared considerably about her wellbeing.

As she was witnessing this, two policemen cordoned off the area, telling the crowd to disperse, go home and individually thank their lucky stars that no one of theirs was trapped under the lorry, as it looked as though the lad "didn't stand an earthly". Indiscreet, to say the least, thought Sister Hope.

'You'd better start praying for his soul, Sister,' said the other policeman in — was in a slightly mocking tone? — as she approached. If so, she was used to it. Her nun's habit ensured that no one actually seemed to have anything resembling a normal conversation with her.

She wandered off, shocked by the tragedy she had by chance witnessed, and made her way slowly to the guest house she had booked previously, which meant another two miles of pavement walking. This was not how her visit was meant to be, and she knew that if there was a relative of hers, however distant, living in that house, it would be hopelessly ill-timed to knock on that front door any time soon.

Hope looked around the dingy room allocated to her, which actually was positively sumptuous compared to her living quarters in the Convent of St. Clare in Ireland. She noticed to her delight that there was a bath and immediately turned on the taps. The clanking water system creaked and groaned into life, and water, at first rusty, spluttered out. Hope took off her habit, underwear, wimple and veil, shook out her short but already unruly curls, smelt the little bottle of bath oil provided and swished it into the water in delight. At first rather furtively, then gaining in confidence, she took a long look at her body in the cracked full-length mirror propped up against the wall. She hadn't seen her body fully for many years. Scrutinizing it closely, she concluded that she was too thin — much, much thinner than when had she donned her habit eighteen years ago at the tender age of twenty. Anyone else observing would have seen a beautiful slender body, well-kept and trim — in fact an altogether striking woman who looked much younger than her years.

'My hair!' she said out loud. 'It's not long since I shaved it either!' Her head had always been smothered in an uncontrollable mass of tight curls, a curse to her as a young teenager, but admired by everyone else, although always cut very short at the orphanage. It had almost been a relief to be required to shave it off completely when she first took holy orders. No more over-large rollers or straightening hair tongs any more, thank God. Now, it was a very short mop but the curls always won.

Hope sank down into the warm water and lay there for half an hour, topping up the water as it cooled. Her body was nicely relaxed from her long walk, although the soles of her feet were grumbling. Her head teamed with a myriad of images: a river sparkling in the sunshine, copious amounts of blood, beautiful south bank buildings, an ambulance, colourful balloon sellers, a boy, barely recognizable as such, and a woman bent low and broken with grief.

CHAPTER 3

Peter Connors, age twelve, barely came out of his bedroom over the next three weeks. Jack, his cousin, had been pronounced dead on arrival at the hospital, Sadie was overcome with grief at what had happened to her only child, and Oliver and Connie were doing their best to support her through what was an appalling situation. The funeral came and went, with the unique juxtaposing of the deepest grief and rivers of tears, with some laughter, streams of memories and a wealth of loving tributes that characterise most funerals.

Thereafter, the home seemed shrouded in a blanket of grey grief which Oliver knew could last for months. Connie, Sadie's sister, had a sharp memory of when their brother, at only a little younger than Jack's age now, had committed suicide and how their mother had appeared to diminish before her eyes in grief. It had seemed that the very bricks of the house were permeated with sadness. Sadie had left home by then, ashamed of her secret pregnancy and the way it had come about.

Two weeks after Jack's fatal accident with the lorry, the police called the vicarage.

'Nothing to worry about, Reverend — er — Lockwood isn't it? May we come in for a few minutes?'

Oliver opened the door wide and showed the policeman and policewoman into his study.

'It's about the wheelchair that the deceased was in,' said the policeman. 'It's routine as you know to investigate every aspect of a fatal road traffic accident.'

'I imagine it is,' said Oliver, wondering where this was leading.

'It seems that the cable leading to the brakes of the wheelchair had been cut prior to the accident, hence the lad was unable to stop.'

Connie stood aghast.

'But how can you tell that? The chair was so damaged and smashed up in the crash. Surely part of the lorry would have severed it?'

The woman policeman spoke for the first time.

'We have had a team of forensic accident investigators working on the case Mrs — er?'

'Lockwood.'

'Are you the mother of the victim, Jack Connors? Presumably, he was from a former marriage? May I express my con — '

'No. Jack's mother is my sister. She and Jack live with us.' She paused, realising the present tense she had used for Jack.

The policewoman suddenly looked awkward. Finally, she said.

'I'm afraid it is conclusive that the victim's chair had been tampered with. Our forensic engineers don't make mistakes. We must speak with — er — is it Mrs Connors?'

'No, she is *Miss* Connors,' said Oliver.

'Hmm. Bit of a complicated household, is it?' she commented.

'It's quite simple,' replied Oliver. 'Jack was born to Sadie Connors. She's always been a single parent.'

'He's Illegitimate, then?' interjected the sergeant.

'If you want to put it that way, then yes, but that really is an outdated word for 1988, Constable.'

'*Sergeant,* you mean,' he replied disdainfully.

'Let's get on,' said the policewoman, embarrassed by the tone the conversation had taken. 'We will need to see *Ms* Connors.'

Connie spoke.

'As you can imagine, she is in a bad space. She's hardly eaten since the accident and she barely talks to anyone, even us.'

'It's important, Mrs Connors, please.'

'You try, Oli,' said Connie, touching his arm lightly.

Oliver left the room, went upstairs and found Sadie in what was now her characteristic foetal position, curled up tightly in a blanket by the gas fire in her living room.

'Sadie, love, you'll have to come downstairs for a minute. The police need to see you.'

'Police?' asked Sadie, looking up finally at Oliver.

'Yes. There's a question or two about Jack's wheelchair.'

'What?'

'Please Sadie, just come down. It's important.'

Sadie slowly took off the blanket, replacing it with an old threadbare navy cardigan that was on the back of the chair. She walked downstairs, shoulders hunched, head down. Connie noticed afresh how thin and pale her sister was as she entered the room, eyes on the ground. Sadie had always been the feisty, healthy one, with her muscular physique and strong dark looks like their father Albert Connors. It had always been Connie, her little sister, who looked as though a puff of wind would blow her away. Not so today.

Sadie sat down slowly. Connie sat at her feet and held her hand.

'Just answer simply, Sadie. Don't get worried by the questions.'

The sergeant explained about the severed cable on the wheelchair and how Jack would have therefore been unable to control the pace of it as it rocketed down the pathway. Sadie wept.

'He must have been frightened,' she whispered.

'Can you tell us a little about Jack,' said the lady officer. 'Did he at any point want not — not want to be here?'

'You mean did he not want to live?' said Sadie, feeling the familiar stirring of anger in her belly. 'Jack may have been disabled but he was more alive than the rest of us, actually. He had inexhaustible joie de vivre,' Sadie crumpled inwardly once more.

'So you would not expect him to — em — ever consider taking his own life?'

'You mean would he have cut the cable on the chair himself? Say what you mean, Sergeant,' she said angrily. 'I don't have the energy to play games','

Oliver interjected. 'Jack was severely disabled. His hands and feet did not work for him. His body was a rogue body that at no stage could be controlled. It has a congenital history. But his mind and his brain were phenomenal. His command of language was amazing. He made up a lot of rhymes.' Oliver glanced at Connie and Sadie. 'Some of them were pretty blue,' he smiled.

For the first time Sadie smiled too, remembering the times she had tried, and failed, to modify Jack's jokes, and the embarrassment they had sometimes caused. Connie and Oliver's three children had always collapsed in helpless laughter when Jack was, as they called it, 'on a roll.'

'So if Jack didn't cut his own brake cable, the big question is… who did?'

He paused. Oliver realised by the sergeant's over-dramatic pause that he was enjoying his moment of power to the full.

'Ms Connors, this is a very difficult question to ask. A boy with such severe disabilities must at times have been a strain on you — limit your life — prevent your freedom. Did you at any time think life would have been, shall we say, easier without him?'

Sadie stood up, her old navy blue cardigan falling from her shoulders.

'If you mean, did I cut the cable, then that is an obscene and insulting suggestion.' She approached the sergeant, thrusting her face close to his, her chin jutting forward angrily. 'You need to learn how to act with a bit of empathy, *Constable*. A course in Human Relationship

Skills wouldn't come amiss either. They run a good one at the Poly. You should sign yourself up,' she said sarcastically, twisting her lips into a sneer. Suddenly she practically spat out.

'My boy is hardly cold in his grave and you come round asking these questions? How *dare* you?'

'Just preliminary enquiries, Miss,' the sergeant replied, backing off and turning away. The female officer spoke more gently.

'The fact remains, Ms Connors, that we have to find out who cut the cable. If Jack did not do it himself, then who did? It could be, you see Ms Connors, that we may be looking at a murder investigation here. Are there any other people living in the house?'

'Just the children,' replied Oliver. 'And —um — '

'And Robbie,' added Connie softly, glancing at Oliver 'Robbie?'

'Yes. He's been living with us for over twelve-years. He runs our church youth club. It's a huge vicarage as you can see, and Robbie has a bedsit upstairs.'

'What did this Robbie do before you took him in, then?'

Connie and Oliver looked at each other. The fact was that they had befriended Robbie after he was released from Wandsworth Prison, having served a sentence for grievous bodily harm.

'Oh, this and that,' said Oliver. 'But it was very clear early on that he had a great talent for working with children and young people.'

'Did he have much to do with Jack?'

'Oh yes,' replied Sadie. 'They were inseparable. Jack loved Robbie.'

'And Robbie?'

'Robbie would have done anything in the world for Jack.'

'I see.' He paused.

'And your children, Mrs. Lockwood? How many have you?

'Three. James is fourteen, Peter almost thirteen and Rosa is nine.'

'Are they at school at the moment?'

'Yes.'

No-one mentioned the fact that Peter was upstairs — disturbed, frightened, angry Peter, who had stayed perpetually hidden under his duvet virtually ever since the accident.

CHAPTER 4

The police returned to the vicarage the next day, this time with a third officer.

'Sorry, Reverend Lockwood, but we need to touch base with your Robbie Taylor. Is he in?'

'Touch base.' What did that mean? Oliver dreaded that Robbie's past would come back to haunt him. He knew other ex-prisoners who seemed to be first in the queue when it came to police suspicions, interviews and on occasion wrongful arrests. Oliver knew he would defend Robbie with his last breath. He had seen the lad grow from someone full of anger with a huge chip on his shoulder into a mature and kind young man. What Oliver did not realise was that it was largely due to his own constant love, influence and prayers that Robbie had turned his life around. Robbie was wonderful in his work with the youth club. 'Worth his weight in gold,' Connie always said, who had shared her husband's loving concern for him in full measure.

'He's not in, Sergeant.'

'We'll wait, if we may.'

Just then, Peter called his father from upstairs.

'Dad! Dad! Can you bring me up a drink?'

Oliver went to the bottom of the stairs and called up.

'No. Come down, Peter. You need to get those leg muscles working. You'll hibernate up there.'

'Who's that, sir?' asked the third constable.

'That's my second son. Peter,' replied Oliver.

'No school today then?'

Oliver was just about to field the slightly tricky question when the front door slammed and Robbie Taylor appeared. Wearing his customary navy blue track suit bottoms and denim jacket, he came breezing into the sitting room carrying a net of footballs and almost skidded to a halt on seeing the uniformed police.

'Oh, sorry, Rev. Didn't know you had company.'

'It's fine, Robbie. Just sit down for a minute.'

'No, no, I'll be off upstairs, thanks all the same.'

'Not so fast, Mr Taylor. It's you we've come to see.'

'*Me?*'

Robbie felt the old familiar feeling of long ago in the pit of his stomach when he encountered the law. It was always trouble, even if there should have been nothing to worry about. He pushed back his long dark hair, took his outdoor denim jacket off, slung it over the back of the chair, rolled up his shirt sleeves with an air of feigned indifference, and sat down facing the three police officers.

'Fire away, Constable,' he said to the sergeant.

The sergeant was just about to correct him when the woman police officer interjected.

'It's about your relationship with the deceased, Mr Taylor. Jack Connors.'

The three police then proceeded to question Robbie in depth about his interactions with Jack, how he felt about him, if he ever got impatient with him, if he had even found Jack a burden, if he often had sole charge of Jack and so on. The questioning went on for half an hour, with Oliver interjecting occasionally to modify or amplify something Robbie had said. By the end, both Robbie and Oliver felt that the police were determined to make the case that Robbie had severed the brake cable in a fit of impatience or frustration.

'See, Rev? Guilty until proven innocent, innit?'

Oliver was just about to answer when Peter appeared in his tartan dressing gown that his aunt had given him. He was blinking furiously.

'Dad..... can I have?'

On seeing the array of police, he backed out of the room immediately and ran back up the stairs.

'Your son, Reverend? Is he ill?

'Peter has been very shocked by the accident. Everyone in this house loved Jack and we are all coping with the grief in our different ways. Peter is rather reclusive. Meeting people has always been a bit of a struggle for him.'

'But he's brilliant on a one-to-one,' said Robbie quickly.

'Well, then,' said the sergeant. 'I suggest we have a one-to-one with him. Officer, could you go and fetch him, please? I think we need to talk to this young man.'

'If you insist, but I'd ask you to tread very carefully. It would be better if I fetched him. He is autistic. He suffers from autism,' he added, seeing the sergeant's bewildered face.

40

'Autism?' replied the sergeant. 'Ye — es, I think I've heard of that. A bit like Schizophrenia, isn't it?'

'*Nothing* like Schizophrenia,' replied Oliver coldly.

Unwittingly saving the day, Connie appeared carrying a tray of tea and biscuits.

'That's very good of you, Mrs Lockwood. Could you fetch your son, Peter, for us please?'

Connie froze.

'Why do you want to talk to Peter? He is autistic and it will frighten him.'

'Yes, your husband told us. But he can still *speak*, can't he? That's not very much to ask.'

Connie realised in one second how the sergeant would have no idea whatsoever how to talk to Peter or understand him. She couldn't even begin to explain to him about the extreme aloneness that characterized her son's internal life.

'Sergeant, is it really necessary, I wonder? He's only just getting over the shock of Jack's death. He witnessed it all.'

'Where was he, then, Mrs Lockwood?'

'At the very top of the slope. He saw the whole thing — chair careering down the slope, getting stuck under the lorry, the squeal of the...'

She stopped abruptly. There was something about the expression on the sergeant's face that made her afraid.

'I'll get him, but I want to be with him all the time.'

'Fair enough.'

Connie disappeared for a few minutes. When the two came down, Peter's hair was brushed and he had a tee shirt and shorts on instead of his dressing gown. Oliver wasn't sure what Connie had bribed him with to get such a quick result, but she knew it would be in the realm of sweets or chocolate.

'There's nothing to be afraid of,' said the woman officer kindly. 'Just a few questions to answer. That's all right, isn't it?'

'No,' replied Peter.

'Well, Sonny, I'm afraid it'll have to be,' interjected the sergeant.

'Now. How sad are you about Jack?'

'That's a silly question,' replied Peter. 'I don't answer silly questions.'

'Was he your friend?' asked the officer.

'He was my best friend,' replied Peter.

'Did he get on your nerves ever?'

'Yes. A lot of the time. Especially his silly rhymes.'

'Did you ever want to hurt him?'

'Yes, I did.'

'In what way?'

'I thought about hitting him or tipping him out of his chair sometimes.'

The officers exchanged glances. Connie squirmed inwardly.

'Did you ever?'

'No, never!'

'Why not, if you wanted to?'

'Because he was my best friend. I told you that.'

The questions proceeded. Peter answered them all with devastating honesty, much to the pride of Oliver and Connie.

They had almost come to the end when the officer asked.

'Are you sad that Jack has died?'

'No.'

'No? Why not? You said he was your best friend.'

'Because he will be in heaven now and able to run and jump and play.'

The sheer transparent innocence and simple faith of the boy left all of them silent.

'Thank you, Peter,' said the sergeant eventually.

As they reached the front door, the Sergeant turned and looked at Peter.

'Did you ever think of cutting the cable of the brake, son?'

'Yes.'

'Why did you think that?'

'Because that way he would get to heaven quicker.'

They left without a word. Oliver put his arms around Peter and for once Peter did not pull back.

'Well done, Peter. I'm very proud of you.'

'Can I have that bar of chocolate now, Mum?'

'You certainly can,' replied Connie, fighting back her tears. 'Let's go and choose the biggest bar we can find, shall we?'

CHAPTER 5

When Peter was happily settled with an eight-ounce bar of milk chocolate, with no rules as to its consumption, Connie came and sat next to him on the sofa. Although convinced her son would never do anything to harm Jack, she had witnessed him become angry and impatient with Jack at times, punching the air in frustration as Jack teased him with his endless silly, clever rhymes. Connie was furious with herself to find that doubts about the current situation crept into her thinking despite doing her best to push them away.

Meanwhile, Oliver was having the same sort of mental tussle regarding Robbie. He had first met Robbie at the Church Army Hostel where the lad was staying after his release from prison. Despite Robbie's self-defensive demeanour of bravado and anger, Oliver had noticed a kind of self-conscious, off-hand kindness coming from Robbie towards Jack, who visited with his mother Sadie from time to time. The two lads made friends with each other and Robbie had a natural manner with Jack, never mentioning, in fact seeming not to notice, Jack's devastating physical disabilities. One day, one of the cooks in the kitchen known for his rough tongue and ill temper called Jack a "fucking freak" in front of Robbie. Robbie's temper flared and he grabbed a knife, whereupon, in defending Jack, he slashed the offending cook's face. Robbie ended up for the second time in his nineteen years with a two-year imprisonment.

Oliver needed to convince himself absolutely that Robbie could not have tampered with the wheelchair. As soon as he sat down with Robbie to broach the subject as subtly as he could, he saw the honest eyes looking questioningly at him. He saw the kindness in the young man's face that had ministered to Oliver's father as he lay dying ten years ago, how he had befriended his own young niece, Kitty, when she had a brain tumour and his easy, relaxed kind of love and commitment to Jack. Oliver could not even begin to question Robbie, and downstairs, in the sitting room, Connie sat gazing at her young son Peter knowing without a doubt that he could never ever tell a lie, even though the truth could be difficult for others to hear.

The police came several times in the next two weeks and were convinced that one of the suspects was guilty. The sergeant said he would put his money on "the odd young lad" who was "insufferably rude" and the woman officer regarded Robbie as "too innocent-looking for his own good". With each visit, Peter became more agitated and his rapid hand-shaking in the air, always a sign of stress in him, became very pronounced. Robbie had the opposite reaction. He became increasingly truculent and offhand, barely replying civilly and it was all that he could do to stop himself from delivering a stream of abuse whenever the police arrived.

Sadie remained more or less immobile in her living room chair, wrapped up in both grief and her old navy blue cardigan, which seemed to have become a tangible symbol of her suffering and increasing depression. She washed neither the cardigan nor her body. She barely ate and only came downstairs once every other day to collect the post.

On this particular day, four weeks after Jack had been killed, a letter arrived from *Fit4Life*, the company from where Jack's wheelchair had been bought. The very sight of the name sent a chill throughout her body. In Jack's case, she surmised grimly, the chair had been 'Fit4Death.' Much as Sadie had tried to dismiss the police sergeant's accusatory questioning, she could not manage to release herself from thinking that someone may have tampered with the brake cable, ludicrous as it seemed.

Slowly, Sadie opened the letter and began to read:

Dear Sir or Madam,

Recall of Fit4Life Wheelchairs

It has come to our attention that a design fault has been noted on our latest design of wheelchair, the A120, involving the brake cable. Despite our rigorous testing and high safety record, we note that in extremely rare cases the brake cable has spontaneously severed without apparent reason. We are therefore urgently recalling all Fit4Life chairs and will issue you with a suitable replacement while we look into this matter.

Please accept our apologies and thank you for your co-operation.

Enclosed within the main envelope, but sealed in a smaller one, was a *Wheelchair Accident Claims and Compensation Form.*

Sadie skimmed the second letter, reading fast.

Accidents with wheelchairs are fortunately usually trivial; however, on rare occasions, they can be catastrophic. If you or someone you are caring for has been involved in an accident, however trivial, please fill in the attached form...

Sadie could read no more. The words "on occasions they can be catastrophic" sent a shaft of fresh pain through her body. Poor Jack. Her lovely boy. How proud he had been of his new chair.

Even though she had mainly been reclusive in her living room, Sadie was aware of the police suspicions regarding both Robbie and Peter. Barely able to reach out from her cocoon of sorrow, she nevertheless knew that this would have been extremely painful for them all. Mentally she had already eliminated both of them from her compulsive internal enquiring. She knew they had both been devoted to Jack in equal measure. Slinging her navy blue cardigan back around her shoulder, she made her way downstairs.

'Auntie Sadie!' cried Rosy. 'Auntie Sadie's down, Mummy!'

Connie ran into the living room and tentatively held her sister. Sadie did not resist, but simply said.

'Read this, Con.'

Connie read both the letters and sat down in a state of amazement to digest the news. No one had even thought that the wheelchair itself might be at fault. Jack had negotiated the front slope hundreds of times without a mishap of any kind. He was very adept at it and had been allowed to go out on his own as long as he let someone know. Sadie had beaten herself up metaphorically since the accident, blaming herself for allowing him to negotiate the slope without an adult. He had been fourteen, although looked half his age, and she had given in to his pleadings to allow him some freedom, backed up by every other voice in the household. In her grief, she had been angry with them all, deciding that left to her own devices she would have stuck to her word and not allowed him out without her or Robbie.

None of that brought him back, though, and Sadie knew her thinking was irrational, and part of her grief, but stop it she could not.

'This is, at last, a proper explanation of what happened, Sadie,' Connie said. She went towards Sadie and took her hands. 'Does it help at *all*?'

'I think so — in a way I can't explain yet, but I do know that everyone else can breathe a sigh of relief. Please tell Oliver, and poor Peter and Robbie. It must have been very uncomfortable for them. On second thoughts, perhaps it is my job to tell them.'

In that moment, Connie saw that Sadie would eventually pull through. She was finally thinking about how others were reacting, and the intense grip of the first sorrow and anger seemed finally to be losing a little of its devastating power.

'Oliver is due in with Robbie in ten minutes. They've been at the youth club. Sadie — stay down and have a bite of supper and tell them the news?'

And so it was that the family that had been shattered by grief finally took the first steps toward healing. Sadie ate a little of the shepherd's pie Connie had cooked and stayed downstairs for nearly an hour. Connie saw how dreadful her sister's appearance was, but said nothing. The next time Sadie came downstairs she was showered, with her hair brushed, with the navy cardigan nowhere to be seen. Sadie had taken the first few small, brave steps back on the slow, winding road of managing her life without her boy.

Oliver took the letter to the police. Within a week Sadie heard that the case had been dropped completely and even the sergeant muttered some words of apology. The next day a large bouquet of flowers arrived on the doorstep for Sadie with the words.

From Southwark Police Station, Borough Road, Southwark:

The Metropolitan police force of Southwark offers its condolences for the loss of your son Jack. May he rest in peace

'And rise in glory,' said Oliver aloud. Nobody deserves it more than little Jack Connors.

CHAPTER 6

Sister Hope O'Neill had decided that she would not ring the front doorbell of the vicarage until a month had passed after the dreadful accident. From the tragic look of the woman who was led gently up the slope to the house by the dog-collared man, Hope knew that sorrow would be lying heavily within the home. It would not do at a time like this to go knocking on the door and enquiring if anyone knew of an Albert Connors, who she had discovered had fathered her towards the end of the war. It might sound incongruously cruel, almost like some kind of sick joke. No, she would bide her time and stem her curiosity for now.

As she reflected on the scene, she wondered if either the man or the woman was related to Albert Connors, her father, however distantly. It was more than she dared hope that there might be a relative somewhere. She had always regarded herself as entirely alone in the world. Her earliest memory was of standing in her cot, probably aged around three, shaking the bars ferociously for attention, her sodden nappy hanging down around her ankles, her bottom raw from urine. It seemed in her memory that no one came to tend to her for a very long time so she screamed and shook the cot more angrily than ever in an attempt for someone to love her a little or at least pay her some attention.

The secret of her illegitimacy had lain hidden for nearly four decades. Was it wise to uncover it now and heap more troubles and questions on the stricken family? After all, it was for her own selfish desires and longings alone to find out if she belonged anywhere. She also wanted to know if her father was as bad as she held him in her mind's eye, which would be painful for the family.

Hope had been granted a three-month sabbatical from her Protestant Convent in Ireland. In her frugal living quarter in the convent (she refused to call it a "cell", although that is in fact what it was), she had plotted and planned where she would visit in London. She had sent off for underground maps and an assortment of information about famous landmarks and had enjoyed imagining how it all might be in reality.

Hope spent hours walking from the guest house in Southwark to the South Bank, over Westminster Bridge and from there to various landmarks in Central London. Always when she arrived back at her guest house, she ran a bath to refresh herself. She had arranged with the landlady that she would be paid extra for the daily hot water. The landlady was at first reluctant, but then, seizing her financial advantage, doubled the price of the hot water tariff, and the deal was done. Under normal circumstances, Sister Hope would have regarded the regular bath as too much luxury for herself, only ever doing her ablutions in cold water back in Ireland. But that was the very point. There seemed something wildly extravagant to her about filling the bath with just the right temperature of the water, swishing the daily bath oil into it and sinking down into its softness. Before immersing herself, she would take another furtive look at her naked body in the mirror, half afraid that at any moment the long index finger of either the hand of God or her *Mother Superior* would point at her accusingly.

'Perhaps I should cover the mirror so I'm not tempted again,' reflected Hope.

Then the whisper of a rebellious voice rose up — the voice that had screamed and shaken in protest to her captivity in her cot.

'There's no harm in it. It's *my* body.'

Once, she ran the palms of her hands down the curves of her waistline, and her fingers strayed, felt the outline of her breasts and cupped them both briefly in her hands.

Hope discovered, that it had felt rather comforting and warming. She wondered what it would be like to hold a baby to her breast. She scrutinized her nipples. They certainly looked fit for purpose, but, she thought a little ruefully, not for *her* purpose, the one she knew God intended for her.

The fact was that Hope was mesmerized by the sight of her own body in the long mirror — not in a narcissistic way, but out of curiosity for what she had become. There were no mirrors of any kind in the convent. Once or twice she had caught her reflection in a window or doorway and always averted her eyes quickly. But as for seeing her own body naked? No. Out of bounds. Forbidden fruit.

Because she had been disturbed by thoughts she felt she had dealt with long ago, she decided this time to have a very brief cold bath rather than luxuriating in it. She knew she must not revisit these reflections, so dressed swiftly back into her black habit, putting the close-fitting white coif decisively on her head and covering it with her veil. She glanced in the mirror for the last time.

'That's much better,' she said aloud, eyeing the fully covered nun who was reflected back. 'And that's enough of *you*!' she added aloud to the mirror as she hung the thin grey towel (which once was probably once white), over it, leaving it looking for all the world like the forlorn drapes of a sail at half-mast.

Tomorrow was Sunday. She had visited Southwark Cathedral on the three Sundays since she arrived, but after the simplicity of the convent services, she found the cathedral with its sung prayers, the choreographed movements of the clergy and the intoned liturgies elaborate and confusing. The reason she had been attracted to Protestantism as a teenager was because of the quiet and simple manner of its worship. She loved the simple understated wooden cross made out of olive wood from Jerusalem that stood on the communion table. Brought up initially in a roman catholic orphanage, as a young child she became used to the rituals of the services, so it was with huge relief (and not a little officialdom), that she transferred her allegiance to the Protestant arm of the church, and was eventually welcomed into Saint Clare Convent at the age of twenty as a Postulant.

Although Hope had quite often walked through the streets of Dublin on various errands and missions of mercy, she never lingered by shop windows. Here, in London, with more time on her hands and very few commitments, she had tried to walk more casually along Oxford Street but felt hideously conspicuous whilst trying to avoid eye contact with scantily clad mannequins in windows displaying arrays of glamorous clothes. For the first time in years, she felt a self-consciousness sweep over her about wearing her nun's habit and veil, and knew she was an alien in this fast and colourful city. A small voice inside had to admit that London felt indecently worldly but wildly attractive. Walking down the Embankment when she first arrived had been different. She was anonymous there, the crowds drifting on their own agenda and the River Thames providing the sight of calm water, which always soothed her and seemed to feed her soul.

Had the viewings of her own body in the cracked full-length mirror changed her perception of everything so soon, or would anyone feel the same in her position? In her evening prayers, kneeling beside her bed, she asked God for a clean heart and that she might not be led into temptation of any kind, particularly those relating to the flesh.

Hope had found out the times of services from the bright blue board which hung outside St. Luke's Church. Eight o'clock a.m. or a ten-thirty family service. She decided to go to both. When she arrived at the church the door was open in welcome and a young male verger handed her an order of service and a hymn book. A simple communion service took place, a hymn was sung, prayers were said, and the elderly priest gave a short address. Sister Hope found again that a feeling of self-consciousness swept over her. In that moment she longed to be back in the Covent of St. Clare in Ireland. It felt safe there, but here, she felt it seemed strangely alien.

'But we're worshipping the same God,' she said to herself. 'The same yesterday, today and forever.' That didn't help one bit, and she found herself scurrying out during the final verse of the hymn and started hurrying back down the road towards her guest house, which was beginning to feel like her place of safety.

She heard running footsteps behind her. The young man who had been giving out hymn books caught up with her.

'I'm sorry, um, madam, er, miss. Sorry, but I don't know what to call a nun,' he said sheepishly. 'I didn't catch you to welcome you to St. Luke's. It's great that you came. I'm Robbie.'

'I'm Sister Hope. It's good to meet you,' she smiled warmly.

'Well I hope you enjoyed the service,' Robbie replied, noticing her gentle Irish lilt. 'If you come at ten thirty you'll find it a much more upbeat kind of thing. We've just started having guitars,' he said and quickly added. 'But it might not be up your street, Sister. We don't run to Plainsong I'm afraid,' he added with a face full of benign cheek.

'I'd love to come,' Hope said, smiling. 'Thank you for asking me — and for running after me,' she added.

She carried on down the road feeling elated. Guitars might not be her "thing" but the warmth of the young man's welcome definitely was.

CHAPTER 7

Robbie left the church and ran up the slope of the vicarage, opened the front door and was greeted by five-year-old Rosy, the longed-for daughter for Oliver and Connie. Rosa had been the name of Connie's beloved mother, so the beautiful tiny baby girl was named after her (abbreviated to Rosy most of the time).

Robbie swung Rosy in the air and she giggled joyfully. He laughed with her, but in his heart, he carried the sorrow of loss. Jack had been his special lad. He had looked after Jack since he met him at Albert Connor's funeral, and Sadie had appeared with him suddenly, without any prior warning. He loved the joyful chat of Jack, with his clever, funny, bizarre rhymes. Robbie probably understood Jack more than anybody else and in some ways combined the role of older brother and the father he had never known. Jack had been the result of a series of rapes that Albert Connors, his maternal grandfather, had hideously inflicted on Sadie, his eldest daughter. Sadie had disappeared in shame and embarrassment when she found she was pregnant, and her little, twisted, misshapen son was the result of the abusive man's greed and wanton wickedness. Sadie had never told anyone about either the pregnancy or the birth until she made a dramatic statement at her father's funeral, denouncing him as he lay sealed in his coffin by wishing him "nothing but the flames of hell that he deserves". She loved her boy Jack with the fiercest of passions. His intellectual ability and use of language had been hugely impressive even if his body failed him, and Sadie and he, they were wonderful company for each other.

Sadie regarded Jack as a gift from God the moment he was born, despite his strange appearance, and Robbie had nurtured and loved Jack almost from the moment he saw him. Everyone now was rightly supporting Sadie through the first dreadful weeks of shock and loss after Jack was killed. No one knew that Robbie spent a long time in his room mourning the loss of "his boy" whilst sifting through photographs and putting them in some kind of order in an album. Jack was the first person Robbie had ever loved, and Jack reciprocated that love in full measure and the two had a forged wonderful, healthy relationship.

Rosy pulled Robbie into the kitchen.

'Come and see what Mummy has made for pudding today!'

On the table was a huge chocolate log decorated with glace cherries and angelica.

'She won't give me a piece,' whined Rosy, making a mock sulky face.

'I should think not!' laughed Connie.

'Is anyone special coming to lunch today, Mum?' asked James, quickly scraping a finger around the remains of the buttercream in the bowl.'

'Hey!' Connie flicked his finger out. 'Don't do that, Jamie. Your hands are never the cleanest. Are you ready for church?'

'But *is* someone coming to lunch today, Mum? You only usually make chocolate log on a birthday.'

'I'm going to see if Auntie Sadie will come down today and I know it's one of her favourite. She hasn't been down for a Sunday lunch since…' she paused.

'Since Jack died. Say it Mum,' he said with the candour of youth.

'It's hard to say, Jamie. It makes it sound so final.'

'It *is* final,' said James.

'Oh no, it's not,' said Rosy loudly, putting her hands firmly on her hips. 'We all know Jack is in Heaven. You said he would have a supersonic wheelchair up there, Robbie!'

They all smiled, but the pain and the sense of loss nevertheless continued to dig deep into them all.

Oliver came into the kitchen looking flustered.

'I can't find my dog collar,' he said despairingly. 'Where's the Fairy Liquid.'

Oliver did what he had done more times than he cared to think. He carefully cut around the top of the firm white plastic bottle until he had a long strip about one inch wide.

'Oh well, if the cap fits…' he said, looking at the back of the strip. 'Here, Rosy, can you read this?' He showed her the writing on the back of the white strip.

'So-ft —and —g-e-n-tle. Soft and gentle!'

'You've got something to live up to, Dad, if you wear that!' remarked James. 'Just make sure you wear it the right way round otherwise it will be all around the parish that the vicar is advertising with Nanette Newman!'

'Mmm, that'd be nice,' said Oliver to himself, smiling.

'That'll *do*,' remarked Connie, flicking him with the tea towel.

Oliver smiled again and pushed the white side of the strip into slip collar.

'There! Perfect!' said Oliver, adjusting the makeshift dog collar and looking briefly in the mirror.

'Perfect, but what about my Fairy Liquid bottle? It's got no top now!'

'All to glorify God,' said Oliver and giving Connie a huge kiss on her cheek. 'Thanks Con.'

'Ugh! What are you kissing mum for in public?' said Peter, walking into the kitchen, kicking the table leg on his way and sitting down heavily.

'What's up, Peter?'

'I'm not coming to church today.'

Oliver put his arm on Peter's shoulders, who shrugged it away impatiently.

'That's fine, Pete. You don't have to come. Anything in particular the matter?'

Peter shrugged again and started to take a cherry from the chocolate log.

'Peter! Don't,' said Connie crossly. 'I've just finished it.'

'I suppose that's for someone *special,* from the *parish,* is it, Mother?'

It was one of Peter's habits to call Connie mother and rarely mum.

'It's just for all of *you,* and for Auntie Sadie,' replied Connie, not rising to the bait of Peter's taunting tone. 'I'm hoping she'll come down today.'

Peter brightened. He found visitors difficult, but always liked Sadie's company. Oliver, seeing the subtle change in him, picked up the glace cherry packet and held it up questioningly to Connie, who received the message and nodded almost imperceptibly back. Oliver held the packet out to Peter.

'Here you are, Pete, have one or two of your own.'

Peter dipped his fingers into the packet and drew out two sticky cherries.

'That's not *fair,* ' screamed Rosie. 'I want one.'

'So do I. Hand over, Dad,' added James loudly.

Oliver shrunk inwardly. Here we go. Another wonderful Sunday morning of family life. He took his Bible from the hall table.

'Just off to wish everyone the *Peace of the Lord,*' he said breezily, giving Connie a resigned smile. She grimaced back and ran after him.

'Pray that Peter will come after all,' she said quietly.

He nodded. Connie had always had a rock-like faith. Oliver noticed that from the very beginning. He loved her more than he could say.

Sunday mornings were always the same in the Vicarage. Oliver envied the honorary vicar, now retired and almost eighty, for the peace and quiet with which he could prepare his sermons. Saturdays were always rather a mixed blessing to Oliver. When he didn't have a wedding to take, he had more space than usual in his day to prepare for Sunday. But the truth of it was that James would clamour for his Dad to watch him playing cricket, Rosy would badger endlessly for Oliver to take her out on her newly acquired two-wheeler bike with stabilizers and Peter would make his own demands simply by being Peter — at odds with the world, generally reclusive but always seeking out Oliver's company in order to bombard him with his strange views on life or vent some pent-up frustration on him.

Connie and Oliver had a vicarage 'open door' policy on a Sunday. It was nothing for Connie to be preparing a roast leg of pork (the cheapest cut she could find), for fourteen, and that didn't count the folk she sometimes scooped up at the church doorway who were either visitors or looking a bit lost.

Eventually, everyone was ready. The meat was checked and the oven turned down, the chocolate log put safely back in the fridge, the cutlery counted and put out to be laid later, James did his usual dash into the dining room with the mustard, cruet and apple sauce, balancing them on one hand and holding them high in the air playfully, Rosy's face was washed, James was directed to wipe the chocolate off his, the dog was told they wouldn't be long (why did the dog never understand that the phrase could mean they could be gone *hours?*), then Connie spoke softly to Peter.

'Pete, you coming? Dad would be so pleased, you know.'

'Nope,' said Peter and dashed off upstairs, his body language, negative and downbeat, as he went. Toby, their black Labrador-cross dog followed him, glad to have company. Peter and Toby were inseparable.

Connie quickly ran upstairs to Sadie's flat and knocked on the door.

'Sadie.' No answer. 'Sadie, do you want to come along to church with me? We can leave before the last hymn.'

Sadie opened the door. It was clear she had been crying.

'Sorry, Connie. I can't face it.'

Connie put her arms round her sister.

'Don't worry. Peter's staying behind. I guess he'll be reorganizing his stones as usual.'

'That's fine,' said Sadie.

'He's very all over the place today,' said Connie.

'Maybe I'll look in on him, Con.'

'Come to lunch later?'

'Thanks. Is anyone else coming?'

'Not that I know of Sadie, but you know Bruce — he may drop round at *just* the right time!'

Bruce was Sadie and Connie's adored middle brother, married with a teenage daughter. He had been the rock of the family when their eldest sibling James had taken his own life as a teenager (Connie's eldest son was later to be named after him). His death had profoundly affected Bruce, but he managed to sublimate his own feelings somehow to support his beloved mother and sisters. In time, he married Clara who was gifted in musical theatre performance and for years had been struggling to make her mark on the West End musicals scene. Now she finally had her opening, having been offered the lead in a brand new musical, and was rehearsing intensely. Clara had always had a tussle over priorities in her life, but at this stage she knew clearly she had to follow her dream, with her family's encouragement. Bruce and Clara had one daughter, Kitty. Clara made it clear from the outset that there would be no more children. Partly as a result of Clara's extended rehearsal absences from the family, Bruce and Kitty grew incredibly close as father and daughter. Kitty was the sunshine in Bruce's life, blessed with an extrovert, warm personality.

It would be no hardship if Bruce and Kitty dropped in for lunch. Connie would simply lay two more places. She always prepared an abundance of food anyway, and their company might help Sadie and lift the general mood of the household.

Sadie herself knew she was beginning to fear the wide outdoors for a number of reasons, many of which had no rational explanation. It might mean she would have to cope with people's sympathy, or perhaps it may be a sunny day outside which would implicitly contradict how she was feeling inside. Everyone else would seem happy in the sun while she was secretly filled with phobic fear. The worst anticipated terror now, though, was that a lorry might come sweeping down the slight hill towards the vicarage, loudly squealing its brakes as it took the curve in the road. Her constant flashbacks were of that fateful day one month ago that took her son. She saw it all over and over and over again in her traumatised mind. The 'What ifs' stretched endlessly towards infinity in her.

In addition, Sadie recognized that she was becoming phobic about meeting anyone who required any emotional effort or resilience on her part. She simply did not have reserves of that kind of energy to cope with them. Soon after she had brought Jack home as a newborn baby to her mobile home in Scotland, she developed what the doctor called "Social Phobia" His answer was a large bottle of diazepam, with repeat prescriptions whenever she needed them, rather than having the knowledge or insight to see that it was one manifestation of a post-natal depression condition. The result was that Sadie became, as she put it, "drugged up to the eyeballs" as she began to double her dose on her "bad days" which became increasingly frequent. It had taken a skilled and kind psychotherapist to support her through a long struggle on both their parts to break her drug dependency.

Her past agoraphobia hovered ominously somewhere above her shoulder now like a threatening storm cloud. It had been a dreadful, crippling experience that lasted all of three years, and she never wanted to travel that route again.

Connie sat in a pew towards the back of the huge, barnlike church having greeted several people. When she first went into the church on a Sunday as a naive vicar's wife she had been ushered to the front to the "vicarage pew" Courteously she had explained to members of the congregation that she wasn't happy taking up residence in one particular pew. She gave the reason that it had the clearest view of the wonderful east-end window, the altar, the pulpit for the sermon, and she would like the seat shared as necessary. Connie did not like anything that smacked of status or privilege, (nor did she want it commented upon if she occasionally missed church).

Rosy loved church and James especially liked it when he could either read a lesson or take up the collection. For Peter, the whole thing was too much of a challenge, and he rarely attended, much to Oliver's sadness. Connie was more philosophical and would say, 'He's in God's hands, Oli. Don't agitate. All will be well. You'll see.'

CHAPTER 8

Sister Hope was excited as she set off again to St. Luke's
Church that morning. She had found the young man who
had run after her very personable. She smiled to herself.
How long was it since a man had run after her? Probably
nearly twenty years. She had entered the convent at the age
of twenty and from then on it had been celibacy all the way
without so much as a hint of anything in trousers — (even
the priests wore frocks). She had handed over her sexuality
happily, even joyfully, believing that in giving everything
to God she was obeying God and gaining spiritual
freedom.

Years ago, Oliver Lockwood had done the same thing:
handed over his sexuality to God before his ordination. He
had found, however, that falling in love had interrupted his
good intentions and as the Bishop had remarked to him,
"The heart is slow to learn". Sometime later, Oliver had
made a wise decision marrying Connie. They were
wonderfully suited.

Occasionally, at night, the memories of Hope's only
boyfriend and their passionate "petting" sessions when
they had both been sixteen, came unbidden to Sister Hope.
She had to pray hard that God would fill her mind with
what she regarded as pure thoughts. Then again, when she
had looked at her body in the cracked mirror in the guest

house, she had felt — what was it? Regret? Quiet pride that she still had curves? Shock at her beautiful body, albeit on the thin side? Then there was the fleeting caressing of her breasts. What was that all about? She knew well enough but did not care to acknowledge it to herself. Feelings of sexuality must be dealt with sternly! Now, here she was, hurrying down the road, black habit flying in the wind like Maria von Trapp's, with the thought of a young man on her mind.

She arrived at the church and was given a hymn book by the said young man, who smiled in recognition.

'Nice to see you again, Sister Hope.'

She was heartened that he had remembered her name.

The church was already almost full, so she took up a seat in a pew at the back and knelt down in prayer — 'Lord, still my heart and cleanse my thoughts.'

The organist began playing and two guitarists enthusiastically strummed out dubious harmonies to the hymn *Dear Lord and Father of Mankind,* not exactly enhancing Hubert Parry's gracious tune in the organist's opinion.

Sister Hope stood up to sing and became aware of two people creeping quietly into the end of her pew: a lad and a woman. She gave a brief smile but both steadfastly kept their eyes on the ground. Sister Hope furtively glanced along the pew again in a few seconds. She recognized the woman as the one who had been at the scene of the crash.

How brave to come to church when her heart must be breaking, if I'm right she's the mother, thought Hope.

They looked a forlorn couple: the boy, tall for his twelve years and with the characteristic stoop of a fast-growing pubescent boy embarrassed about his height, and the woman, somehow shrivelled and bent as though bracing herself against the world and its slings and arrows. She was strong and striking with her dark hair and rounded figure, but forlorn indeed, thought Sister Hope. Hope had a strong instinct to hold her and comfort her, but as the context was inappropriate she decided to spend much of the service in silent prayer for them both.

She was surprised to see that it was not the elderly gentleman taking the service as before, but a nice-looking youngish clergyman standing and singing at the front. Oliver Lockwood was aware of his son Peter and Sadie creeping in at the back, and he glowed inside. He adored his troubled boy and he and Connie spent many hours discussing and praying about how best to handle and support him. Oliver was very pleased to see his sister-in-law Sadie had made it to church, but it was Peter's presence that made his heart sing. Maybe this was a new beginning, perhaps prompted partly by Jack's untimely death. Peter was feeling empty and bereaved, but he seemed not to have an avenue for expression other than to kick the table and make angry or cynical comments to Connie and most particularly to Oliver. It seemed as though he set out deliberately to hurt his father. The school had arranged for Peter to see an Educational Psychologist, saying that his behaviour was 'disturbed and worrying.'

Nevertheless, here was Peter now, and he and Sadie seemed to gain courage from each other — enough to face people, albeit from the back of the church.

During the last hymn, the boy and the woman crept out. Robbie moved swiftly to the church door, put his arm for a second round the woman as they were leaving and then gave the lad a playful punch. Afterwards, Robbie slid into the pew next to Hope and sang the remainder of the final hymn loudly. When the service had ended the clergyman walked quickly and unceremoniously to the door at the back of the church to say goodbye to people.

Robbie took Hope by the arm, surprising her with physical contact — the first in many years — and steered her towards Oliver.

'Hey, Rev. Come and meet my new friend. This is Sister Hope.'

'Good morning Sister Hope, how lovely to have you here.'

'Yes, not every day you scoop up a Nun, is it?' said Robbie cheekily.

Hope might have been embarrassed, or even slightly affronted if anyone else had said this, but her face lit up with laughter, much to Oliver's relief. Robbie could overstep the mark sometimes. However, in that moment, both he and Robbie saw in front of them a woman of considerable beauty despite her face being somewhat concealed by her veil; or did that make her beauty rather more enigmatic? Oliver found a verse from *Twelfth Night* flying into his head:

Lady, you are the cruell'st she alive If you will lead these graces to the grave and leave the world no copy.

He had not recalled it since his "A" level English days and quickly banished the inappropriate and ill-timed thought.

Hope was wrestling with what she regarded as an inappropriate thought too as she stood talking to the clergyman. She had come to see if she had any family, and find out about her father. All her research had led her to this place. Could it possibly be that this rather attractive clergyman was related to her in any way, however distantly?

'I'm Oliver Lockwood,' he said, smiling, confounding her thoughts when she realised he did not have the Connors surname. 'Let me introduce you to my wife. This is Connie.'

Sister Hope saw a rather fragile-looking woman, very slender and rather pretty, approach her. She greeted Hope with a warm smile. In a heartbeat, Hope sensed — what was it? She had never met this lady before and yet there was something vaguely familiar about this woman. Or was she imagining it? It was easy to indulge in a flight of fancy in this situation.

'It's very nice to welcome you here,' said Connie. 'I presume you're just visiting?'

Connie had a lovely open face, one that would invite confidence. In a trice, Hope wanted to tell this young woman why exactly she was there, but Connie continued.

'It would be lovely if you felt able to come over to the vicarage and have a bite to eat with us, Sister — er — '

'Hope,' interjected Robbie quickly. 'Connie makes a mean Sunday lunch. You'll not want anything for a week. Shouldn't turn it down if I were you, Sister!'

Hope had been extremely frugal with all her meals since arriving in London. She had spent most of her spare cash on hot water for her baths, so had lived off meagre rations. She had shunned the seductive eating places in London, buying instead a bread roll and nothing much else for lunch. Supper usually consisted of heating up some soup with more bread, some cheese, and an apple or banana if her self-imposed daily allowance could run to fruit. The thought of a hot roast lunch was irresistible; but more than that, there was an intrinsic loveliness about these people. She wanted to get to know them for their own sake, and not just because they represented the last stage of her mission or a good hot meal.

CHAPTER 9

As Sister Hope entered the house, she was greeted by the delicious smell of roast pork. Connie showed her into a sitting room, which had a comfortable squishy brown sofa in it belonging originally to Oliver from his theatre chaplaincy days, and three slightly battered-looking but comfortable arm chairs. Nothing in the room quite co-ordinated with anything else, but Hope was overwhelmed by the homeliness of it. In Ireland, she had gone from sparse orphanage to bare convent, where she had a room smaller than a single bedsit, with a narrow single bed, a small desk, a wash basin and stand and one hard chair. Even her room in the English guest house, although with more furniture and a bath and wash basin, was nevertheless sparse with its thin carpet and skimpy curtains that did not meet in the middle. Now here, in this vicarage, was positive luxury! In actual fact, the living room was far from luxurious, but it was warm, colourful, welcoming and, Hope sensed immediately, a "lived in" home in which everyone in it was loved.

'Would you like a drink, Sister?' asked Connie. 'What will it be? Coffee? Tea? Fruit Juice? Or we have some white wine?'

'I'd love a little fruit juice,' replied Hope.

'Jamie, Rosy, you'll keep Sister Hope company, won't you, while I just fetch her a drink?'

While Connie was gone, Hope noticed an array of framed family photographs on the mantelpiece. Rosy looked at James. They had never met a nun before and were dumbstruck.

'James, Rosy. It's lovely to meet you and very kind of you to have me for lunch. I know — I wear funny clothes,' she said. 'You're allowed to laugh.'

Jamie and Rosy smiled. Sister Hope had broken the ice for them.

'And these must be your relatives?' she said, taking a photo down.

Hope was burning to know about the family of six staring out at her. How could she ask questions without seeming intrusive? She needn't have worried. Rosy was full of joy and energy now she was relaxed and started talking immediately — like a babbling brook, Hope observed, smiling inwardly.

'Well, that's my grandma. She's got the same name as me. Rosa. She died before I was born. And that's James. He's my uncle but he died too. And that's Uncle Bruce. He's coming soon. He's a man now. And that's my mummy. She's pretty isn't she? And that's Auntie Sadie. She's upstairs. She's sad because Jack has died. *Everyone's* dying,' Rosy said dramatically, using her arms and hands to good effect.

'And that is?' said Hope pointing at the man who was standing next to Grandma Rosa.

'Oh, that's my grandfather. He wasn't a very nice man. Auntie Sadie told me.'

'Oh dear,' said Hope. 'I'm sorry to hear that.' She stared hard at the picture.

Connie came in with a tray of glasses and an unopened packet of orange juice.

'Oliver will be back in a minute. He's sometimes caught up with the verger who — who can go on a bit. Sorry, but he can,' she added, suddenly aware that she was in the presence of someone who must be very holy. 'Now I expect Rosy is filling you in with *all* the family details,' she laughed. 'There are no secrets while Rosy is in full flow! We call her Gabbling Gertie!'

'Yes, I've heard all about your family, Mrs Lockwood,' said Hope, smiling.

'Oh, *Connie*, please,' said Connie quickly.

'And I'm Hope.'

'I like the name Hope,' said Rosy.

'Do you, Rosy? My mother named me before she died.'

'Your mummy *died?*'

'Yes. As soon as I was born, so I was told by the nuns.'

'Oh no, not *another* death!' exclaimed Rosy, holding her head in feigned despair.

Hope hadn't meant to share that with the little girl; in fact, she had not anticipated divulging anything much about herself at all. But there was something about Rosy's open face, the glow of the fire, the warmth of the home, the smell of roast pork and Connie's sweet manner that made her feel expansive and comfortable.

'No *Mummy*! That's sad. Who looked after you then?' Rosy sidled up to Connie and held onto her skirt.

'I was looked after by some kind people in a very large home.'

'What was that? An orphanage? What about your dad?' interjected James.

'I didn't know my father,' said Hope quietly.

'Oh — are you looking for him? He might be lost,' said Rosy, still fingering the material of Connie's skirt.

Everyone went quiet. Connie looked hard at Hope, worried that Rosy and her innocent remarks might have hurt her.

Sister Hope spoke very quietly.

'That is why I have come to England. I want to trace the father that I have never known. He may not be alive, but I need to find out who he was.'

'There must be lots and lots of daddies in England. Do you think you will ever find him?' said Rosy.

'I can try,' replied Sister Hope.

'Where on earth do you start? Do you just stick a pin in a map and go there?' asked James. Sister Hope, unsure of her ground suddenly, started to formulate a reply when the front door banged Oliver entered, carrying his robes over his arm.

'Sister Hope, it's lovely to have you.' He kissed Connie and Rosy, hesitated in front of Hope and then impulsively gave her a kiss on the cheek. Hope looked embarrassed but pleased.

'The peace of the Lord be with you, Sister. We're blessed to have you here,' he said, giving a little bow.

'Well, you'd better tell me that after I've been here a wee while!' she said with a laugh.

Everyone visibly relaxed.

'Excuse me,' Oliver said, pulling the plastic that had served as a dog collar out of the neck of his black shirt and tossing it on the sideboard.

Rosy picked it up and ran over to Sister Hope.

'My daddy's all soft and gentle! Look!'

Rosy spelt out the letters on the back of the plastic to Hope.

'S-o-f-t and g-e-n-t-le.'

'My goodness,' said Hope. 'So he is, how wonderful!.' She clapped her hands in the air and threw back her head in laughter. 'And you're a very good reader, Rosy.'

'But you should see him sometimes,' said James, 'particularly when he's trying to fix the chain on my bicycle! The air is blue!.'

They all laughed. Oliver playfully clipped his son over the head with *The Church Times* that was lying on the coffee table. Connie disappeared into the kitchen and appeared a few minutes later announcing that the meat was ready for carving (Oliver's domain), and the vegetables were on the table. Would they all please come? She went to the bottom of the stairs and shouted for Sadie, Peter and Robbie.

After a minute, Sadie appeared. Connie saw again how diminished her sister looked. She welcomed her, noticing with relief that as Sadie had brushed her hair and made an effort with her clothes, she might get through lunch for the first time since Jack died without disappearing up to her room half way through the meal. Peter came down looking more cheerful than often, but almost skidded to a halt when he saw Sister Hope. He went up to Connie and whispered angrily.

'Thought you said no one was coming to lunch, *Mother.*'

Connie chose to ignore the remark and asked Peter to fetch the chocolate roll from the fridge and put it on the side ready for serving after the main course. It was all a case of diversion tactics when managing Peter. He went to the fridge, carried out the chocolate log and put it on the side, taking the central glace cherry off and eating it, smirking at Oliver. He was relying on Oliver not making a scene in front of Sister Hope. Oliver glowered a warning which Peter knew meant, "Just you wait till everyone's gone!"

Finally, everyone was settled at the large farmhouse-style table. Two places were left empty in case brother Bruce and his daughter Kitty appeared. Sister Hope couldn't believe the lunch that was served: roast pork, crackling, tasty stuffing, roast and mashed potatoes, carrots, sprouts, peas, creamed leeks and a huge jug of gravy. Connie served this up every Sunday and no one ever got tired of it. She put aside two lavish meals, presumably for Bruce and Kitty.

Hope was the happiest she could remember being for years. There was something alive and natural about this family. Her heart warmed towards Peter, who she could see was a troubled lad. She found the depth of Sadie's grief, clearly etched on her face, moved her deeply. Everything in her wanted to reach out and say something, but she could tell from Sadie's body language that she was turned in on herself and would not welcome any intrusion into her grief. She decided that Connie was the loveliest of women and Oliver was what in her traditional eyes a husband should be: kind, warm, with a touch of firmness and with a love for his wife and family transparently clear. Rosy was irresistible and James was trying very hard to be an adult, intent subconsciously on replicating his father, whom he hero-worshipped. Robbie was as he had first appeared to Hope: cheeky, attractive, warm and jokey. She had never been in a family before — only the convent family, full of serious-minded women seeking to serve God. They laughed a lot, but Hope could not exactly describe the atmosphere as "light" by any stretch of the imagination. There were some very happy times, but always in the controlled atmosphere within the granite walls.

While she was relishing the delicious meal, and chatting with the family, Hope decided she would not pursue her enquiries about her father today. It felt dishonest now as if it might seem that her sole purpose of accepting the lunch invitation was to make her enquiries. She had even felt bad about asking Rosy who the man was in the photo. It would wait for another day. Even if she never found out about her father, she had met a family who had extended warmth, friendship and hospitality to her in the most natural and unaffected manner. It filled her with profound joy. She could not believe that she was actually fitting in somewhere. She had no idea family life could be so rich and so beautiful.

The family was going to an infant baptism ceremony that afternoon in the church. Sister Hope quickly prepared to leave. Thanking them all profusely, she was assured that she would be welcome at the vicarage *any time at all* — and most certainly to another few meals before she went back to Ireland. Her offers of helping with the washing up were firmly but politely turned down.

'We'll do it when we get back,' said Connie as she and Oliver, together with James and Rosy, left for the church. Connie didn't even ask Peter to come. He had made a huge effort to go with Sadie this morning, but enough was enough. Anyway, why should he? It wasn't a family baptism unless you counted the family of God, Peter had thought cynically, remembering a conversation he had recently had with Oliver.

Sister Hope wanted to show Sadie how sad she was for her loss. Somehow she could not find the words, especially as she hardly knew Sadie. On impulse, quite suddenly, she hugged Hope tightly to her and whispered.

'God will honour your grief, Sadie. He has you in the palm of his hand.'

Hope stepped back quickly, fearing she had been inappropriately intrusive in her desire to express her sorrow for Sadie. From someone else, Sadie might have drawn away or resisted. Sadie was not a believer, but she accepted Sister Hope's words gratefully with tears and a smile. The beginnings of a special bond was forged in that moment. Neither of them would forget it.

CHAPTER 10

Hope wanted a walk before returning to her guest house. She was happy and relaxed and, after the final course of cheese and biscuits at the vicarage, had decided she had never felt so full, in fact satiated, in her life.

She decided to go via Southwark Cathedral and experience Borough Market on a Sunday. She knew it would be closed, which would give her a chance to sense the vastness of the place without the crowds. When she had first arrived in Southwark, she was swept along by a jostling crowd of people and had virtually been buffeted into the famous market, finding herself amongst huge piles of colourful spices — a vibrant medley of turmeric, saffron, paprika, cumin, the smells as well as the sights overwhelming her senses. Visually, it was reminiscent of an exotic shiny oil painting, Hope decided. She walked up and down the aisles of undulating seas of fruit — powdery oranges, waxy lemons, bunches of fresh mint and tarragon, piles of shiny green and black olives, then past roll upon roll of fabric of every colour and texture imaginable. Sister Hope had been dizzy with it all and relieved to find her way out of the maze and breathe deeply where the air was marginally fresher. It presented a vast culture shock to her. She had spent all of her adult life within the confines of the convent of St. Clare and the city of Dublin. As she walked back to her guest house she felt strange with disorientation and culture shock.

Now, today, this Sunday afternoon, the place was deserted. It was like another land, another country. The only tell-tale sign of the market of the previous day when the market was in full swing were the huge mountains of litter that had been gathered into corners ready for collection the following Monday morning. Sister Hope meandered happily on the outskirts of the quiet market, feeling that life was very good.

A group of young men, five in all, clearly bored and disconsolate, eyed the nun. She looked them clearly in the face, as she passed them, refusing to feel intimidated, although in fact, she was. She was familiar with stares and whispers. Two of the men had Mohican hairstyles, she noticed, and another slicked-back bleached white-blond hair. One of them talked furtively to the rest of the group, clearly hatching some kind of plot. They sauntered up to Sister Hope. The one with the blond slicked-back hair spoke:

'Watcha, darling. What's a nice lady like you doing out on 'er own then?'

'The same as you, I would imagine,' replied Sister Hope. 'It's Sunday and it's a lovely day for a walk.'

Another picked up part of the hem of her black habit, fingered it and pulled it up alarmingly high.

'What d'ya wear this fancy dress for then?'

'Strange, isn't it?' she said, feigning an attitude of nonchalance. 'It's a kind of uniform in a way. Like a clergyman wears a dog collar. You're all wearing Denim.

I suppose that's *your* uniform,' she said, forcing a smile, but beginning to feel extremely uneasy.

'You ever 'ad it then?'

'Will you please leave me alone' Hope said emphatically. 'I need to get back.'

'D'ya fancy it then darling? We can show you *exactly* what to do, can't we lads?'

They laughed mockingly.

'She'd be a nice little number, her being a virgin and all. Nice and... you know... tight.' He made an obscene gesture. 'Know what I mean?'

More mocking laughter.

Hope began to walk away very fast.

'Leave me alone, I said.'

'Or what?' said another, catching up with her and twisting her round roughly by the shoulders to face him.

'Shall we show her what it's all about lads?'

With that, two of them pinned Hope against a huge pile of rubbish, lifted up her voluminous garments, and tugged down her underwear greedily. The blond one unzipped his jeans and was egged on by the rest of the group. Sister Hope, a good woman, an innocent woman and a servant of God, was viciously and aggressively raped, first by one, then another, then a third. She cried out in shock and pain whereupon a filthy handkerchief was stuffed into her mouth to silence her.

She felt something ripping inside and she started to bleed. The fourth man, champing at the bit and unzipping his jeans, leered.

'Ever had it in the missionary position, love? That would suit her wouldn't it, lads? Made for it, I'd say.' Raucous laughter. 'Down with 'er then!'

Two of them pushed her flat into a pile of fly-ridden rubbish and one after the other raped her while the remaining three, satisfied, clapped rhythmically in time.

'Go boy — go boy — go boy — go boy!' they chanted.

All having helped themselves, they began to leave the scene, nonchalantly swaggering as they went. Twisting Hope's knickers round his index finger, the blond one shouted.

'Look! We've got these, Sister! A nice little souvenir we can remember you by.'

Another shouted.

'Nice was it love? Bet you've never had it so good!'

'Bet you've never had it *at all* — until now.'

'Like the buses, none come and then five come at once!.'

More raucous laughter.

'Don't get cold without your knickers!'

One of them made an obscene sign to her as they left, saying,

'Don't you worry. We'll be back for more, love. Got the taste for it now, ain't ya?'

There was not a soul around on that Sunday afternoon. Hope lay in the pile of rubbish for many minutes in a state of pain and shock. Her face and head were bleeding, first when she was thrown against the cans and bottles, and then as she was pushed further in. Her habit and rough cotton underslip were still pulled up beyond her waist and her veil and coif had been tugged off so that her short, tousled tight gold curls were showing. She was throbbing and hurting from top to toe, most particularly where she had been roughly violated and stretched, not once but five times. Finally, she curled up foetal-shaped amongst the litter and rotting market debris and wept, remaining there for several minutes.

When she could think a little straighter, she knew she must get help — find a phone box — quickly — phone the police. But all she could think of was somehow getting back to that warm and loving household. It was a ten-minute walk away. Could she make it? She stood up in the vile rubbish, pulled her underskirt down and smoothed her habit over it. She tried to straighten her hair, picked up her mutilated veil and coif and walked shakily and slowly back past Southwark Cathedral and round and down to the Vicarage. A few people stared at her and then averted their eyes, embarrassed. A man asked if he could help in any way, but she shied away immediately, terrified.

At last, she was at the slope of the vicarage. She suddenly remembered that the family would be out. What about Sadie? Robbie? Would anyone answer the door? If not, she would just wait there until Oliver and Connie returned. She yearned to be near them. She needed their kind and soothing physic for body and soul.

She rang the bell and then called through the letter box.

'Help me — please. *Please* help me. Can someone come? *Please.*'

CHAPTER 11

When the Connor family had gone to church after lunch for the Christening, and Sister Hope had left the vicarage household, Sadie looked at the sea of washing up. It was a daunting pile. She vowed inwardly that she would buy the family a state-of-the-art dishwasher. She felt suddenly as though someone had pulled the plug on her energy, draining her from top to toe. She had enjoyed lunch surprisingly much, but the result was deep fatigue from the effort. All she wanted to do was retreat to her bed.

Sadie reflected on the state of the kitchen. Connie and Oliver had been so good at supporting her in every way ever since Jack and she had arrived all those years ago. She had a lovely two-bedroom flat upstairs in the vast vicarage, and Connie had often cooked meals for Jack and herself. All of them had shown them huge love and understanding from the word go. Sadie gave herself a stern talking to, rolled up her sleeves purposefully and called Robbie and Peter. Robbie came bounding down the stairs two at a time, although as usual there was no response from Peter.

'Robbie, give us a hand with all of this?' She waved towards the washing up. 'Let's get it done before they arrive back from church. It's not fair to leave it'

'Sure,' said Robbie. 'Have you called Pete?'

'Yes,' replied Sadie. 'But perhaps we should just leave him to it.'

She started to collect dishes and put them in piles.

'No. On second thoughts, I'll go and see what he's up to, and try to entice him down.'

Sadie went up one flight of stairs. Peter's bedroom was first on the left of the large square landing. She knocked.

'It's me — Auntie Sadie. Can I come in?'

'Yes.'

Peter was sitting in the middle of his bed, with his collection of minerals and fossils laid out on the cover, categorising them for the hundredth time.

'Peter, your room looks amazing! How long have you been tidying it?'

'About a week,' replied Peter. 'It's never tidy enough.'

'Pete, it's immaculate! And these are beautiful,' she said, carefully picking up a tiny fossil.

'Don't touch it!' cried Peter. 'No-one is allowed to do that. What did you want, Auntie Sadie? Is it important or —'

'Is it important enough for me to be disturbing you, you mean,' she smiled. 'Come on, Pete. I need a hand downstairs. Let's give mum and dad a surprise. Come and help?' Reluctantly and with several sighs Peter carefully put his collection of minerals and fossils back in their case, replaced it on the sideboard and after a few minutes came downstairs. He would do anything for Sadie.

The three of them had a convivial time, instigated by Robbie. He put radio music on full volume: Phil Collins, Billy Ocean and then The Pet Shop Boys blasted out one after the other, while Robbie proceeded to dry the plates Sadie was washing, throwing each one in time to the music across the kitchen to Peter shouting.

'Catch, Pete! No butter fingers allowed!'

Pete caught them all, avoiding any breakages on the quarry-tiled floor, and laughed in a way he hardly ever did. Sadie smiled at their antics and Robbie noticed that it was the first time since Jack had died that there was any sign of laughter in Sadie.

Quite suddenly the front door bell rang, followed by a voice calling through the letter box.

'Help me — please. I need help. Can someone come? *Please?*'

They looked at each other, knowing that the call sounded desperate. Robbie ran through the long hall, tea towel in hand, followed by Sadie and Peter, and opened the door.

There, collapsed in a heap on the doorstep, was Sister Hope.

'Oh *NO!*' said Sadie, as Robbie bent down to her.

'Pete, take the other side of her. Let's get her on her feet then we can take her inside. Really gently. She's been hurt,' instructed Robbie.

'What on earth has happened to her?' questioned Sadie, but as they carried her into the hall, Sadie could guess: torn habit, veil and coif obviously wrenched off her head, gold curls wet, and the most tell-tale sign of all: a sinister leakage of liquid seeping through the back of her habit and forming a large dark patch of blood on the black material.

Sister Hope had been raped.

What Sadie could not have known was that she had been raped not once but five ugly times.

'You can bring her up into my room,' said Peter in what was for him an act of supreme altruism. 'I can cover my bed with towels,' he said, eyeing the blood. 'And it's opposite the bathroom.'

Even as they helped poor, violated Sister Hope up the stairs and onto the bed, Robbie and Sadie realised the significance of this moment. To help, *Peter* had offered his precious sanctuary which he cleaned, tidied, polished and tidied again every half an hour to try to subdue his obsessive compulsion need for order and cleanliness.

'Thank you, thank you so much,' said Hope weakly.

'Don't try to talk yet' said Sadie. 'Just lie there quietly.'

'I'll get you a cup of tea,' said Robbie, knowing that the story that would unfold was essentially one where Sister Hope would probably need a woman.

'Come on Pete. With me.'

As they went downstairs, Robbie put his arm around Peter.

'That was a smashing thing you did there, mate. Great of you to offer your room.'

Peter said nothing but smiled sheepishly up at Robbie, who felt in some small way he had witnessed a minor miracle and it was as if Peter felt the shift within himself and for a minute was pleased.

Hope shut her eyes, trying to blot out the terrifying images that were insisting on filling her mind with every graphic detail. She saw the young man with blond hair bearing down on her. She felt the hideous pain and tearing as one after another penetrated her violently. She heard the jeers and the lewd comments and the rhythmic chanting of the rest of them as they watched. She clasped her hands over her ears and screwed her eyes tight shut, trying to banish the pictures and the sounds and the pain that she knew would haunt her for the rest of her life. The trauma had been so profound that Hope felt the best she could pray for was that, eventually, it would recede into a ghastly dim and distant memory.

Sadie said nothing, but gently washed Hope with warm water and Jack's special hypoallergenic soap and dabbed her bleeding head and hands with a soft towel. She did not touch anywhere else in case the police wanted to gather samples for evidence. Besides, Sadie felt that Hope's "private parts" were just that, despite what she deduced had been a violation of them. She did not even hold Hope's hand but just sat on a bedside chair and waited. She felt strangely privileged to be the one who was tending her.

She watched Hope and saw her covering her ears and tossing her head this way and that. After a few minutes, Sadie said.

'Sister Hope, can I ask you? Have you been — raped?'

Hope started weeping a little.

'Yes.'

'Sister Hope, I think we must call the police.'

Hope slowly sat up.

'Not yet. Please,' she replied.

Sadie was silent. Just then, Robbie brought up the tea. Sadie indicated to put it on the bedside cabinet and then made it clear that he should leave quickly.

'You *must* report it, Sister. He must be caught.'

'They,' she corrected.

'*They?*' questioned Sadie.

'Yes. There were five.'

'*What!*' Sadie exclaimed, aghast. 'A gang rape?'

'Is that what it's called?' said Hope weakly.

Sadie heard the family returning. Robbie filled Connie and Oliver in on the situation downstairs and within minutes Oliver was knocking at their door.

He whispered low.

'Sadie, come to the door.'

'Shall I come in?' he asked Sadie in undertones.

She hesitated.

'I'm not sure. She's very frightened and has been brutally raped,' she whispered. 'It's terrible. Five thugs, one after the other.'

The colour drained from Oliver's face in shock.

'*What!*'

He crept hesitatingly around the doorway.

'Sister Hope,' he whispered. She turned slightly towards him, then pulled the pillow over her head.

'I'm sorry,' she mumbled in muted tones. 'I can't talk, Reverend — Oliver.'

'This is terrible, Sister. We need the police. I'll ring them.'

'I'm not up to questions,' mumbled Hope. 'Can you leave it a little while?'

Oliver wanted to swing the law into action. This was a heinous crime and it had happened in his parish so he felt partially responsible. He was determined to seek justice for Sister Hope and root out the wicked perpetrators, but he knew he must respect her wishes and wait. She looked utterly broken.

When Oliver had gone, Sadie sat on the side of the bed.

'I want to tell you something, Hope.'

It was the first time Sadie had dropped Hope's "Sister" title. This had to be woman to woman, not woman to nun. Or was there any difference?

'Hope,' she spoke in a whisper. 'Hope, I want to tell you something,' she said again.

Hope turned her head, pulled the pillow from her face that had been shielding her and looked Sadie straight in the eyes.

'I've been raped too,' said Sadie.

Hope sat up, leaning on one elbow.

'*You* have, Sadie? When?'

'Seventeen years ago.'

Hope gasped.

'That's dreadful. Was it — was it one person?'

'It was one.'

Hope was silent. One or five — it was still a violation of the most dreadful kind.

After a pause, Hope said.

'Did you know the man who did it?'

'I knew him well,' replied Sadie.

Silence.

Then Sadie, trusting Hope completely with the information, said.

'It was my father.'

CHAPTER 12

No words passed between them, but Sadie and Hope wept a little together. Finally, Sadie held Hope's hand and stroked it gently as Hope buried her head back in the pillow, eventually falling into a fitful doze. Sadie sat upright but soon leaned her head on her arms on the side of the bed where she too drifted into a light sleep for a few minutes. With a jerk, she pulled herself back to consciousness and realised that all the while she had been concentrating on Hope and her dreadful trauma, she had not thought of her own loss of Jack. The distracting pain of Sister Hope was such that she put her own feelings aside and became engrossed in tending to her traumatised and damaged patient. Although the circumstances were dreadful, she found it comforting to be able to care for someone other than herself. In that few minutes of self-realisation, she had a brief glimpse of a way ahead out of her deep grief. Here was someone who needed her, someone with whom she had shared an intimate secret. Sadie knew at that moment that she must stay by Hope's side for as long as she was needed. She realised she was growing to love Hope.

Connie knocked at the door and crept in, placing a cup of tea by Hope's bed, with two plates — one of the delicately made egg sandwiches and the other of segmented oranges and slices of finely cut banana covered with a dusting of soft brown sugar. Hope heard her and put her hand out.

'Thank you, Connie. That's very kind. Tell your lovely boy that he can have his room back very soon. I must get back to the guest house.'

'Sister Hope,' said Connie gently but firmly. 'You'll do no such thing. We want you to cancel your guest house and stay here. We've talked to Peter and he is very happy for you to have his room — as long as you don't touch his stones,' she added, smiling. 'He's going to sleep on a camp bed in with Jamie.'

'I don't know what to say,' said Connie.

'Don't say anything. We will all be so glad to have you.'

Hope looked at Connie and saw great kindness in her face. No wonder Oliver loved her. She had something particularly special about her. There were one or two nuns and sisters like that. She regarded it as their auras — a holiness that seemed to emanate from them and around them. Connie was like that.

'Now, about the police,' said Connie. 'This terrible crime must be reported, Sister Hope. Do you feel you can manage that now if they come to your house?'

'I suppose so,' she said. 'I'm not used to talking about anything like this. I won't even know what language to use to describe what happened.' She winced again at the thought of it and despite her best intentions to suppress her feelings, tears ran down her cheeks.

'We can be here to support you,' said Sadie. 'Don't worry, I know all about how rough the police can seem.'

'Yes,' said Connie quickly, but that's only the minority. 'They will have someone specially trained to support rape victims.'

Hope turned her head away. The phrase cut through her like a knife. Was that really what she would be called? A rape victim? How on earth could she begin to explain things to the Abbess and sisters when she returned to the convent? The whole scenario was hideous.

Hope nodded in assent then buried her head under the pillow again.

That evening a policewoman and trainee, neither uniformed, arrived at the house. The policewoman, as Connie had said, specialised in supporting rape victims and her questioning was gentle and sensitive. She was clearly taken aback to see a nun, still in full regalia, and took Sadie outside the door, whispering.

'How do I address her?'

'She's Sister Hope.'

'Thank you.' The policewoman returned.

'Now, er, Sister Hope, you've clearly had a very bad experience. We're here to help you,' she said gently. 'I'm Detective Inspector Maureen Lewis and this is my assistant P.C. Angela Pearce.'

'Thank you,' replied Hope.

'Can you tell us a little about yourself so we can gather some background notes, please Sister Hope? May I ask where were you born, and I'll need the names of your parents and your current address.'

Hope took a deep breath, wincing as she felt her ribs groaning in protest at her lungs filling up more fully than from the shallow breathing adopted to protect her from pain. She didn't see the relevance of the questions but complied nevertheless.

'I was born in St. Brigit's Hostel for Fallen Girls in Northern Ireland in 1948. My mother's name was Erin O'Neill and she died in childbirth. I hardly know anything about my father except that he was a sergeant major and he paid my mother visits during, and for a while after, the second world war. He had a family already who lived in London apparently and he abandoned my mother when he found out she was pregnant.'

'That was unfortunate,' said the policewoman.

Connie and Sadie looked at each other. That was the understatement of the year, wretched man that he must have been.

Hope related her childhood as if she was reading a dull paragraph out loud from a book. She had long ago ceased to feel any emotion when speaking of it. It was ancient history now and could no longer hurt her. She failed to tell the police woman that her reason for coming to London was to track her father down and that the trail, rightly or erroneously, had led to this place. She would not tell the Lockwood family now of her reason for coming. It almost seemed irrelevant in the light of what had happened and it could only upset them.

'Your place of childhood?'

'St. Frideswide's Orphanage, Dublin.'

'And your current place of — um — '

'Work. Yes, we work.' Hope finished her sentence for her, and couldn't help raising a small smile inside herself. The Convent Sisters were working nuns rather than purely contemplative, and Hope had been on all sorts of missions of mercy within the community, including teaching at the orphanage. There was much misunderstanding about what went on behind some convent walls. Yes, the sisters all prayed and contemplated and reflected a good deal, but it certainly wasn't the whole story and the vows they took were different from those of contemplative nuns.

'I've been a sister at the Convent of St. Clare in Dublin for nearly twenty years and before that, I worked as a cleaner and teacher in the orphanage from the age of fifteen.'

Hope's head reeled as she thought of her convent and returning there. She lay back on the pillow.

'Sister Hope, let's just run through the tests you will have when you come to the hospital tomorrow, shall we? We need to catch the perpetrators of this crime and we need concrete evidence. Do you think you will be able to describe the men?'

Hope shuddered inwardly. She could remember the Mohican haircuts and the one with the slicked-back bleached white-blond hair. She could recall the stench of them — one full of aftershave, another of body odour, the blond one of sickening, pungent hair lacquer. She could feel again and again the agonising and prolonged thrusts of them but she could not recall any of their features, just putrid breath coming from each of them as they helped themselves to her body.

Hope shut her eyes as the policewoman outlined the course of action. Each statement, although gently delivered, was as if Hope was being hit in the solar plexus. The phrases raced around her head like a diabolical litany: internal examinations, swabs, specimens, forensic tests, signs of sexually transmitted infections, etc. etc. — the list seemed endless. All these years she had kept herself a virgin, having vowed solemnly and sincerely to be the bride of Christ alone. Now, in one fell swoop all that had gone. How would she look God, the Abbess, the other nuns or herself in the eyes ever again? She would rather she had been brutally assaulted with fists or knives than violated in this way.

The police left. They had both been kind and gentle, but they were adamant that she needed without fail to be at the station by eight o'clock the next day and please not to bath or wash down below. A nurse would take a vaginal swab first thing in the morning.

When they had gone, Oliver came up to her room and put his head round the door.

'Sister, If it is all-right with you, Connie and I will go round to your guest house, settle up with the landlady and pack your things so that you have everything here; would that be in order?'

Even though Hope knew that Oliver was a kind and honest man, she nevertheless pulled the sheets and blankets up to her chin over her habit. The sight of a man was making her feel like retching. She turned towards the wall. Sadie understood and gently ushered him out.

'I'll get Connie, Sister Hope,' he said. 'You just relax here with Sadie.'

Hope gave Connie her key gratefully, saying.

'Tell Revd. Oliver 'Thank you' please. I didn't mean to be rude.'

Connie understood and said as much with a gentle stroke of Hope's hand.

It was going to be a long time, Hope knew before she could look at a man in the eyes again with any degree of comfort again, whether he be a priest or pauper.

CHAPTER 13

When Connie and Oliver arrived home from the guest house, having settled everything with the rather disgruntled landlady, they found to their relief that Hope was finally deeply asleep. Sadie was still by her side. Connie took the suitcase into the double bedroom and Oliver went to see the children, who had been very patient over the whole episode.

Connie opened her jewel box where she kept particularly treasured items. There was a beaded brooch that had been her mother's and a plain tie pin that her dead brother James had worn for school. Connie took out something wrapped in several layers of tissue paper. In it was her Rosary that she had kept from her days as a Roman Catholic. She treasured it, and had found it an invaluable lifeline to prayer, but when she married Oliver, an Anglican priest, she converted to Anglicanism so quietly tucked it away.

Connie fingered the rosary lovingly, spent a little time with it, then wrapped it in fresh tissue paper and put it in an envelope. She wrote a letter to Sister Hope and tucked the letter and the envelope in the suitcase. Her heart ached for Hope and she knew that it was a long journey towards inner healing that Hope alone could travel. Connie had seen the suffering of her own sister Sadie which psychologically affected her life. Their father's abuse was a stain on both their lives. Connie also was used mercilessly as a young child by their father and as a consequence had brought into adulthood a fear of sex. To her, the sex act until that time had seemed in her mind to be something simply to be endured. It was only through Oliver's patient and special love and understanding and the fact that Connie adored him, that she found herself both healed and released. She knew that the sex act would not be a practical issue for Sister Hope as she had made a vow of chastity, but the pain and the memory and the psychological damage done to her would last a lifetime. Her Rosary was the most precious thing Connie could give Hope, and even if Hope never used it, Connie knew it would be accepted in the spirit in which it was given — a gift of love with a promise of prayer.

Connie saw the children and then went to Sadie, who had fallen asleep in the chair next to Hope. She put the suitcase at the end of Hope's bed and gently shook Sadie awake.

'Sadie, go to bed. You'll be exhausted. I'll listen out for Hope. You've been wonderful the way you've looked after her. I'll bring a hot chocolate up.'

Sadie looked at Hope and saw that she was finally peaceful.

'Thanks, Connie. We can remember what it was like, can't we? But this is so much worse. At least our father loved us in a strange kind of way, even though he abused us. What happened to Hope was brutal and animal.'

'But our father was in a position of trust, Sadie. Don't forget that. It's all dreadful, isn't it?'

Sadie nodded in agreement and slowly went upstairs to her room. Suddenly her maternal sorrow crashed in. No Jack, she thought heavily. No Jack to go and check on or pull the duvet up around. No Jack peacefully snoring a little. No Jack asking for a drink or needing the loo at some ungodly hour. Simply, no Jack. Sadie wept with loss and fatigue. She was not particularly a believer in God despite Olive and Connie's gentle discussions and the light that shone out of both of them; nevertheless, she thanked God that for a little while there had been some respite from her deep grief. Once more she promised herself that she would try and look outwards more towards others and that in its turn would lead to a forgetfulness of self.

Hope woke at three-thirty a.m. She hurt all over and one of her head wounds was still bleeding slightly. She lay in the darkness for a few minutes thinking hard, then got to her feet with the resolve of someone who has hatched a plan and is intent on seeing it through, defying the pain that screamed out, 'Rest!'

She couldn't endure the thought of any more prodding down below that the tests and examinations would inevitably involve. Neither could she cope with more questions. She had given the police all the relevant details — how many men, rough descriptions of them, where she was when it happened and so on. There was nothing more to say. Regarding sexual transmission of disease, she had prayed for healing for many others, and seen quietly transforming results. She would pray with fasting for healing for herself, that she would be protected from any grizzly outcome of the rape. Wasn't rape enough on its own for her to endure? Would her loving God test her yet more? Even as she was asking herself these questions, she knew that her answers were self-made and that, as ever, God would move in His mysterious way. Whatever the outcome, she was prepared to trust him completely to protect her.

She washed very carefully everywhere that hurt, and with relief found clean underwear in her suitcase. Straightening herself down, she brushed her hair and knew, with a tinge of regret this time, that within twenty-four hours it would be shaved off again. Her coif and veil were damaged but passable. She found her journal in her suitcase, tore a page out and wrote:

Dear lovely family. Thank you more than I can ever say for your wonderful kindness. I will write and explain. I will never forget you. God bless and protect you all. Sister Hope O'Neill.

She crept downstairs, worried that either Toby the dog or Rosy, who the family had said was a very light sleeper, would hear her, but she managed to reach the front door unobserved. She had seen when exploring the area that there was an underground station servicing Southwark called Borough on the Northern Line. That would take her into London and then it was another short underground journey to Euston. She thought about the difference in her spirits now from when she had arrived: then, full of hope and excitement, now, filled with shame and dread.

The sky was just lightening as she gingerly opened the front door, and anyone out at that time of the morning would have seen the figure of a nun dressed in full regalia wheeling a suitcase and hurrying as best she could, with her head down, and moving nervously past Borough Road Market. Already there was activity there, with stall sellers unloading their goods from parked lorries and refuse lorries collecting huge piles of garbage from the various entrances. For Hope, it was an act of courage simply to pass the spot where the rape had happened. She prayed her way forward until she reached the underground station.

She was dreading going back to Ireland yet knew that she should inform the Abbess of what had happened. She was sure it disqualified her from staying in Holy Orders. She was now soiled goods. Soiled goods indeed, yes, imperfect, ruined, violated, unclean — any of those words would be suitable to describe her now, she thought; *Sister Hope*, who no longer deserved that name. Dante's Inferno would be more appropriate: *Abandon All Hope.*

She had come to England in search of her father to satisfy her curiosity and to tell him how ashamed she was to be the daughter of someone who could abandon her mother so easily. At the Convent, Hope always lit a candle daily in memory of the mother she had never known. Its flickering light called Hope to pray and remember her and the insults her mother bore when her lover if he could be called that, abandoned her. She identified vividly now with her mother in the abuse she had suffered and the depth of despair to which she had been reduced.

The longing in Hope to have known her mother was carved deep into her being. She had met many children and adults who had never known their mothers. These children and adults carried their sorrow and loss like a quiet, invisible badge that singled them out by their deep inexpressible yearnings. Hope yearned to have her mother to talk to now.

The early underground train was eerily empty. It whisked through the darkness, stopping only briefly at stations where one or two people boarded. She knew she should have waited to explain properly to the family to whom she owed so much, but the thought of any one of them trying to persuade her of a different course of action was too much for her to cope with. She knew they would be disappointed in her, but that was a little less important than her need to escape the ordeal that had threatened to overwhelm her later that morning. She doubted she would ever see them again once the grey granite walls had swallowed her up on her return and made demands on her that would, fortunately, take all her energy.

Arriving at Euston, she was lucky to catch the early train to Liverpool. It was only when she had settled in a carriage in a corner seat all to herself that she broke down and silently wept all the way to Birmingham.

CHAPTER 14

Sadie went quietly downstairs to make two cups of tea — one for herself and one for Hope. It was very early, but something had woken her. The hole left by Jack's death always threatened to overwhelm her in the early morning when she would have been busy with personal chores with him. This morning had a different focus. She crept downstairs from her flat with the tea, knocked gently at Hope's door and went quietly in.

Sister Hope had gone.

Sadie saw immediately the note on the bed. She woke Oliver and Connie, who were already stirring, and showed them. Oliver leapt out of bed.

'I'm going to see if I can catch her up! She mustn't go so soon after such a shock. She's so fragile at the moment. We can see her through this, can't we?'

'And she really must have those tests,' said Connie.

'I'll drive up to Euston. The roads will be quiet,' said Oliver, dressing at top speed.

He grabbed a few sips of the tea that was meant for Hope and disappeared out of the front door, pulling his sweater on as he went. He drove fast, breaking every speed limit in the quiet early morning city, and jumping two sets of red lights. The only other time he had done that was when third baby Rosy insisted on putting in a dramatically quick appearance and was threatening to be born in the car on the way to the hospital. This morning, Oliver parked the car on double yellow lines at Euston Station and raced across to the correct platform just in time to see the five-twenty-five a.m. train to Liverpool Lime Street making its sluggish way slowly out of the station.

He stood staring and pushed the over-long quiff of his dark hair back out of his eyes. Damn! They had no address for Hope either, he remembered, but perhaps simply "Sister Hope, The Convent of St. Clare, Dublin" would reach her. He even thought, momentarily, of catching the next train to Liverpool and stopping her there but realised this would be folly.

'What's the point? This is what she *wants* to do.'

Oliver couldn't help but feel a little disappointed. Could they have done anything more for Hope? But it was less than twenty-four hours since the rape so he wasn't sure what else they could have done in that time. And what had made Hope suddenly go?

Connie had shared with him the descriptions Sister Hope had given of the rapists. She recounted how Hope could remember two of them with Mohican hairstyles and a third with, as she described it "slicked back bleached white-blond hair". His task now was to see if he could track down the offending lads. Yes, it was the police's task, but it happened in his parish on his watch, so to speak, and the least he could do for Sister Hope was bring the offenders to the notice of the police. Maybe Robbie, in the course of his youth outreach work on the streets had come across them?

Oliver walked slowly back to his car, cursed that there was a parking ticket and knew he had a job ahead of him. Mostly, though, he was sad for Sister Hope. He had noticed that a lovely light seemed to radiate from her. He sensed it even when he was first introduced to her, much as he had noticed coming from Connie when he had met her as a young Nannie. Just think how Sadie and his troubled son Peter had responded to her! Sadie had been able to forget her sorrow for a little while and Peter — miracle of miracles — Peter had given up his precious pristine room for her. That must be saying something about Sister Hope and the warmth she generated from two damaged people.

Oliver concluded that both his wife and Sister Hope seemed special women in his eyes and there was definitely something similar about them. There was some kind of physical likeness that Oliver had noticed at the Sunday lunch table. It was to do with the way they both smiled. But it was more than that, decided Oliver. It was something indefinable — a goodness that seemed to shine out of both of them. Connie had often talked about her mother Rosa in this kind of way as she endured the slings and arrows of Albert Connors and his behaviour.

He remembered again Mary Baker Eddy's writing, which he had recalled when he was falling in love with Connie:

When angels visit we do not hear the rustle of wings, nor feel the feathery touch of the breast of a dove, but we know their presence by the love they create.

CHAPTER 15

Bruce Connors was thoughtful. He hadn't visited his sister Sadie since Jack's funeral, which he knew was remiss of him. Bruce did not always find Sadie easy. She was forthright and, in his eyes, had become rather hard, with a sharp and unpredictable tongue. He assumed it was because of Jack and her tigress-like care for him, defending him in every difficult situation. Who wouldn't toughen up with that challenge? He remembered with pleasure, however, a sunlit day in their garden after his father's funeral, when Sadie brought Jack round for the first time. Kitty, their daughter, was three years old and a ball of energy. The way Jack and she related to each other had delighted everyone. His deformities and strange little ways were irrelevant to Kitty, who collapsed in a fit of giggles whenever Jack told his quirky rhymes. Bruce remembered how Sadie's face shone as she watched her son throwing his head back and peeling with laughter at his own jokes as he struck up a firm friendship with his feisty little cousin.

Kitty, now fifteen, had been very shocked and extremely angry and saddened by Jack's sudden death. For the funeral she made a cushion out of his favourite sweets and chocolate bars instead of the usual flowers, and wrote a heartfelt poem, insisting both were buried with him so that could "eat his way to heaven". She had cried copiously at the funeral and for forty-eight hours afterwards, then picked herself up, seemed to pull herself together and carried on with life as before.

Seeing Kitty's recovery, Bruce realised afresh the resilience and optimism of youth and was glad. Kitty herself had a close brush with death when she was five. She had been diagnosed with childhood leukaemia and was saved by a bone marrow transplant from Bruce's body, so their bond was particularly close. Kitty was a joyful teenager now, academically bright, with creative arts gifts in abundance like her mother Clara, and was a treasure to her parents. Bruce knew that sooner or later the problems that often characterised the friction between adolescent girls and their fathers might rear their ugly heads, but for now, his relationship was close and happy and he basked in it.

Kitty came into the kitchen as Bruce was making sandwiches for Clara for her sustenance during the run-up rehearsals to her big opening night in the West End. He was intensely proud of Clara. She was not easy to live with. She could be temperamental, moody and offhand. Bruce knew she was selfish; Clara knew it too, but somehow after a very shaky start, with infidelity on Clara's part due perhaps to Bruce's early impotence, the marriage now worked and both partners seemed to be happy with the other. Kitty, chestnut-haired and lovely looking, with an hour-class figure, was the apple of her father's eye. Clara, although not blessed with an abundance of maternal instinct, without a doubt loved

Kitty but left most of the day-to-day caring and practicalities of having a daughter to Bruce.

'Dad, me and Beccs want to go to Borough Road Market this afternoon. Is that OK with you?'

'As long as you bring me back some of those Pontefract Cakes!' he replied. 'I'll give you the money. Here you are,' he said, delving into his pocket. 'Take this.' He gave her a five-pound note. Treat you and Beccs to a MacDonalds or something.'

'Oh *thanks,* Dad!'

'Bruce, you spoil that girl!' said Clara, then she went into her leather shoulder bag and brought out another fiver.

'Here you are,' she said. 'Get yourselves a hot chocolate with cream afterwards.'

'Oh *Mum!*' Kitty said, her eyes shining. 'Now that's what I call good parenting!'

She whisked out of the door and left them both smiling.

'I should think I'll be back by eight o'clock, Dad,' she called.

'No later,' called Bruce back, 'because it's pretty dark by then.'

'O.K.' With that she was gone, slamming the front door with joyful abandon as she went.

'That's one happy daughter,' said Clara.

'We *are* lucky,' said Bruce. 'When you think of that little shorn lamb full of chemotherapy and given less than a twenty percent chance of survival.'

113

'Bye Bruce,' she said, unable to cope with his sudden display of sentimentality and pecking him on the cheeks. 'Thanks for the sandwiches. They'll be life saver.'

'Bye Clara. Hope it goes well.'

Bruce climbed the stairs to his home workshop, which was a converted room at the top of the house. He had developed his considerable carpentry skills and built up a thriving business with four partners and a couple of secretaries. He still worked mainly from home but had a central workshop and office just out of Richmond upon Thames where the family lived.

Kitty met her friend Rebecca at the underground station to journey to Borough Road station for the market. Both girls loved it there, and their particular joy was rummaging through various bric-a-brac stalls, finding quirky belts and scarves. Thanks to mum and dad they would round their afternoon off with a Macdonald's Burger and a hot chocolate with cream and marshmallows on the top. This was their idea of heaven.

After a longer than usual browse, they were rather late leaving the market, having lost track of time. The market was beginning to close down and the place took on a different character in the dusk. The girls had to walk from the market exit along to McDonalds near London Bridge — about a five-minute saunter. A group of lads stood at the entrance to the market indolently kicking litter and smoking. They watched the girls. At a signal from one of them, they began slowly to follow them. The girls were nearly at the entrance to MacDonalds when the five lads caught up.

'We're coming in with you,' said one of them. 'Fancy a bit of company, darlin?'

The girls ignored him.

'Hey, don't be like that,' said another. 'We can give you a good time.'

'You gonna buy us a burger then, sweetheart?'

'Nice goodies,' said another, coming too close to Kitty and twirling her bag. 'Watcha bought?'

The girls tried to enter McDonalds', but the lads pushed roughly in front of them, barricading the way, their backs to the door.

'We thought you'd like a bit of fun,' said a fourth. 'Come on,' he said, tugging at Rebecca's jacket. 'Come for a laugh.'

The proprietor had seen the intimidation going on. He pulled the door open sharply, and the lads fell backwards into the shop.

'Get off my premises or I'm calling the Fuzz,' he shouted. 'Don't you do nothin' to these girls! You're a load of louts. Now *go away! Scarper!*' he bellowed, red-faced, looking as though any second he might have a heart attack.

The lads looked at his face, then at the customers who were all watching, and slowly and sullenly moved away.

'Keep your hair on, mate. We was only havin' a butchers.'

They shuffled off, pretending to be unconcerned, but alarmed by the mention of the police. They knew they were on the watch list of the law.

Kitty and Rebecca nervously made their way to the counter. Unbeknown to them, one of the lads, with bleached white-blond hair slicked back, had slid into the restaurant when the rest left. He stood eyeing the girls as they placed their orders. His eyes rested on Kitty.

''Ere. Let me,' he said, pulling a five-pound note out of his denim jacket pocket. 'I'll make it up to ya. We didn't mean any 'arm. Just a bit of fun. Now. What will you be having?'

He pushed the five-pound note down on the counter.

'Go and find a seat and I'll bring it over,' the lad said.

The girls moved away and found a seat, slightly bewildered by the lad. They couldn't work him out. He had a friendly face, but...

'What do you reckon, Beccs?' said Kitty. 'He's quite nice, isn't he?'

'He obviously fancies you, Kitty. Better watch it!' said Beccs, smiling. She knew Kitty was the envy of all her school friends with her stunning looks.

'Don't be daft!' laughed Kitty. 'He's much older than us.'

'So?' replied Beccs.

The lad returned with his tray piled high with burgers and drinks.

'There,' he said. 'That's to make up for what happened back there.'

'Thanks,' said Kitty. 'We don't even know your name. I'm Kitty and my friend is Rebecca — Beccs for short.'

'Gary — that's me,' he replied.

'Thanks, Gary,' both girls said in unison and they all laughed.

The burgers went down well. After a while, Beccs excused herself and went to the ladies toilet. Gary immediately homed in on Kitty.

'How old are you, Kit?'

'Sixteen,' Kitty lied.

'Kitty, I'd really like to go out with you. You're nice. Classy girl. Meet me at the market next Sunday?'

'But it's shut on a Sunday.'

'That's the point. We can have a nice wander round, just the two of us.' He eyed Kitty greedily. Kitty had never had a boyfriend and was flattered by his advances.

'OK but don't mention it to Beccs. I'll have to think up something to tell Mum and Dad. They'll wonder why I'm coming here on a Sunday.'

'Oh just tell 'em your friends are having a party in McDonald's.' The lie tripped off his tongue. Kitty blushed with pleasure.

'Yes, that'll do nicely!

'Four-thirty outside here. Next Sunday then,' said Gary. 'I must go. Gotta meet someone. Say goodbye to Beccs for me.' He pecked her on the cheek and was already undressing her in his mind.

Beccs arrived back at the table.

'Where's Gary?'

'Oh, he had to go.'

'That's a bit sudden,' said Beccs, slightly hurt. 'He could have waited to say goodbye to me. Anyway, Kitty, it was you he was after. Clear as daylight. I think it might

117

be a good thing he's not hanging around. There was something a bit shifty about him.'

'Course he doesn't fancy me,' said Kitty, blushing, and in one fell swoop demonstrated the art of female deception. 'Come on, mustn't be late, Beccs.'

With that, they walked to London Bridge Underground station, Beccs happily thinking about what she would wear her newly purchased belt with, and Kitty in her mind already scheming a way to manipulate her parents.

CHAPTER 16

While Kitty was out, Bruce decided to visit the Lockwood household and see Sadie in particular. He realised that he could have accompanied the girls on their underground journey to the market if he had thought of it in time, but then decided he would be cramping their style. It would be lovely to see his sister Connie as well and the children. He had a slightly tense relationship with Oliver, although respecting and admiring him. There was history there over Clara but it was now water under the bridge.

He wondered how Sadie was after losing Jack and her visible and intense expression of grief at his funeral. He felt again a pang of guilt. Why did he not have a better relationship with her? Was it him or was it her, or was it, as he eventually decided, just a complex chemistry between them that siblings could sometimes have. He stopped at a flower stall and bought Sadie twelve vivid multicoloured carnations — red, yellow, orange and there were even two blue ones. Clara would have hated them and called them "tasteless" but she wasn't there so Bruce bought them with impunity.

Rosy as ever flung her arms around Uncle Bruce and Peter hovered in the hall wanting Bruce to take notice of him but not having the confidence or social skills to greet him.

'Hi, Pete boy. How you doing?' said Bruce, going up to give him a light and friendly punch in the chest. Peter backed away immediately from the physical contact but smiled broadly.

'How long are you staying, Uncle Bruce?' he asked.

'Till I get kicked out,' teased Bruce.

'Lovely to see you, bro,' said Connie. 'Cup of tea?'

'Love one in a few minutes, Con. I'll take these up to Sadie first. I presume she's upstairs? How is she?'

'Well, there's been quite a lot to take her mind off poor Jack just now. I'll fill you in when you come down, unless Sadie does first.'

Bruce bounded up the stairs three at a time, watched in awe by Rosy and Peter. To them, Bruce was a tall and mighty hero figure with his strong physique and athletic ability.

James came out of his room to greet his uncle.

'Hiya Jim. Howdy pal,' said Bruce in an American accent.

'Howdy partner,' replied James. 'I'm damn well fine splendid!'

'Now, now, language Jimmy boy,' said Bruce laughing and carried on to the top landing. His eldest nephew was so *easy*. He knocked on Sadie's door.

Sadie came to the door looking dishevelled and sleepy.

'Hi, Bruce. Where've you been? You could have come a bit sooner' she said reproachfully. 'Thought my little brother had forgotten all about me.'

'Here you are, Sadie' said Bruce, thrusting the gaudy flowers in her hand. Sadie looked at them and was about to make a derogatory remark, then thought better of it, simply commenting that she had never seen blue carnations before.

'Thanks, Brucey. Nice of you to bring the flowers. Cup of tea?'

'Thanks, Sadie. How have you been?'

'Oh you know,' said Sadie. 'The hole inside me will never mend, Bruce.'

'I know, I can imagine, Sadie. It's awful. So sorry. He was the most wonderful chap. We'll all miss him terribly.'

'He was, and we will,' replied Sadie quietly.

'Connie said there'd been a lot going on. Fill me in?'

Sadie found she wanted to tell her brother about Sister Hope. Bruce had always been gentle apart from the very occasional display of fiery temper if provoked — too gentle for his own good, Sadie thought, with that witch of a woman bossing him around and taking him for a ride. Sadie could rely on him to understand, she knew. She found herself filling Bruce in with every detail: how the family had first met Hope, the Sunday lunch conversations, Hope finally setting off for home and then the pained call through the letter box. She told of her shock at realising that Hope had been raped by five brutal young men, talked about the subsequent visit from the police and finally the trauma of Hope's decision to leave without telling anyone.

Sadie looked at Bruce. She saw tears in his eyes as she related how this innocent and holy woman had been violated. Bruce and the sex act had always had a complex relationship thanks to how he had witnessed Connie as a small child being abused by their father. What Sadie did not know was that it had taken several years into his marriage before he found his way out of his impotence. Now, hearing of the aggression and violence inflicted upon an innocent victim he recoiled in horror and suddenly became deeply distressed. He could not control the tears and felt angry with himself for it, but something had touched a memory that he had chosen to bury long ago.

Sadie realised afresh the damage that had been done to him her brother. The sins of the fathers were in Albert Connors' case, very grave and far-reaching. She went across to Bruce and put her arms around him and stayed there.

'I know, Brucey, I know,' she said softly.

Through the most unplanned of conversations, both older sister and younger brother sensed the rift was beginning to heal between them. Their dark and painful memories of childhood became intertwined in that moment. Sadie witnessed from her brother's tears just how painful his memories were and the information she had shared about Hope's rape had clearly touched a deep chord in him. She saw afresh the pain he carried through life, the legacy of witnessing the activities of their paedophiliac father. Her own memories were black and dreadful, but the gift that came from the direst of circumstances had been Jack.

'What's happening to the case now?' asked Bruce finally.

Sadie slowly let go of Bruce.

'The police are onto it, but as Hope failed to turn up at the police station the victim of the crime is deemed absent so the case has lost its impetus,' said Sadie. 'Bastards are going to get away with it,' she said bitterly. 'Except good old Robbie is doing his best to track them down. As you know Robbie has loads of contact with the youth of Southwark and beyond and he's asking around and doing a reconnoitre himself. Hope gave a sketchy description of the vile bullies.'

'It makes you think nowhere is safe, doesn't it?' said Bruce. Where exactly did the rape take place?' he asked.

'Just inside Borough Road Market.'

'That's where Kitty is. I must get her.'

'Oh Bruce, she'll be OK. You can't clip her wings because of one incident. She's a sensible girl. Don't worry. Come on, let's go downstairs and see the others.'

She stopped Bruce at the door and gave him a brief kiss on the cheek.

'Brucey — thanks for the carnations. They're beautiful and the colours will cheer the room up. I'll enjoy arranging them. They're a lovely thought — and it's great to see you. Come again soon?'

'Absolutely, I will,' said Bruce, meaning it and pushing her thick hair off her face. 'You're still a good looker, Sadie. Love you.'

'Love you Brucey,' she replied.

CHAPTER 17

Kitty was unsure how to broach the subject of going again to Southwark Market so soon after her last visit. It had seemed so easy when Gary was telling her what to say, but now she was back in the home environment, where she was trusted and loved, she found it hard deliberately to lie. She couldn't ever remember doing so before to her parents. She decided that Clara was the better one to approach in the first instant.

Clara came home from her all-day rehearsal at about eight o'clock, having had a nine-thirty a.m. start. It was a week until opening night and this was the pre-dress run.

'How did it go, Clara?' asked Bruce.

'It's touch and go whether we pull it off. It's nowhere near ready.'

'You say that before every performance, big or little.'

'But this time I *really* mean it.'

Bruce smiled inwardly. He'd heard that every time before as well.

His wife drooped herself over the green velvet sofa. Even though Clara looked so tired, Bruce thought yet again how beautiful she was. He went up and kissed her on the lips.

'Not now, Bruce. Sorry, but I just need space'

'Would you like a drink? Whisky?'

'Yes please, with ice and lemon.'

Kitty waited till Clara had had several sips of her drink and Bruce had left the room to serve up Clara's supper.

'Did it not go well, Mum?'

'Oh the usual, Kit. It's always chaos at the first dress rehearsal.'

'Mum, can I ask you something?'

Now. Say it nonchalantly as a throw-away line or put in the heavy persuasion? Kitty was unsure.

'What is it, Kitty? You're not usually lost for words. What are you squirming around for?'

'Mum I've been invited to a McDonald's party at London Bridge. Next Sunday afternoon. It's a friend's birthday.'

'Which friend, Kit?'

'You don't know her. She's a friend of Beccs. From her old school.'

Oh, how the lie tripped off her tongue so terrifyingly easily!

'Sounds nice. You are coming to my opening night the day before, aren't you?'

'Course I am, Mum. Can't wait' replied Kitty.

'You'd better check it with Dad, because I'll probably be called in for a post opening-night debriefing.'

Bruce came in with Clara's supper on a tray and one red rose in a vase.

'Here you are, Clara. Home-made Lasagne. Hope it's O.K'

'Thanks, Brucey. No salad?'

'Sorry darling, no. The lettuce had wilted in the fridge.'

'Tomato Ketchup?'

Bruce disappeared to the kitchen. Clara's wish was his command. It was almost as if unconsciously he was spending his whole life atoning for the early years of his marriage when he was such a disappointment to Clara. He came back with the sauce.

'I'll put it on for you. All over?'

'Yes please, Bruce. It's a wee bit on the dry side. The rose is nice' she smiled. 'Thanks Bruce.'

'Dad. Next Sunday I've been invited to a McDonald's party. Is that OK with you.'

'I don't see why not. Where is it and what time is it?'

'London Bridge. You know, it's the one near Borough Road Market. 4.30 onwards.'

Bruce froze. Borough Road Market on a Sunday at dusk. It had an ominous ring.

'You can, Kitty, but I'll come and collect you by eight o'clock in the car.'

It was Kitty's time to freeze. How was she going to manage that with Gary? Instinctively she thought it would be a bad idea for Bruce and Gary to meet, and anyway, her lie would be found out in one fell swoop.

'O.K. Dad. Thanks. But there's no need. I can get the underground. There's bound to be someone else coming back this way.'

'NO Kitty' said Bruce emphatically. I will collect you. End of story.'

'OK Dad. Thanks.' Kitty left the room.

'You do fuss over that girl, Bruce. Why can't she come home on her own?'

Bruce filled her in sketchily about the rape of Sister Hope at Borough Road Market.

'They probably saw her as a challenge' said Clara, 'A virgin and all that.'

'Well, presumably our daughter's a virgin, so wouldn't she be just such a challenge?'

'OK Bruce. Point taken. But she doesn't wear a nun's outfit and advertise the fact, does she?'

'No, but she wears a ridiculously short mini skirt.'

Clara raised her eyes to heaven. Bruce was *so* over-protective.

'It's up to you if you want to trundle up to London on a Sunday Night. I think it's over-the-top but you're her father'

'I am' said Bruce, 'and all I care about is that our daughter is kept safe.'

'Yes of course' said Clara. 'Brucey, fetch me another whisky, please, and some more Lasagne' she said, holding out her plate. 'You'll see. She'll be fine. She's got to grow up some time.'

Bruce nodded but was filled with a sense of danger for his daughter, having heard what happened to Sister Hope.

CHAPTER 18

Bruce set out early that evening to meet Kitty, unable to subdue his anxiety. He wished he hadn't heard about the rape of Sister Hope. It was now dusk so within half an hour would be dark. Bruce wanted to avoid Kitty seeing him hovering anxiously in his car. He had no wish to cramp her style, so parked opposite Borough Road Market, intending to walk to London Bridge at the allotted time to collect Kitty and then walk back together to the car.

He sat reading the thick sports section of the Sunday paper and soon became completely absorbed in the cricket score details — a passion of his. Had Bruce looked up from his paper he would have seen in the distance a youth with blond hair half-dragging his daughter Kitty along.

'Come on, Kitty, Kitty,' he mimicked as if calling a cat. 'You didn't think it was just about having a McDonalds, did you? I need a good reward for paying for you — and the other night. Bet you haven't done it before, 'ave you?' He made a gross gesture. 'I'll show you what it's all about, you little Jezebel. Beggin' for it, in't you?'

'Please, Gary. I don't want to. *Please* let me go. My dad will be along in a minute and then your game'll be up. I didn't reckon on any of this. Anyway, I'm under age.'

'You told me you was sixteen,' sneered Gary as he dragged his unwilling victim along.

'Well, I'm not. I'm *nearly* sixteen. I'm fifteen now and under age.'

'Even better,' said Gary with a leer. 'I love 'em young and virgins.'

He kept dragging her along until they reached the spot in the shadows where Sister Hope had been raped. He pushed Kitty hard against the wall and began kissing her violently. Then he ripped her blouse open. She struggled and kicked, bringing her knee up towards his crotch, but he had the whole procedure down to a fine art.

'Ha! Easier than that Nun woman. Not so many layers,' he said as he worked his way down. He then reached under Kitty's skirt and began pulling her briefs down and then quick as a flash, unzipped his trousers.

Somehow she managed to let out the most enormous yell as he pulled her skirt up round her waist.

'No! Gary. No! Help! Help! Someone come!'

Bruce heard the cry and leapt out of the car and looked up the road. About thirty yards away, he made out his daughter pinned against the wall and a brutish lout forcing himself on her. Running at the speed of light, he reached the pair and with enormous force pulled Gary off and started punching him violently to the ground. Quick as a flash, while avoiding as many blows as he could, Gary pulled out a knife from his inside jacket pocket and brandished it at Bruce, trying to slash him as he was being pummelled.

'Dad, dad, leave it, Dad,' cried Kitty. 'He's going to kill you.'

'Not — before — I — kill — him,' panted Bruce, each word accompanied by another punch at Gary. Kitty cringed in a corner sobbing.

'It's all my fault,' she wept.

Suddenly the dynamic changed as Robbie from the vicarage appeared apparently out of nowhere. He threw himself on Bruce and tugged him off Gary. Once standing, Bruce rushed to Kitty and threw his arms protectively around her while she sobbed into his sweater.

'Sorry dad, sorry. It's all my fault.'

Robbie started to haul Gary up on his feet. Gary was bleeding on his head from Bruce's blows, but strong enough to point the knife in Robbie's face.

'Not a good idea, mate,' said Robbie as he pulled him up. 'You're in enough shit as it is, without adding GBH with Intent to the list.'

But Gary lashed wildly out and with one mighty effort dug the knife into Robbie's shoulder. Robbie yelped loudly but continued to hang on to Gary. After a minute, though, the pain and debilitation got the better of Robbie and he sank to the ground. Gary raced away, and Bruce went to chase him.

'No, no, Dad. Please don't! Let him go. We can report him later. Robbie needs an ambulance.'

But Bruce's blood was up and he was intent on capturing the lout who had been molesting his daughter. Kitty knelt down to Robbie who was bleeding profusely and beginning to look ashen.

'I'll run for help, Robbie. Stay as still as you can. Don't attempt to move.'

Kitty dashed over to the pub across the road and a few yards down. 'Get an ambulance. Quick! To opposite' she shouted. Then she dashed back to Robbie.

'It's OK, Robbie. You'll be OK. You were a hero coming to our defence.'

'I know that Gary,' Robbie whispered weakly. 'He's big trouble. How did you get mixed up with him, Kit?'

But before she could offer any kind of an explanation, he had passed out. Kitty sat on the pavement cradling his head and trying to soothe him. Robbie had been a part of her life for all of her life — ever since he had moved into the vicarage at the invitation of the Connors.

A police car arrived quickly, followed by an ambulance. Kitty was asked for a description of Gary. As soon as she had described the hair, one of the police said.

'Ah Yes, Gary Johnson. We've had our eye on him for a while now. Which way did he head off?'

'My dad is chasing him. Gary's got a knife.'

'We can see that, love,' said the policeman eyeing the pool of blood that was painting the pavement red.

One of the police called for back-up, instructing them to go and tour round London Bridge area looking for Gary and Bruce.

'He was really nice to begin with,' said Kitty. 'Kind and good at chatting.'

'If it was Gary Johnson the chatting up had just one ulterior motive, love. Did he, did you — sorry to ask you this love, but did he — um — actually have sex with you — you know, get inside? Sorry to ask.'

'He was about to,' said Kitty.

Bruce arrived back, panting wildly.

'He disappeared at London Bridge. I lost him completely. No idea where he went.' Bruce pushed his damp thick brown hair out of his eyes.

'The bastard was within a second or two of raping my daughter,' said Bruce. 'I saw it all. If I hadn't arrived when I did he would have raped her.'

'Who started the fight between you, Sir?'

'I had to drag him off my daughter.'

'Did you punch him in the face?'

'In order to protect Kitty here. She was about to be raped.'

Kitty looked at her father. He was generally a kind man with an enviable strength of character but his Achilles Heel was known to be his occasional red mist temper flare-ups which had once or twice led him into trouble. Kitty saw how Bruce was losing control in defence of her and thought he would have pummelled Gary to death had not Robbie intervened.

Robbie was being put on a stretcher and was gradually coming round.

He whispered, barely audibly, 'Someone needs to locate Gary. He took one hell of a beating.'

What was Robbie like! Here he was, thought Kitty, worrying about the attacker who had just stabbed him hard in the shoulder. Most people would have said, 'Make sure you get the bastard!'

The Paramedics tended to Robbie and then whisked him off to the hospital, their blue lights flashing as they raced through the streets of Southwark.

Robbie had learnt kindness the hard way. Brought up in a run-down state children's home virtually from birth, he was appeared very tough and hard and unable to receive any kind of love when Oliver first met him in the Church Army Hostel. Both his parents had been heavily involved in a life of crime, locked up more times than they had been free.

Little by little Oliver had worked on Robbie, showing him love in the face of aggression and surliness, and turning the other cheek at much of his abuse. Eventually, slowly, a remarkable change began to take place in Robbie. So great was the transformation that Oliver became known as rather a miracle worker. Oliver, however, believed that if it was anything to do with him, then it was the spirit of God working within him.

When he came out of prison after his two year sentence for Grievous Bodily Harm with Intent, having stabbed the cook at the Church Army Hostel in defence of Jack, Oliver and Connie gave him a home in their vicarage. In the fullness of time Oliver offered him the post of Youth Worker within the parish and it was this heartbeat for the youth of Southwark that prompted Robbie to ask someone to see if Gary was all-right.

Connie had spent many hours into the night over the last few years chatting with Robbie. Having been so damaged herself as a child, she could empathise with him on a deep level. The difference, however, between their upbringings was that Connie's mother had loved her fervently. Robbie only knew that his mother abandoned him and went her own inebriated way. Connie had been sexually abused by her father, but Robbie was discarded by his. The cruelty and damage inflicted on each of them as children was very considerable. Connie spoke of having felt guilty and responsible for her father's actions. Robbie felt the same — not worth staying for — guilty at not being the child his parents might have been able to love, abandoned by them. Connie gradually persuaded Robbie, through the influence of her loving and forgiving nature, that there was a better path to follow towards healing than the one of anger and aggression, and it was about finding ways in the heart to develop forgiving and loving attitudes. That in turn led to a gradual realisation, Connie had said, of one's worth as a child of God. Robbie was attracted to the path of healing and inner change mainly through the love and example that shone out of both Oliver and Connie.

Robbie had twenty-two stitches in his wound and stayed in the hospital for four days. Meanwhile, Bruce was interviewed by the police and eventually was free to go. Kitty was deeply ashamed of her deceit and both her parents were wise enough to know that she had learnt her lesson and needed no further punishment. To see her father so angry and in a vicious fight, and Robbie her friend so wounded, was enough. Kitty was covered in shame and regret.

Bruce and Kitty went to Clara's opening night of the spectacular new musical at Her Majesty's Theatre in London. Both of them sank back in their theatre seats in the darkness with relief at the escapism the show afforded. Clara was brilliant as predicted. She came home afterwards on an adrenalin "high", but when she finally tucked into bed with Bruce, she murmured in his ear.

'Brucie, you were right to collect Kitty. Thank you. Think what would have happened had you not been there. You were a brave warrior, you know. I'm sorry I thought you were fussing. You saved our daughter yesterday evening.'

'And you were wonderful *this* evening, Clara,' he said, folding her in his arms. 'How about not going to sleep just yet?'

'Let's not,' replied Clara. 'The night is young, isn't it?' she said, slipping her nightdress off.

***

The police tallied the description they had from the nun of the gang rape with Kitty's "near miss" and noted that in both cases each described the rapist, more or less, as having "bleached blond hair slicked back". Gary Johnson. He had been known to them for over a year but had somehow avoided being caught. The police did not catch up with him despite hotly pursuing him. He was a very slippery customer. They even wondered if he had escaped by means of the river at London Bridge. He was known to them as a strong swimmer as he had fooled them once before by swimming as far as Westminster Bridge when the current happened to be favourable.

In the hospital, Robbie decided with absolute certainty that when he was better he would seek Gary out. He did not want that young man sliding further down a slippery

135

slope as Robbie himself might have done had not he been rescued by the Lockwood family. Maybe, thought Robbie, with his own history of violence and imprisonment, he might be able to indicate to Gary Johnson that there was a route out of this toxic alpha male behaviour that caused so much havoc.

CHAPTER 19

It was nearly five months since Sister Hope's return to Ireland. She had climbed the Convent steps with more than a little trepidation, knowing that she was a different person from the carefree woman who had set off to England with such high hopes. Her mission to find out about her father had not been fulfilled, and she had experienced the worst ordeal of her life, thanks to five brutish louts who raped her. Hope knew she had acted in a cowardly way by running away from more questions and physical examinations by the police physician. She had prayed through the months for protection from sexual disease and permanent damage, and most of all for the healing of her vivid memories of the abuse.

The Abbess welcomed her back but could see that something had changed in Hope's demeanour. She questioned her a little, but Hope had decided not to say anything about the rape. Initially, she had thought it would be a comfort to share her story but having experienced the warmth of truly empathetic listeners in England, she did not wish for the cool, detached listening of the Abbess, nor for the lengthy sessions of prayers for healing that would follow. She would deal with it in her own way.

Hope knew that her periods had been scanty since the rape, but assumed that would be the effect of the shock to the system, both physically and emotionally. She had felt strangely weary since arriving back, and the daily chores took on more of a challenge than they had done previously. She also found that she craved carbohydrate food, and often took an extra slice of rations at breakfast and secreted any spares away for a mid-morning snack. She could explain every change, every symptom. This was a deep-seated emotional reaction to the trauma she had experienced, she decided.

This was not denial. Hope simply had not thought of pregnancy.

But this morning was different. She had been lying on her back staring at the ceiling and willing herself to get up. In the quiet and stillness of the moment, she felt a tiny flickering inside her abdomen, like a butterfly's wing tapping gently inside her. There. Again. She put her hand down and realised that there was a small swelling towards her pubic arch. She never normally stroked her abdomen. Ever since what she regarded as the self- indulgent scrutinizing of her body in the landlady's long mirror in what seemed a lifetime ago, she had refrained from any further investigations. It had shocked her. Also, the rape had made her feel tarnished, unclean and guilty.

Now she sat bolt upright as the realisation swept over her. Could she possibly be pregnant? She knew the answer was a resounding yes. Five young virile men spilling their seed into her meant that there was actually a strong likelihood that certainly two or three of them would be fertile. Also, she knew her periods up until recently had been as regular as clockwork, so she assumed her ovulation time would have been as well. She did some mental calculations. She had her period when she travelled from Ireland to England and had silently cursed the fact (in her own particular fashion), hoping she would have been free of all that hassle for the journey. The rape had happened two weeks after she had arrived.

Two weeks. Most probably at the peak of her fertility.

Hope got out of bed and stood upright, feeling the shape of her body slowly and carefully. She examined her breasts and realised they were fuller than before, slightly sore to touch and the nipples were darker.

Finally, she had to acknowledge that she must be nearly five months pregnant, and within a month the pregnancy was bound to show. Her head raced; so much so that she felt dizzy and sat down heavily on her narrow wooden chair. She must think what to do.

In all of her confused thinking, she never once considered what would, by this stage of her pregnancy, amount to a late termination. It would go against every fibre of her moral being to have countenanced it for a second. Rather, her head teamed with practical questions. Where would she have the baby? What would she do? How could she afford it? Once the Abbess knew about the pregnancy she would be duty-bound to ask her to leave, for the sake of the reputation of the convent. She knew that was how it worked. The Abbess would probably suggest she went to the Hostel for Unmarried Mothers in another part of Dublin — the very one in which her mother had given birth. Sister Hope was very aware that it had a dangerous history. She had heard of babies being secreted away from mothers at birth, even as late as the 1980s and either placed for adoption or dying in mysterious circumstances. She had been inside it once and it was a chilling place despite the potential for new life within it.

Hope realised she would have no option but to take up a place there. She had no known family and her life in the convent had precluded her from making friends in the world. The friends she had made in the convent were committed to their lifestyle, which would mean that once the convent doors were shut, with her on the outside, it would be the end of her contact with them. Hope trembled. The thought of the disgrace and the dismissal from the convent was troubling in the extreme, but the thought of giving birth in a hostile environment was *terrifying*. She lived with the nightmare vision in her head of the leering rapists, and the thought that any one of them could possibly be the father of the baby was repulsive and repugnant to her. She recalled more than anything else their breath polluting her face and the smells of each one of them as they had their way. The one with the slicked back bleached blond hair, she remembered again, was particularly obnoxious. He smelt of a toxic mixture of strong cheap aftershave and alcohol.

She looked up at the cross on her wall made out of simple olive wood and knelt down in front of it and pleaded out loud, 'Father. Help me.' She remained there for a few minutes, silently laying her heart and soul open to God. Towards the end, she put her hand on her abdomen again and at that moment felt the baby like a delicate feather moving inside her. Quite suddenly she was filled with a rush of joy, briefly but definitely, as she thought of the new life inside her. She had long ago dismissed any idea of having children. That was the hardest promise she had made during her vows. Now that she was carrying a child, she swore in that moment that she would protect it if it took her last breath.

Her last breath. Hope thought of her mother dying in childbirth. She had learnt that as a newborn baby herself, she had been taken to St. Fridewide's Orphanage, where she was lucky to have more than the statutory feed and change of soaking wet nappy but nothing more. She had no memory of feeling loved, and it was only when she had worked for a brief while as a cleaner in a local school that she had felt some semblance of warmth and friendship, particularly from the children. She remembered again how, at the age of three, she had violently shaken the bars of her cot in an attempt to get someone to notice her. That was *not* going to happen to her baby. Somehow, she must make provisions for him or her in the event of her death.

'Lord, please help me protect this infant in every way possible,' she prayed again, and hastily dressed for Matins.

CHAPTER 20

Sister Hope knocked on the Mother Superior's door a little while after the service had finished. Entering cautiously, she saw that the Abbess was standing on a chair trying to mend one of her scanty blinds that was refusing to be closed. She cautiously inched her way down.

'Stupid blinds! The one and only thing we lack a man for is these practical tasks! Ah, Sister Hope, I'm glad it's you. I have been meaning to speak with you. Do sit down.'

She paused, then fixed her penetrating stare on Sister Hope.

'I'm a little concerned about you. You have not been quite yourself recently. Have you been feeling well?'

'Well, yes I have, thank you Mother but…'

The Abbess interrupted her.

'—Because I can always ask Dr Wyatt to run some blood tests for you. You may be anaemic, my child. You really have been looking pale. Don't think I don't notice things, because I do,' she said, smiling slightly at Hope. 'I even wondered if something happened in England to upset you?' she said, with a second penetrating stare.

'Yes,' replied Hope, her legs shaking under her habit. 'Yes it did, Mother.'

'Ah. I thought as much. Not much escapes me when it comes to the welfare of my flock,' she said, slightly smugly. Hope pushed down a wry thought that this particular secret had very much eluded her eagle eye.

'Are you going to tell me about it, Sister?'

Hope had planned how she was going to break the news. She had constructed various sentences, and then deconstructed them in her mind, reworking them into various formats. She was going to present the news little by little, step by step, so as not to give the Abbess too much of a shock, (she wasn't in the best of health). Hope certainly had not intended to blurt it out the way she did. She looked the Abbess full in the face.

'I was raped.'

The Abbess swayed slightly for several seconds. Finally, she sat down heavily and stared at Hope.

'You — *what?*' The Abbess put her hand to head, and looked as though she was going to faint.

'I was raped,' Hope repeated. 'By five men. A gang rape.'

'Why — why have you not said anything about this before?' she asked breathlessly, trying to regain some kind of inner equilibrium. 'It is our duty under God to bring everything before His family for loving prayer.'

'I know,' said Hope. 'But would you have been able to if it had been you?' Hope challenged her. Despite the violent shaking inside, Hope found herself more defensive and confrontational than she had intended.

The Reverend Mother, holy and prayerful as she was, was not the kind of person who could possibly imagine herself in that situation.

'It is our duty under God,' she repeated. 'To share both the good and the bad things with our Convent family that we experience.'

The Abbess was looking very shocked and quite pale, and it was clear she had no idea whatsoever how to handle the situation. She had seen 'her children' in various states of upset during her long ministry at the convent, but this situation for her was unprecedented.

Hope pressed on. She knew it was now or never. She would not find the courage again to face the Abbess with her shocking news.

'That's not all, Mother. I'm pregnant as a result of it.'

Silence. After what seemed like an eternity to Hope, the Abbess put her head in her hands again. She remained there for another minute without moving. Was she simply horrified, or praying, thought Hope. Most likely, both. Eventually, without looking up, she spoke.

'Sister Hope. I am afraid it is impossible to raise a child in a Convent. Have you thought about what you will do? We will have to lose you, which we will all regret.'

'As you know, I have no family that I know of.'

'You are entitled to a severance package from the diocese, but it is not enough to support yourself and your child.'

Hope was silent. She really had no idea at all what to do.

'I will contact St. Frideswide's Home for Fallen Women and see if I can secure you a place. I'm sorry, I should say "for Unmarried Mothers". The terminology has changed but,' she paused and gave a wry smile. 'The

144

clientele remains the same. Let me know what you want to do, sister. We can provide medical attention while you are making your decision,' she paused again and leafed through some papers. 'Leave me now, please. I must pray and sort out the paperwork for your departure.'

That was all. That was the entire encounter with the Abbess. Hope was bereft. No word of sympathy, no sign of understanding, no enquiry about how she was; just a dismissal. Hope went to the door and opened it, the heavy wood creaking eerily. She felt she was leaving the Headmistress's study after being expelled. She walked down the cold and echoing cloisters numb with pain and distress. Suddenly, she heard a voice calling her,

'Sister Hope! Sister Hope! Wait!'

Hope turned to see the Reverend Mother running heavily after her, her habit lifted in the wind that often whipped around the cloisters. She reached Hope, said nothing, but threw her arms around her and held her tightly for many seconds. She then turned and made her way slowly back the way she came without a word. Hope felt a warmth flood through her body. It was a hug she would never forget and she knew it also lovingly embraced the baby she was carrying.

That night, however, a cloud of deep depression descended on Hope and she was filled with an agonising dread of the future. It seemed she had not a friend in the world. In the darkest of moments, she felt God too had abandoned her. In the early hours of the morning, she woke with a start from her fitful sleep and sobbed for her mother.

Quite suddenly she remembered the beaded rosary that Connie had secreted into her suitcase. Hope had been touched deeply by this loving gesture and kept the rosary wrapped carefully in its tissue paper. Now, she went to the drawer, took out the package and carefully unwrapped it. Picking up the rosary, she touched the cross within the beads lightly and prayed the Apostles Creed fervently. She ended the prayer by pleading to God.

'Lord, you know the secrets of our hearts. *Please* help me. I know everything is always in your good time, but I can't help that. I need the help *now!* '

CHAPTER 21

Sadie and the family had received three letters from Sister Hope. Sadie knew that the nuns were limited with their allowance on letter-writing, so it came as no surprise that letters were few and far between. The first one from Hope had been very full, explaining and apologising for her swift exit from the vicarage in Southwark. It was also profuse in its expression of thanks for the care and love she had received. The second letter had mainly been describing life in the convent and Hope's reflections on being back in Ireland. The third letter was addressed to Sadie alone. The envelope had simply said, 'Sadie at The Vicarage, Southwark.' Clearly, reflected Sadie, Hope did not know that her surname was Connors. She must let her know the next time she wrote.

This third letter had been different in tone from the previous two. It was short, more succinct with news, or rather a lack of news, and much less communicative generally. Sadie pondered over it. She had developed a close rapport with Hope when they were together and had begun to feel real affection for her. Having tended to her wounds and talked about the intimate issues of the rape, it would have been difficult to remain detached. Anyway, mused Sadie, she was not looking after her in a professional capacity; it was as a friend, so it was quite in order for her to feel rather like a sister towards her.

What perhaps Sadie had not fully realised was that her capacity for loving and caring were left unfulfilled and unrequited since Jack had been so dramatically wrenched from her life. Sister Hope was not only someone who needed her but for a little while provided a channel for Sadie's full attention, which was a welcome and much needed diversion from the intense grief that enveloped her in her deep loss.

Soon after she had received the third letter from Hope, Sadie woke with a start at two a.m. She sat bolt upright and for a second thought it was Jack calling from the next room. He had often needed her in the middle of the night. She realised almost immediately her mistake and the grim reality of her loss pounded into her as it always did when she first woke. She had gone to sleep with Sister Hope on her mind, having re-read her letter of a week ago, and a few minutes after waking had a very strong sense that Hope was in deep trouble. Sadie was perplexed by the strength of her intuitive feeling and vowed she would somehow connect with the convent the following morning either to either speak to Hope or to make enquiries as to her well-being.

She began to think again about Hope's predicament. She could identify with it in as much as she herself had left home suddenly with nothing more than a note by way of apology. Sadie was regularly abused by her father, whom she had grown to hate with a passion. She was not sure if it was accurate to call it rape, as there came a point where she simply lay back and acquiesced to her father's demands. But always she felt her stomach knotting and her body tensing and every time she heard her father whispering hoarsely, 'Relax for your daddy, there's a good girl.' Again and again, Sadie wanted to tell her mother, but she knew it would crucify Rosa's feelings. Sadie's father, in her eyes, was a devouring monster from whom she had no escape. In her mother's eyes, her husband was the breadwinner and an indispensable part of keeping the family solvent as well as the father of her children. She was prepared to turn a blind eye to many of his faults for the sake of a quiet life.

Unlike Hope, Sadie, who had cut herself off from her family, had realised she was pregnant within one week of missing her period. Her whole body seemed to change within that short time, and she had felt nauseous. All she wanted to do was escape before her mother started asking questions and began noticing small changes in her daughter, which Sadie knew she would. She hatched a plan, therefore, and within three weeks had left home to stay temporarily with her maternal great aunt, who kept her secret and financed a mobile home in Scotland for her. Sadie had decided to move as far away as possible to avoid being traced or followed. Her great-aunt visited Sadie when Jack was born, looking after them both as well as she could for two weeks and breaking her heart at the sight of her little great-nephew who would need so much medical attention in his childhood. Whatever happened, she knew she must prevent her dreadful brother from wreaking havoc on his daughter and his family. Sadie kept it to herself that he was the father of her baby and that he was the result of an incestuous relationship. She felt responsible and ashamed.

Sadie reflected on this in the middle of the night and suddenly was overwhelmed with a feeling that she must urgently go to Hope. Oliver and Connie would have called it the Holy Spirit nudging Sadie into action. Sadie had no such language or belief. What she did realize with horror was that it was quite possible that Hope might be pregnant by one of the monstrous males who had raped her. If so, she would be feeling utterly bereft and quite alone. Maybe that accounted for the change of tone in Hope's last letter? Was she sitting on a secret? Sadie knew exactly what that felt like. Terrible and terrifying and unutterably lonely.

One thing was holding Sadie back from her desire to go immediately to Hope. Her old enemy Agoraphobia was hovering somewhere over her shoulder waiting to pounce and dominate her at the least provocation. Since Jack died Sadie had hardly gone out, and she knew from all the "self-help" books she had read during the bad times and latterly a couple of counselling sessions, that the worst thing she could do would be to avoid going out of the front door, down the slope and past the corner outside where Jack was killed. To reach Euston she not only had to walk through Southwark but then endure the underground to reach the train to Liverpool and thence over to Dublin on the ferry. She broke out in a sweat at the very thought of it. Her counsellor was right when she said that Sadie's trouble was fear of the fear, rather than the fear itself, but that did not help her when she was on the edge of a panic attack away from home. It sounded like an over-simplistic formulaic thing to say.

Sadie knew despite everything that it was as if she were being compelled to follow her instinct and go to Hope and that she must not give in to any avoidance tactics. She shook herself down, gave herself a stern talking-to, showered, and gathered a few things together in a small suitcase. She would track the Convent down and find Hope, presuming Hope could meet her somewhere in Dublin, or better still invite her inside the Convent. Sadie had no idea if visitors were allowed.

She told the family of her intentions. Connie gasped.

'Oh, Sadie. That's a brave thing to do, but you can't go over there all on your own.'

'Why not?' replied Sadie. 'Sister Hope has done the journey there and back, and just think what a shock to the system that must have been for her. After all, most of her life has been in the Convent and she had barely negotiated any transport systems, for a start.'

'Are you well enough, Sadie?' asked Oliver, concerned. It's a very short time since Jack died. What you've been through shocks the whole system, mental, emotional, and physical doesn't it? I've seen it often and you're no exception,' he said kindly. 'Bereavement hits everyone one way or another. Give it a few days to think about your decision.'

'No. I've thought hard, Oli. I need to go.'

Connie and Oliver were silent, seeing the determination in Sadie's eyes and fearing this was several steps too far for her. She had never in their eyes been a fragile person but coping with the shock of sudden loss brought with it its own distinctive and distressing fatigue. Normally, Sadie's physical looks, conversely, spoke of strength. She had the well-rounded, muscular frame of her father, together with the inheritance of his strong dark hair, which in Sadie's case fell in waves way past her shoulders and was generally hoisted up in some kind of a makeshift bunch. She never wore any make-up, but her eyes looked permanently highlighted with eye liner and her skin was dark and rosy. She was a very striking woman; nevertheless, for months her brother and sister had seen her broken and fragile.

Finally, after thinking about the week's commitments and what he could rearrange, Oliver asked.

'Would you let me accompany you, Sadie.'

Connie stared at him. Was that practical? He had two funerals to take within the next few days as well as an important Parochial Church Council meeting that evening, none of them easily cancelled. She wondered if she should go instead, but that brought its own set of problems, particularly with Peter, who became disturbed if his routine was upset.

'No thanks, Oli,' said Sadie lightly, not quite taking in what a magnanimous gesture this was on Oliver's part, and the rearranging that would have to be done.

'Connie, let me at least phone and book you a train ticket quickly. You don't want to find yourself standing all the way to Liverpool,' said Connie.

'And I'll drive you to Euston so you can avoid the underground rush hour,' insisted Oliver.

'Thanks,' said Sadie. 'Both of those things would help me on my way.'

Suddenly, she started crying.

'But I'll feel as though I'm leaving Jack behind!' she said. 'While I'm here I have his things around me and can imagine him. When I go to Ireland I will lose him.'

Connie knew exactly what Sadie meant. When their mother had died, both girls were bereft, but for Connie most of all it turned her world upside down. She sobbed for nights remembering her mother's warm touch and sweet fragrance. The first time she went away from home, she found she could not recall her face, much to her distress.

Connie went to Sadie and hugged her closely.

'It sounds silly,' she said. 'But tuck Jack's little grey rabbit in your bag. It will help. He took it everywhere, didn't he?' She paused. 'Sadie, you're very brave. It's a great thing to be doing.'

Sadie reached for a piece of kitchen roll, dried her eyes, put her shoulders back and said,

'Half an hour then, Oli?'

'Half an hour it is,' replied Oliver.

Instead of clearing away the breakfast things, Connie reached for her bible, thumbed it open at the First Epistle to the Thessalonians, chapter three verse three, and read it over and over for Sadie:

The Lord is faithful and he will strengthen you and protect you

'Amen to that,' she said aloud. 'Amen to that.'

153

CHAPTER 22

The only normal day clothes that Hope had were those that were put aside for her twenty years ago when she first arrived at the convent. There was a short-ish pastel skirt and a cream blouse. Both looked well-kept, having been wrapped in tissue, but she knew that neither would fit. Hope had lost more than three stones in weight over the twenty years and although she was now five months pregnant, her bump was only just visible. The skirt was way too big round the waist and the white blouse drowned her. Hope felt extremely disconnected and embarrassed as she tried them on, and decided that with her small allowance from the diocese she must at least buy one set of reasonable clothes. She remembered the beautiful shop windows in Oxford Street with the amazingly clad mannequins wearing clothes such as she had never set eyes on. She had no desire whatever to have anything extravagant (the money wouldn't allow it anyway), but it would be nice, she decided, to have something with colour in it after wearing black and white, rather like a penguin, for twenty years.

The Abbess had acted fast, partly so that Sister Hope might settle somewhere quickly for her own sake, and partly to maintain the good reputation of the convent and the diocese. She visited St. Frideswide's Unmarried

Mother and Baby Hostel and found it somewhat bleak, but nothing as bad as she had imagined, or had been led to believe from rumours that were flying around about the place. She did know that at least eighty percent of babies were put up for adoption. She reported back to Hope that there was a place reserved for her, and that if she wished, the Nuns who ran it could organize for Hope's baby to be fostered out soon after birth, and then adopted, depending on her plans.

Hope was silently outraged that anyone should think she would want her baby adopted. She did not know which of the five young men had fathered her child, but nevertheless she now regarded this baby as a child of God and he or she would be treated as such and looked after and loved by its own birth mother and no one else. She knew her mother would have done the same had she not met an untimely end. Hope had never needed or longed for her mother more. At the thought of how she imagined her mother would have been with her as a daughter and as a grandmother, Hope broke down and dissolved in tears.

Her doorbell was ringing. She rapidly dried her eyes and then mumbled, 'Come in.' She kept her eyes to the ground for fear the Abbess would see she had been crying. No one spoke. After a few seconds, Hope looked up. There in the doorway, silhouetted against a shaft of light that was streaming in from the tall narrow window behind her, stood Sadie.

Hope gasped. Sadie stood quite still. Eventually Hope found her voice.

'Sadie? Are you a vision? *Is* it you, Sadie?' Her excitement mounted. 'I can't believe it.'

'Sister Hope,' said Sadie softly. 'I've come to see you.'

The two women suddenly flew to one another and hugged closely for a long time. As they held each other, Hope wept for joy and Sadie slowly became aware from the slight but definite firm swelling of Hope's abdomen that her guess had been correct. Yes. Hope was pregnant.

'What made you come?' asked Hope. 'This is too wonderful for words.'

Sadie told Hope how she had imagined very vividly two nights ago that Hope might be in trouble and from then on she was compelled to find her in case she was in need.

'This is beautiful,' said Hope softly. 'Sadie, this is answered prayer.'

'Is it?' said Sadie. 'I call it good old female intuition.'

'Maybe God was part of the intuition, Sadie.' Hope clapped her hands joyfully.

'Whichever it is, it's beyond my wildest dreams to see you here. Come down to the kitchen and I'll make you some tea. How was your journey?'

Sadie could not begin to describe the journey; how she had almost turned back several times in panic; how one minute she had felt very brave and the next a total coward; how she almost missed the ferry because she had mislaid her suitcase for a few panicky minutes at Liverpool Lime Street station, having left it in the Ladies' toilets. So she simply said.

'It was quite an adventure, Hope. Yes, I'd love a cup of tea. We've a lot of talking to catch up on.'

'We have,' said Hope.

Sadie looked down at Hope's abdomen and said in her forthright manner.

'I needn't ask how or when this happened, you poor thing.'

Hope stared at her.

'I didn't think it showed much. How did you guess?'

'Call it woman's intuition again, Hope, or —' she said with a smile full of cheek.

'—Or your God might have tipped me the wink!'

They broke into laughter and both women knew that maybe that was the case.

Hope had not laughed for a very long time and she gazed again at Sadie. This indeed was a miraculous happening.

'A cup of tea,' said Hope, handing Sadie the statutory institution green up and saucer.

'You have this little kitchen you can use then?' said Sadie, surprised.

Hope laughed.

'It's not a prison camp, you know! People have got the wrong idea about nuns and convents. It's only the cloistered nuns who have taken a vow of silence that lives in isolation. Some things are reasonably relaxed here, but basically, above all else we're a praying and serving community.'

It didn't look very relaxed to Sadie, with its narrow bed and stone floor and a one-bar electric fire for heating.

In addition, Sadie had undergone something akin to the Spanish Inquisition before she was allowed through the huge and terrifying wooden gates.

'Will your baby live here with you?'

'No,' answered Hope simply.

'Oh — not *that* relaxed then?'

Hope didn't reply. She could see that, lovely as Sadie was, there was a general hardness in her about Christianity in general and religion in particular. Oliver and Connie hadn't managed to soften her then, she speculated. Perhaps it was to do with Sadie's history with her father and having to fight for her son.

'Where will you have the baby and bring it up, Hope?'

Hope paused, embarrassed that she should be institutionalised in such a place as the unmarried mother and baby hostel.

'You must have thought, Hope?' she urged.

'I will go to the Unmarried Mother and Baby Hostel near Dublin'

'*What!* Hope, you *can't*. Some of them have terrible reputations — babies being put up for adoption without the mother's consent, or even in some cases dying because of lack of care. I've read that there is a lot covered up that we are only just beginning to learn about.'

Hope put her hand on Sadie's shoulder.

'Sadie, how long ago did you read this?'

'I suppose I did most of my reading up on it was sixteen years ago when I was pregnant with Jack and wondering what to do.' Sadie stopped. She realised she had not thought of Jack once since she alighted from the ferry at terminal three at the port of Dublin and now almost felt like a traitor. Fighting back tears, she stroked the little velvet rabbit in her bag.

'Sadie, I'm so sorry. I didn't mean to touch such a raw nerve.'

'It's OK,' replied Sadie. 'You're right. My knowledge is probably out of date.'

She looked Hope squarely in the face.

'Hope. Come home with me. We can be your family now.'

Silence. Hope stared at her.

'I mean it. When Oliver took on the role of a vicar he knew he and Connie both wanted to fill that vast vicarage with people who needed the comfort of a home and family life. They were insistent on it as part of his accepting the job. Honestly, Hope, they saw it as their calling. That's why Robbie has a bedsit upstairs, and Jack and I have a self-contained flat with two bedrooms. We just pay for heating and lighting.'

Hope was silent.

'Hope, there is *room!*' Sadie urged, then suddenly hesitated, full of pain, but wanting so much to say what was on her mind. Finally.

'Hope, you and the baby could have — could have my Jack's room.' She blurted out the last few words rapidly so as to skim over the intense pain. 'It's six months now, and Oliver says it might be time I stopped thinking of it as a shrine. It would be good to feel there was life in it again, I guess. Please come. Maybe I could even help you with the baby?'

Hope was thinking hard and praying under her breath.

'Unless you don't want to?' added Sadie, suddenly wondering if she was forcing the pace.

Hope burst into tears.

'Don't want to? I can think of nothing in the world I would love more. I've never in my life experienced family life and I felt so enveloped by everyone's love and welcome. Sadie, do you really mean it? What would the family say — the children — Peter?'

'I really mean it, and the family would be *delighted,*' assured Sadie. 'Rosy will smother your baby with love,' she added, smiling. 'She keeps on to Connie to have another one!'

'You are a walking miracle, Sadie — um...' She stopped mid-sentence. 'How strange. I don't even know your surname.'

'Connors,' said Sadie. 'I'm Sadie Connors.'

CHAPTER 23

Albert Connors. Rosa Connors. James Connors. Sadie Connors. Bruce Connors. Constance Connors: those names had become seared in Sister Hope's brain.

When she was researching into who her father might be, those names, she discovered, belonged to the wife and children of Albert Connors, the man who had used and abused her mother. Her research had eventually led her to The Vicarage, Southwark, S.E.1. Unsure how to approach it with the family, she was subsequently thrust into a terrible gang rape situation and left without broaching the subject.

Now, here, before her very eyes, was living proof that the surnames of Sadie and Albert were one and the same. She stood mesmerised, staring at Sadie.

'Hope, what's the matter? You're staring at me as though you've seen a ghost. Are you feeling a bit faint?'

'Sit down, Sadie. I need to talk to you.'

Sadie could see that Hope was very serious about whatever she was to divulge. She sat on the edge of Hope's hard bed. Hope went to her small desk and brought out a file of papers. She sat on the bed with Sadie, putting the file between them.

'I want you to look at this please, Sadie.'

They spent the next two hours thumbing through papers, laying them out, re-reading them, and occasionally Sadie would gasp aloud. Hope showed her a photo she had wrapped in tissue paper and then polythene.

'This is my mother, Sadie. It's the only photo I have of her. Erin O'Neill.'

Sadie gazed for a long time at the photo. Hope was so like her mother — slim, slightly fragile-looking, curly golden hair, pretty. In addition, there was a hint of Connie in Hope, particularly the smile, she thought.

'You're very like your mother, Hope.'

Above all other reactions, Sadie was devastated yet again by her father's behaviour. To think that he could have betrayed his wife Rosa in such a way was shocking. Sadie thought of his appalling record: sexual abuse of both his young daughters, a vicious temper and tongue that had been instrumental in driving their beloved older brother James to suicide; his wife Rosa's head mysteriously hit against a wall in dubious circumstances causing her death; and now the discovery that he had fathered a daughter and walked out on a mistress.

Sadie wept copiously. It was as if all the anger, the hurt and bewilderment of her father's behaviour suddenly overwhelmed her. Jack had been the result of her father's regular rapes of her. She remembered the feelings of guilt over Jack's little deformed newborn body, which almost certainly had been the result of genetic mismatching with her father. Sadie had been offered genetic counselling after Jack was born, but she had declined it. She knew she would never ever have another child. She had found that

162

she shunned men and everything they stood for including their physical appearance, preferring to trust only the company of women. Oliver was the exception for Sadie. His gentleness and quiet concern warmed her heart. She could not turn her back on him, nor her brother, but every other male filled her with alarm. She thought of the many nights where she had lain in bed as a child dreading the creeks of the floorboard as her father crept into her room. She would never forget the way he lumbered heavily onto her bed and her pain and endurance as he helped himself to her body. Afterwards, there was always the gift of a stick of barley sugar as a bribe to ensure she kept their secret. Worst of all was her feeling of shame and betrayal of her sweet, kind mother Rosa who, in Sadie's eyes, did not seem to have a bad bone in her body.

Hope enfolded Sadie in her arms. Sadie melted into her and felt the solace of a woman's warmth and touch. It reminded her of her mother. After a few minutes, she gently released herself and looked straight at Hope.

'My sister,' she said, smiling at last.

'My sister,' replied Hope, and they hugged each other for a long time again.

In the secret place of her heart, Sadie was relieved to find that they were related, quite apart from the shock and subsequent joy of the revelation for its own sake. She had worried that in her grief and bereaved frame of mind she had developed unfamiliar feelings for Hope that had shocked and disturbed her as she tended her after the rape.

Now all those feelings were justified. Maybe, she reasoned to herself, deep down there was a recognition of a blood tie that explained it all.

CHAPTER 24

The next day was a flurry of activity. Hope had to collect her money from the diocesan offices, cancel her place at the mother and baby home, say goodbye to her sisters in Christ, sign paperwork, and finally sort out clothes for returning to the "real" world. That was Sadie's phrase, not Hope's. Several people had expressed strong feelings when she was about to become a novice, saying that she was escaping "the real world". Hope never really understood this and always wanted to take issue with those thoughts. Living in a community, with fewer means of distraction or diversion meant that she and her sisters developed a heightened sense of the deep issues of life: amongst them, poverty, suffering, bereavement and the weight of sorrow in the world, and Hope always felt that an empathetic and imaginative connection with those elements meant that actually she was very much in touch with what was going on outside the walls and her prayer life became all the more real and urgent because of it.

Sadie was urging Hope to come into town with her and choose that one set of garments in which to travel home. Hope was overwhelmed by the tasks in hand and Sadie had booked an early afternoon ferry across to Liverpool, so time was at a premium. Hope therefore asked Sadie to go and buy some simple garments for her, bearing in mind that she would like her bump to be disguised. While Sadie was out she would find the gardener. Hope had taken great delight in working alongside him planting bulbs every spring and watching their handiwork blossom. She wanted to say goodbye to him personally.

Sadie wandered round the shops, finding it an overwhelming task. If she was buying for Connie, or her niece Kitty, or even her sister-in-law Clara, she would have more of an idea of their taste. Connie's would be unsophisticated but pretty and Kitty's would be verging on punk in style — the statutory torn jeans and bright neon oversized shirt, or an exotic Ra Ra skirt when she wanted to dress up for an evening out. Clara's — well, Clara's could be anything from black tights or jeans and a tight top through to either a flouncy or slimline and sexy beaded dress — usually black with a low cut neck to ensure her cleavage showed to maximum advantage.

But as for Hope? There was absolutely no hint of her taste from a black-and-white habit! There was not a splash or even a streak of colour anywhere. Sadie could not decide whether Hope was yearning to wear vibrant colours or would wish for more subdued clothes. She decided the latter would be less of a shock to the system so she finally bought a loose pale turquoise smock-style cotton blouse with coloured embroidery, and a pair of navy blue trousers with a stretch waist designed as maternity wear. She wasn't sure what nuns wore under their habits. Should she buy any underwear? She bought a few basic pairs of white briefs and one white stretch bra, estimating Hope's size, and left it at that.

Nervously she spread her purchases on the bed. Hope was astounded. All of it was, as Sadie had guessed, a shock to the system, but she was thrilled with everything Sadie had chosen. Sadie sensitively left the room while Hope took off her Nun's clothes and donned her home ones. It was a hugely significant moment for Hope. Her habit and accompanying uniform had become an intrinsic part of her identity. They had indicated a life of prayer and self-sacrifice and she realised that a further facet of her life in the convent had been the gradual healing of her scars of abandonment and neglect from childhood.

Hope took off her veil and coif. She ran her hand through her hair. Since arriving back in Ireland from England it seemed to have grown thicker and it was certainly longer. It was, she imagined, still the unruly mess of old with its curls that had a will of their own, defying any kind of discipline that a brush or comb might proffer. She took off the shorts that had become her regular underwear and slipped on a pair of white briefs. They just about came up to her waist and covered her bump, and Hope felt the rounding swelling of her abdomen through the smooth material. She felt a wave of excitement as she realised that the stress of being pregnant had largely been taken off her thanks to her wonderful half-sister. The birth of the baby held some fear for her in view of what had happened to her mother, but Hope knew that she would be safe in a London hospital with Sadie to support her. If she had any say in that, Hope would ask that Sadie would be in attendance at the birth. In a sense, with Sadie's agreement, they would be mother *and* father to this infant.

She had spent long hours in prayer for the healing of her memories of the rape, and most particularly for the obliteration of the thought that one of those louts was the father of her baby. Perhaps Sadie was the answered prayer.

She put on the navy blue trousers which were much too big for her round the waist. She couldn't believe that her tummy would ever grow big enough to fill them, but the label said they were suitable for women who were between six and nine months pregnant. The turquoise blouse pleased her greatly and she could sense that it might look rather nice on her. She smiled wryly. Oh, the ways of the world! Already she was imagining what she looked like. What *would* the Abbess say? Hope decided that more prayer was needed to guard her against vanity and worldly thinking. It didn't help when Sadie came back in and exclaimed,

'Oh my goodness, Hope, you look *beautiful!* The colour suits you so well. And your *hair!* It's so *golden*!'

Eventually, and not a moment too soon, the women boarded a taxi (Sadie insisted on paying), and arrived at the docks. Hope gazed back at the receding port feeling the most exquisite kind of agony: joy, sadness, excitement, fear, but above all a sense that finally, she was going home.

Eventually, after a long and rather tortuous journey, the two women arrived back in Southwark. Sadie had not got her front door key with her, so she rang the bell of the vicarage. Both women waited and Sadie reflected that she had walked up the slope without the terrible memory of Jack's accident flashing in her mind. She was excited by Hope's arrival home.

Eventually, Connie came to the door, her hands still dusted with flour from her baking session. She stared. *Was* it Sister Hope? She couldn't believe it. She was hardly recognizable, and certainly, the lady in front of her was gently pregnant.

'Connie, brace yourself for a shock.'

Connie held on to the sturdy handle by the door that had been put up for Jack and steadied herself. Historically, Sadie's "shocks" had the potential to be life-changing.

'Connie,' said Sadie with a broad smile. 'Meet your other sister. She's come home — for good. This is our Sister Hope.'

Connie looked bewildered but nevertheless went up to Hope and hugged her. She assumed Sadie was talking figuratively.

'I'm not sure I'm understanding yet, but come in and sit down and I'll make you a cup of tea. I've just made some shortbread biscuits. You both look worn out. Oh yes, and perhaps I should say, 'Welcome home Sister Hope!'

As she led them in, she whispered to Sadie,

'Sadie, you need to fill me in. I've no idea what's happening.'

'I will,' replied Sadie. 'I promise. Meanwhile, I'll take Hope's suitcase up to Jack's room.'

Connie looked perplexed.

'*Jack's* room, Sadie?'

'Yes,' replied Sadie, 'It's time to bring it to life again. Jack would want that.'

Connie felt a wave of pure relief and joy flood over her. Whatever had gone on in Ireland, she knew it was a good sign that her sister was beginning to come to terms with the loss of Jack, and was glimpsing some kind of a future at last. This was certainly a rather extraordinary homecoming, she thought, but then Sadie had sprung surprises on them all her life.

END OF PART ONE

PART TWO

CHAPTER 25
August 1989: three months later

Kitty Connors had recently mastered the art of persuasion. Every day now there seemed to be an "issue" with her parents, particularly her father, over what she was allowed to wear, how short her school skirt could be, how late she could stay out and so on. She had quite rapidly changed from being a compliant, good-natured youngster to an argumentative and truculent sixteen-year-old. Bruce was amazed how quickly she seemed to have changed. Clara was more philosophical, saying she knew it would happen.

'It always does with girls. Bruce. We have to learn to use our weaponry otherwise we'd be defenceless in a man's world. Anyway, it's *hormones,*' she would say with a coquettish "know-all" sort of a smile.

'Man's world!' Bruce smiled grimly to himself. It was hardly a man's world in *his* home, he concluded. Recently, he had felt dominated by women who always had to have their own way and the last word. He feared that slowly but surely his beloved Kitty was changing into her mother. He loved Clara very much, but the thought of *two* Claras in one household was rather daunting.

Kitty seemed to have been quite resilient over the Gary Johnson episode and was more upset about her father's fight with Gary than the fact that he was near to raping her as he had Sister Hope. It took Kitty a few months, nevertheless, to re-visit Borough Road Market. No one had seen anything at all of Gary Johnson and that included the police, despite their best efforts.

Kitty had been trying to secure a part-time job for herself. She was increasingly fond of clothes and accessories of all kinds and needed extra money to finance her growing passion for them. She had gone first to the local supermarket, then the newsagents, followed by the local grocers' stores and even braved her feelings and asked the stall holders at Borough Road Market if they needed an assistant. Everywhere she drew a blank, even though she was personable and would have done any of the jobs well. With signs of a recession looming, there did not seem to be any spare cash around to pay for assistants.

Bruce and Clara increased Kitty's pocket money, giving in to her constant cry of 'all my friends get more than I do,' the oldest trick in the book, Bruce knew. Both he and Clara adored their one and only daughter, but both agreed that the worst thing they could do would be to spoil her. She had been getting her own way rather a lot recently.

One evening, Clara came home from her show in a particularly buoyant mood.

'Brucie, I think I've got Clara a job.'

Bruce turned over sleepily in bed.

'Can it wait till the morning, baby?'

'No. Wake up, Bruce. It's exciting.' She shook him. 'You know Matt, the Musical Director?'

'Yes,' said Bruce sleepily.

'Well, he and a few friends have been invited to a birthday party on board a pleasure steamer on the Thames. Matt wondered if Clara would like some work on it as a one-off. It would be paid very well — way above the odds.'

Bruce eased himself up on one elbow.

'Would it be a daytime job? What about school? Or is it on a Saturday?'

'It's a night time Sunday morning job, starting at twelve-thirty a.m. — for a few hours, but... '

She heard Bruce's sharp intake of breath at the timeline.

'Matt will be there and he's promised to look after her. She'd be serving drinks and canapés. It's a great opening for her.'

'But Clara, do you honestly think she'd be safe in that sort of set-up? It sounds highly *un*suitable. She's only sixteen. Won't they all be swigging back the alcohol with gay abandon? '

He couldn't resist a smile at the unintended double entendre. Matt was a dear friend of Clara's and known for his sexual preferences for men (much to Bruce's relief).

'Oh Brucie! You really have got to drag yourself into the twentieth century. This is a one-off. Anyway, Matt says they're a really decent set of people. You mustn't think of stereotypes. They are mainly from the theatre and arts and business world.'

Bruce raised his eyebrows. It had just got worse.

'She'll love it. Matt says they're all great fun. He knows them well. Come on — it's such an opportunity and she only ever kicked over the traces once, hasn't she? Let's see what she says in the morning. I absolutely know Matt will guarantee her safety.'

Bruce could feel that he had already lost the argument. His two women, plus the myriads of reassuring quotations from Matt ('Matt says this,' 'Matt says that') were more than a body could cope with.

'What steamer is it, Kitty? Not one of those rickety old things that look as though it should have been in the scrap yard centuries ago? You know. We've watched them — the ones that trundle up and down the Thames overloaded with sight-seers and looking as though they are going to conk out at any second? Some of them have been in action since the 1920s you know, and that's exactly what they look like.

'Rubbish, Bruce. They've all been renovated and I know they have to pass stringent safety checks. Matt told me.'

'Hmm. OK,' he said reluctantly. 'Let's talk to her about it in the morning, but we mustn't get her hopes up too much in case we decide it's unsuitable work for her'

Clara raised her eyebrows.

'Oh Bruce, I wish just for once you weren't so danger-aware over Kitty. You really must start letting her go.'

'What, starting with a pleasure steamer up the Thames all through the night, Clara? Let me sleep on it. What did you say the boat was called?'

The Grand Duchess,' replied Clara.

***

Meanwhile, Gary Johnson, who was incredibly adept at dodging the police, was settling down for another night of sleeping rough. His bed was an old duvet he had found at a recycling tip and someone had taken pity on him and recently given him a shabby tartan plaid travel rug. His home for the next couple of nights would be in the tunnel on the south side of the Southwark Bridge. He kept moving his portable bed around in order not to be tracked down and had found that tunnels and disused warehouses on the south bank of the Thames were the most anonymous of places. There was no worry about keeping warm in the summer, and tonight was a particularly soft and friendly sort of a night. He settled himself down and opened a sandwich that someone had given him.

Gary Johnson's history was a tragic one. All his life he had been forced to fight for survival. Both his parents were in prison for bestiality crimes. At a young age, Gary had been made to commit low-grade sexual crimes with animals so that his parents could film him and sell the resulting myriad of photographs on the black market. When eventually he was placed in a school for Emotional and Behavioural Difficulties the teachers were appalled when they read the reports on Gary and his background. They were incredulous that a child should have been abused to such depraved depths. Gary was seriously disturbed as a result. His form teacher noticed, for example, that when he went to the lavatory he was gone a very long time. Eventually, they realised that the poor lad was masturbating furiously, even at the tender age of nine.

From thereon in he had to have a 'minder' with him every time he visited the loo to prevent his obsessional behaviour.

Gary was sadly highly charged sexually as a young child as a result of his early experiences. Staff also noticed that he was often cruel to animals. While some of the pupils clamoured to take the class hamster home for the holidays, Gary would poke fun at it and secretly torment it through the cage with his freshly sharpened pencil. Furthermore, while most other pupils sought out the school's friendly black cat and enjoyed stroking it, Gary would find opportunities secretly to throw stones at it, sending it leaping away, terrified, at the very sight of the boy.

Eventually, the law caught up with Gary's parents. They were put into prison on animal bestiality charges and given the maximum sentence. Gary went to a secure children's home, but his behaviour was such that it warranted the judgement of "Coercive Violent Behaviour" with which he was sent to a secure youth custody centre. His parents continued their life of crime when they were eventually released from prison, and, so damaged and depraved were they themselves, that they did not worry to find out what had become of their son, and never bothered to track him down again. They regularly went into prison for spells, then came out, moving frequently to avoid recapture.

Small wonder, with this sad history, that Gary ended up on the streets, stealing where he could sometimes quite large amounts pick-pocketed from unsuspecting customers in Borough Road Market in particular, and committing violent sexual acts when the opportunity arose, to mention Sister Hope and Kitty Connors but two, and he was always on the lookout for more possible unsuspecting victims.

He was a driven and obsessed young man and regarded as extremely dangerous by the police.

CHAPTER 26

Bruce dropped his daughter off at Charing Cross Pier at twelve-thirty a.m. precisely, in order for her to board *The Grand Duchess*. Clara had persuaded her father, of course, that it was a safe job and therefore it would be churlish to refuse Kitty as she had been seeking work since her sixteenth birthday. He had to hide his feeling of foreboding in order not to convey any fear to Kitty. He kissed his daughter goodbye, arranged a picking-up time with her and waved to her jauntily.

Clara had been wildly excited ever since her mother had suggested the job and her father had finally acquiesced. Clara and Kitty had gone shopping together and Clara bought Kitty a short black dress, black tights and a white lacy waist apron. Kitty looked very grown up and sophisticated in the clothes, and Bruce took a sharp intake of breath when he saw her; so like Clara, so beautiful, so instinctively provocative.

Kitty was welcomed, as promised, by Matt the musical director, who was standing at the foot of the short gangway leading to *The Grand Duchess*. Quite suddenly, Kitty felt her stomach churn and her heart pound fiercely. Would she cope with the job? Would she be amongst friendly people, and, yes, she had to admit the next question was — would she be safe? Suddenly the Thames looked dark and foreboding.

Kitty was led below deck, introduced to the team, including the captain, and was shown where the bar was and how to arrange the refrigerated canapés onto plates with napkins. *The Grand Duchess* was due to leave Charing Cross pier at one a.m. but for some reason, it set sail late at one-twenty-five a.m. probably due to the delayed arrival of guests, Kitty surmised. She was grateful for this as even arranging the canapés on plates took her longer than she'd imagined. However, by one-twenty-five she had put the glasses on trays ready to serve the party guests, including those on the upper deck.

The disco music had already started as they drew away from their moorings. London looked stunning with the illuminations on the river bank and nature's own lighting from the moon, which had been at its fullest three nights ago. Bruce's research into river conditions for Kitty's event indicated that it would be a full spring tide with little wind. He had to quash a rising fear when he read that the current of the Thames that evening would be swift and therefore the undercurrents strong. He dare not tell Clara of his secret fears. She would laugh him to scorn and tell him to get a grip on his anxiety levels, adding that Kitty wasn't going swimming! She was serving as a waitress, Clara would say. Bruce could write her script in his head. Occasionally, he wondered what it would be like to have a wife who would meet his fears, talk to him about them and put her arms around him instead of forever putting him down, albeit in a teasing manner. He had battled with irrational fears ever since his painful childhood.

The clarity of the sky and the river itself that evening were magical. Kitty looked up at the stars. This was spellbinding! She then quickly refocused on the task and started circulating around the deck with her tray of canapés. Some of the partygoers were downstairs and others wandered up and began eating, plate in one hand, drink in the other. They were very pleasant and friendly to Kitty, who thought immediately what a great bunch of people they were. Her father need not have worried. There was nothing riotous about these partygoers. They were out to celebrate a birthday and were enjoying a thoroughly good time. Dancing started on the upper deck and Kitty had to pick her path carefully between the couples, making her way to the forward deck and grateful that she was no longer carrying the tray with glasses on it.

The previous evening she had looked at a map of the various bridges across the Thames. She knew they would sail downstream against the tide and would be going under Blackfriars Bridge very soon.

Sure enough, within minutes they were passing through the central arch of the bridge. More partygoers came up on deck, many gazing at the passing landmarks and commenting on the beauty of the night. The music of the disco below was in full swing. The wine flowed and the atmosphere was celebratory. Kitty loved it and already was thinking that if she did really well she might be able to secure another job on, *The Grand Duchess*.

They were approaching Cannon Street Railway Bridge. Kitty became aware of a group of partygoers on the top deck who were pointing towards the stern. Kitty couldn't hear what they were saying, but they were clearly concerned. There was apparently a dredger vessel travelling very fast behind *The Grand Duccess* and rapidly catching it up.

Suddenly, as they were approaching Southwark Bridge, the group of people watching let out a huge scream as *The Stepney Tarzan* dredger struck *The Grand Duchess* in the stern. *The Grand Duchess* swung violently to port but remained upright. Kitty's tray of canapés went flying, glasses flew in the air, people clung to each other in shock, the band stopped playing. Kitty was terrified. Suddenly *The Grand Duccess* was rammed again and all Kitty knew was that the boat felt as though it was pivoting round on the bows of *The Stepney Tarzan* and turning rapidly on its side. It was sinking. Fast. The lights cut out and in the nightmarish darkness people on the top deck began jumping overboard in desperation into what had been moonlit and romantic water but was now the dark, ugly and lethally monstrous jaws of the Thames. The sound of screaming was spine-chilling.

There was nothing for it. Knowing she was taking her life in her hands, Kitty leapt into the water. She sank down almost to the bed of the Thames. Her instinct for survival immediately kicked in as, holding her breath and thrusting her arms into a diving position pointing upwards to the surface, she swam vertically. As she came to the surface she was aware of calling and screaming, of people around her in the water, but worst of all were the muffled cries of those trapped below deck and unable to escape. Some on the top deck had frozen to the spot in terror, too paralysed by fear to attempt to save themselves. Others clung to each other.

Kitty was a good swimmer, but that was little use as the tidal flow was at its strongest and would sweep anything in its track along with it within seconds as it flowed relentlessly downstream on the tide. She managed to grab a large piece of wood for a few seconds but had to release it as someone stronger and equally desperate pulled it away. At that moment, Kitty knew for certain that she was fighting for her life with nothing and no one to support her. She was familiar with that area around Southwark Bridge and knew that if only she could reach Bankside there was a beach of sorts there where she could scramble up.

The river's flow was merciless and Kitty was swept under several times. She was overwhelmed suddenly by a sense of futility and weakness and resigned herself to die. 'Love you, Mum, Love you, Dad. Sorry Dad' she reiterated in her head over and over. An empty beer barrel was being swept by the tide, bobbing like a toy almost in front of her. With a last-ditch effort to save herself, Kitty managed to cling on to the end of it and was content simply to flow with it wherever it went, grateful that the immediate struggle for survival had lessened although she felt weaker and weaker as the cold of the Thames began to penetrate her body. She was not far from death and she knew it and she no longer minded.

Gary Johnson curled up comfortably on his duvet near the entrance to the tunnel on the south side of Southwell Bridge. He was always roaming around the city until gone midnight, and tonight he was later than usual as he had found a girl who he had intimidated enough to comply with his need. He had heard the crash on the Thames near Southwark Bridge, although because he was in the tunnel the sound that reached him was dull and muffled. He was used to various night time noises. London never slept, the saying went, but on this occasion, Gary wanted to. He turned over and pulled the duvet up round his ears with the intention of drifting off again, but the unfamiliar sound of the dull, ominous thud played on his mind, so after tossing and turning for a few minutes, he decided to see what it was all about.

Years ago, Gary had stolen a pair of pocket binoculars from an unsuspecting sightseer and these had remained his prize possession. Nothing else much mattered as long as he had them and he had spent many hours watching the river activity through their magnifying lenses. From his vantage point on Southwark Bridge, he looked out across the river.

There was a huge amount of activity out there tonight. He could see several small boats riding the waves upstream with the tide, and another pleasure steamer was in the vicinity. There had obviously been a major incident. What particularly caught his eyes through the binoculars, though, was a floating beer barrel rushing down the centre of the Thames which looked as though it had someone clinging onto it. Quick as a flash, Gary dashed to Bankside where he knew he could access the river. He was there within two minutes. Ripping off his tee shirt and jeans, he had another look through his powerful binoculars to locate the barrel again. He saw it had already travelled fast, so tucked the binoculars under his pile of clothes, waded into the murky water and swam hard. Gary knew he could reach the barrel even with the fast-flowing tide. He had complete faith in his own ability. He had swum illegally in the Thames many times, and from this very beach, the water serving as his weekly bath.

With an enormous effort, he was reaching the barrel and saw the girl's head dipping in and out of the water. She looked almost lifeless, but miraculously, with the buoyancy of the water, her head was more above the surface than below it. Immediately he weighed up the situation and decided his best course of action was to swim behind the barrel and girl and push them along and up to Bankside, the barrel acting as a kind of float apparatus.

'Hold on,' he yelled. 'Don't let go. Just do as ya told.'

Kitty barely heard him. She was hypothermic and fast losing consciousness. Gary swam behind, pushing the barrel. He managed for a couple of minutes, but then realised that they were all going fast downstream and past the beach and the barrel was not actually helping. He had never done any lifesaving of any kind, but knew now that it was a case of survive or both die. He shouted at the girl to let go, but she was beyond obeying instructions so he managed with brute force to prize her fingers off the barrel.

In a flash, Gary decided that the best way to move with her was for him to swim on his back with the girl holding onto his shoulders and leaning on his body. He instructed her to hold on but realised immediately that the girl was no longer able to hear anything. He grabbed her under the arms and with superhuman strength managed to swim with her, using his legs only. By now the girl was completely limp so although she was taking in mouthfuls of water (Gary somehow managed to keep her head up), it also meant that she did not struggle, which made the manoeuvre slightly easier than it might have been.

Somehow Gary made it to the beach and flopped down on the hard rocky shingle, exhausted. The girl's lips were turning blue. Mustering up the last dredges of energy, he turned her onto her side and with no knowledge of survival techniques whatsoever, thumped her on the back until she spewed out water. A flicker of recognition crossed his face.

A police launch was steaming up to the shore, having seen Gary and Kitty in the water and witnessed the courageous young man who had undoubtedly saved the girl's life.

'He's a bit of a hero, that lad,' said one of the navel police officers.

'I should say so,' said the other. 'Wonder who he belongs to?'

The answer, in Gary's case, was no one.

CHAPTER 27

The police pulled their launch up onto the shingle, secured it and leaping out with blankets, ran over to Kitty, who was dipping in and out of consciousness. Wrapping her in a blanket, they reassured her that everything was all-right, she was safe now and they would soon have her shipshape (an unfortunate turn of phrase under the circumstances).

One of the river police put a blanket around Gary and congratulated him on his magnificent effort in the water. Gary shrugged the compliment aside, wanting to escape as soon as possible as he knew he was a wanted man by the Metropolitan Police. He was wet and bedraggled, but even so his blond hair, although a couple of shades darker from its river soaking, was distinctive. He vowed to try and nick a dark dye from the supermarket as soon as he was able. He didn't know why he hadn't thought of it before.

An ambulance arrived which had been summoned by the river police as soon as they had caught sight of Gary and the girl battling against the tide to reach the beach. The paramedics tended to Kitty and told her that the hypothermia from which she was suffering, together with symptoms of shock — her pupils were enlarged and her lips were still bluish — needed careful handling and that they were conveying her to Charing Cross Hospital for treatment and observation. Kitty was unable to answer their questions so she could not articulate her home address.

Gary was pulling up his jeans and putting on his tee shirt that he had left in a pile on the beach and was relieved to see that his binoculars were safe. He was about to make a quick exit when one of the river police stopped him.

'Hey, laddie, not so fast. You've been in a state of high adrenalin and you've saved a life today. You can't just go off like this. You need to come with us as well and get properly checked over. Besides, the lassie's parents will want to see the person who saved their daughter's life.'

'No, I must be getting home,' Gary lied. 'Me mum and dad will be worrying. Said I'd be back by one o'clock.'

'You're very cold, son. I really think you should come in the ambulance with us for the once over at the hospital. You can phone your parents from there.'

'I'll be fine, thanks Officer. Me mum'll run me a nice hot bath and make me a cuppa. She's keeping me supper for me. I'll be right as rain.'

'Dream on, Gary Johnson,' Gary said to himself. These were things for which he had long ago stopped yearning.

'Come on, Fergus, we need to get this one to hospital. She's away with the fairies again.'

'OK,' he shouted. 'Listen, laddie, just promise me you'll report into the station tomorrow so that we can get your name and address and pass it on. What you've done tonight shouldn't go unrewarded, even if it's just a thank-you. You've been one hell of a hero. That river's flowing at over three knots and you were swimming against the tide to save the wee lassie.'

'Thanks,' mumbled Gary as he stumbled as quickly as he could up the beach. His legs felt like lead and he was freezing cold, but he was away from the Fuzz, which was his top priority and the last thing on God's earth he was going to do was report to them in the morning. That would be tantamount to handing himself in.

***

Robbie Taylor was an insomniac. He lived "on the edge" nervous energy-wise and was not usually asleep until the small hours of the morning. Robbie had a perfectly adequate, large bedsitting room at the top of Oliver and Connie's vicarage, complete with a comfortable bed. He never heard Rosy and her famous nocturnal wanderings, however, but nevertheless, sleep often eluded him. He had been glad sometimes to take a turn to relieve Sadie when Jack called for her in the night. Now that distraction had sadly gone and once more, he was willing the hours away. It didn't really worry him; he was used to it and always tuned in to Channel fourteen on his radio, which was one of the International Marine VHS channels. He found that if anything was to lull him to sleep, it would be the soft monotone voice of the announcer giving out news of the tides, the weather and the activity on the Thames in central London that night. It made him feel safe.

Suddenly he sat bolt upright. The man's monotone voice had become uncharacteristically animated and urgent sounding, plus several shades more treble in tone. He was reporting that news was coming in of an accident on the Thames near Southwark Bridge. Apparently, he continued with growing energy, a pleasure boat The *Grand Duchess* had been rammed by a dredger, The *Stepney Tarzan*. Southwark Bridge was just a few minutes' walk away from the vicarage. Robbie put on his clothes at lightning speed and then crept down the stairs with cat-like stealth. He was going to see what was going on, oh yes he was, and what a welcome distraction it would be from the proverbial counting of sheep! Whatever it was, it sounded exciting. Maybe he could be of some help. He wasn't a bad swimmer, after all.

He ran all the way to Southwark Bridge and immediately saw that the river was a hive of activity. Several police launches were heading downstream with their blue lights flashing and air ambulance helicopters were roaring their noisy way towards Charing Cross Hospital. Robbie saw that a large vessel was winching people from the water who were floundering close to an almost submerged vessel, presumably the stricken pleasure boat. Robbie felt a rush of excitement through his body. This had been some incident! He watched for about half an hour, enthralled and appalled in roughly equal measure by the scene.

Finally, Robbie climbed down from his vantage point on the bridge and made his way to the tunnel. In his capacity as youth leader, he often went there to see if he could chat to someone and entice them along to the club. Normally, there were a few vagrants, often young, lining the bridge, but this time Robbie nearly tripped over a body that was in the middle of the path at the entrance. The fact was that Gary had just about made it to the tunnel and then collapsed, water seeping from his wet clothes and hair. He had also lost control of his bladder, he presumed from the cold or shock, so the puddle was turning a dull yellow.

Robbie knelt down.

'What's up, mate? You look like a drowned rat? Can I help? I can find you somewhere warmer than this.'

'It's OK,' replied Gary. 'I'm just a bit done in. Pulled a girl out of the Thames.'

He said this without the faintest hint of pride, relating it as though it were an everyday occurrence for him.

'*What?* From the accident?'

'Yeh. Bit tricky. She's gone off in the ambulance now.'

Robbie realised with amazement that this was Gary Johnson who had lashed out and stuck a knife in his shoulder when was defending Bruce and Kitty at Borough Road Market. He also knew that Gary was on the 'wanted' list. Robbie had been on the lookout for him ever since his altercation with Bruce and his own stabbing, and here he was in front of his eyes, going absolutely nowhere.

Robbie had no ulterior motive when he said to Gary,

'Look, mate. Come with me. My home is only a few minutes away and I can lend you some warm clothes, then you can come back here. No strings attached. I just want to help, mate — warm you up a bit and all that. For all I know, I might be looking at a hero,' he smiled.

Still, Gary did not recognise him.

'Thanks, mate. Wouldn't mind a hot drink,' he said through chattering teeth. 'I'm freezing.'

'You can have a warm bath as well, mate, if you want.'

That sounded beyond Gary's wildest dreams.

'Don't mind if I do, then. Thanks. Then I'm coming back 'ere.'

'Fine, if that's what you want,' replied Robbie.

Robbie knew he had to think hard about this scenario. Here was a violent rapist in front of his very eyes; one who had violated Sister Hope, who was now living at the vicarage, and who had almost succeeded in raping Kitty Connors — Oliver's and Connie's precious niece. Robbie never forgot that he had once been rescued from a life of crime by Oliver, mainly through the power of his acceptance and, yes, his love, which Robbie had known was something to do with Oliver's faith.

Everything in Robbie knew that he must hand Gary over to the police, but that would mean a betrayal of what he had just said to Gary Johnson. It presented a distinct moral dilemma for him, even though he would never have couched it in those terms. The immediate task was to get Gary up the hill and round to the vicarage before he smelt a rat, recognized Robbie, and changed his mind, immediately mistrusting his motive

Gary walked slowly up the hill and was clearly very cold, even though it was a warm August night. He was beginning to shake violently. Robbie guessed that he was suffering from delayed shock and knew that he must warm him quickly. They arrived at the vicarage and Gary stumbled up the slope, looking more and more in need of some rapid action to be taken to keep him safe from increasing hypothermia and shock. Inside, Robbie whispered for him to be quiet and led Gary up the three flights of stairs to his bedsit at the top of the house. There, he turned on the light. Gary gasped at the sight of Robbie.

'I know you.' He put his hands up to his head in despair. 'Bloody hell. I've done it now,' with which he went to open the door and escape. Gary put his hand on his shoulders.

'OK, Gary. There's no plot here. I want to help. That's all. I swear to you that once you're warm you can go and I'll not say a word. Either you believe me or you don't. It's up to you.'

Gary looked Robbie full in the face.

'Well, thanks mate, but I never trust people. They just shit on you.'

Robbie reached for a blanket, and putting it round Gary's shoulders said.

'Not this one doesn't. I was shat upon on a regular basis throughout my childhood. I swear I was. Ended up in prison twice. You can't tell me anything about people letting you down. I could write the book.'

Gary stared at Robbie.

'You been in the nick 'ave ya? What for?'

'*Grievous Bodily Harm* — twice — once was "GBH with intent" and I'm not proud of it.'

Robbie started making a cup of tea and a cheese sandwich for Gary.

'But you've done good now. Seen the light have ya?' said Gary, the hint of a cynical smile playing on his lips.

'I was rescued by this family,' Robbie said simply. 'I learnt from them that people can actually love you as you are, no strings attached, no ulterior motive.'

'Blimey. Well, *I've* never met anyone like that.'

Even as Gary said this, a thought entered his head about the man in front of him who had given him a warm drink, made him a sandwich, put a blanket around his shoulders, offered him a hot bath and didn't seem to be judging him.

'Have these, but first take your wet togs off.' Robbie threw Gary his well-worn navy-blue towelling robe that was hanging on the door. 'Hurry up, 'cos you're half dying of cold. My bathroom's next door if you want. I wouldn't have the water too hot if I was you. Too much of a shock to your system.'

Gary stripped off in front of Gary, before putting the towelling robe on.

'Oh, that's better. Thanks mate. What's your name, by the way?'

'Robbie Taylor.'

'Well Robbie Taylor, I gotta thank you for this — and these,' he said, eating the sandwich voraciously and taking great gulps of the sweet tea.

'How was the girl when you got her out?' asked Robbie after Gary had devoured one half of the sandwich.

'Now she *was* dying of cold I reckon.'

'How did you see her in the water?'

'I got these binoculars, you see. I'll tell you the truth as you told me the truth about your GBH stuff. I nicked them like I nick me food, me gear, money, pretty much everything. I saw her through me binocs clinging onto this beer barrel in the water. Going under again and again — nearly drowning she was, so I swam out.

'Then what? How did you get her back? The current is lethal in the Thames tonight. I heard it on the Thames channel news.'

'I life-saved her,' said Gary simply. 'Unconscious she was by the time I reached the beach. She kept going under. Tricky holding her head up.'

'No wonder you're done in,' replied Robbie. 'What after that?'

'The ambulance came and took her off.'

'S'pose that would be to Charing Cross Hospital?'

'Yep. I 'eard the para-wot-nots say that. They wanted me to go too.'

'I suppose you didn't catch the girl's name?' asked Robbie, thinking Oliver would want to follow it up.

'Yeh, I know it. Pretty sure I recognized her,' replied Gary. 'But I'm not sure I should tell ya. Don't know what you'll do with the info when you hear it.'

'OK,' replied Robbie. 'Whatever. Just thought we could let her parents know if we can trace her.'

Gary thought for a second.

'Well, seeing as you've been pretty good to me, I'll tell ya.'

'OK,' said Robbie, glad that there was a modicum of trust beginning to build up between them. 'What was her name then?'

'It was that Kitty something. The one I was gonna have it off with in the market when you and her dad barged up. I didn't recognize her till I got her on the beach.'

'Kitty Connors?' said Robbie, aghast.

'Yeh, that's the one,' replied Gary, taking his final bite of the cheese sandwich. 'By the way, how's your shoulder where I knifed ya? Sorry about that, mate. Me blood was up.' Gary held up his mug. 'Any chance of another cuppa, mate?'

CHAPTER 28

Robbie, who was normally full of ideas and solutions to problems, was not sure how to handle this situation. He knew he had to tell Connie that her brother and sister-in-law would be urgently needed at the hospital. God willing Gary's rescue had not been too late for their daughter Kitty. He wondered what time *The Grand Duchess* had been due back at Embankment Pier, presuming that was from where it had left for its pleasure cruise — which tragically had turned out to be anything but. Bruce would soon be there to meet his daughter. Someone had to intercept him so that he could go straight to the hospital. What was the time? He reached for his watch from the bedside cabinet. Four thirty-five. He guessed Bruce would be setting out from Richmond-upon-Thames to collect Kitty about now. The pleasure cruise would probably have been perhaps four hours in total, which made it due back to the Pier any time from five a.m., depending on its disembarkation destinations along the Thames. He decided he must tell Gary that he was going to wake Oliver and Connie so that they could phone the unsuspecting Bruce and tell him about his daughter.

When Gary came out of the bath, he was looking better, with some colour back in his cheeks.

'Look, Gary, I've got to wake Oliver and Connie. You understand that, don't you? If it was your daughter, you'd want to know.'

'Oh blimey. I'd better go quick then. S'pose they'll tell the police.'

'Gary,' Robbie looked Gary straight in the eyes, and Gary did not avert his. 'I really *promise,* the police won't be called. You've saved Kitty's life, please God. None of us would want to do you in just now, would we? We'll have to live with the fact it's a bit wide of the law, but it's what I call "extenuating circumstances" (learnt that phrase from the Bill). Get into my bed and stay there and leave it to me. Honestly, I swear nothing will happen to you. You have my solemn word.'

Just as Robbie had felt all those years ago when Oliver had rescued him from becoming a lifelong criminal, Gary now had a strong feeling that he really *could* trust Gary.

'O.K. mate. But if you're lying to me and you do me in, I swear I'll kill you.'

'Fair enough,' said Robbie, unphased. 'Now get into bed and I'll go and wake Oliver.'

Oliver and Connie were, of course, appalled. Connie immediately telephoned her brother, but there was no answer. He had obviously left for the pier to collect Kitty. Clara slept with earmuffs on as she didn't like to be woken, and this evening she had chosen to sleep in the spare room which had no phone in it, so she did not hear either Bruce creeping out of bed or the telephone ringing insistently. Connie had her own opinions about her sister-in-law but being ever mindful of the damage the tongue can do, she kept her thoughts strictly to herself, even from Oliver.

Connie was beside herself when she imagined Bruce arriving at the pier and discovering there had been a tragedy on the Thames involving the vessel on which his daughter had been working that night. Oliver decided that his only course of action was to drive down to Embankment Pier and support Bruce as he received the devastating news.

Neither Sadie nor Hope had woken, so neither knew of the drama that was taking place in the house.

***

Bruce had only cat-napped fitfully in the few hours between dropping Kitty and going to collect her. He had tried to bury the fear that insisted on rising up inside his head. He had suffered like this before when Kitty had the diagnosis with childhood leukaemia when she was three years old. Once he had eventually donated his bone marrow for her, his fears had begun to subside a little. At least he felt he was doing *something*. This fear now was different. It was what the doctor had once described as "free-floating anxiety" — in other words, he had explained to Bruce, the fear has nothing specific to latch onto, so it will focus on anything that is a vague worry at the time and blow it all out of proportion.

That was it, Bruce had decided at about three a.m. He was suffering from free-floating anxiety and must deal with it with the strategies he had been given by his psychotherapist all those years ago. Except, Bruce argued to himself, this was not 'free floating.' This was about Kitty on an unknown vessel with an unknown group of partygoers in the middle of the night on the fast-flowing, rather than a free-floating Thames.

He set off early for the Pier. It was a clear run from Richmond-upon-Thames to Embankment Pier, although as he approached Charing Cross, he noticed what he thought was more police around than usual. As he approached Embankment Pier and was about to park the car, a policeman knocked on his window.

'Good morning, sir. Can I help you?'

'I'm here to collect my daughter, Officer. She's due in on *The Grand Duchess* very soon.'

The policeman's face was grave.

'You'd better park your car and go and talk to the officer in the booth at the entrance to the pier, sir.'

'Is everything all right, Officer?' asked Bruce, seeing the policeman's reaction.

'Just do as I say, sir,' said the officer noncommittally. The feeling of foreboding that he had managed to overcome since giving himself a good talking to flooded over Bruce again. He parked quickly and ran over to the booth.

'What's going on, Officer?' he said to one of the two policemen who were standing in the booth.

'Have you come to collect a passenger off *The Grand Duchess*, sir?'

It was then that Bruce noticed that there were a few people waiting around, with one or two holding each other.

'Yes, I have,' replied Bruce.

'Name of passenger?' asked the other policeman.

'Kitty Connors,' replied Bruce.

The man consulted his list.

'Sir, we have to tell you that there has been a river incident near Southwark Bridge involving *The Grand Duchess* I'm afraid the steamer was hit by a dredger conveying gravel. A huge vessel. It crashed into *The Grand Duchess* and there have been — casualties. I have to tell you that the steamer sank, sir. Many are still missing. I'm sorry.'

Bruce felt his legs collapsing under him and steadied himself on the outside of the booth. He thought he was going to be violently sick.

'What now?'

He felt a strong pair of hands on his shoulders and turned to see his brother-in-law Oliver standing behind him.

'Bruce, we think Kitty might be OK. She was rescued by a lad who is now at our house. She's been taken to Charing Cross Hospital. You need to get there quickly.'

'Oh, thank God, thank God. Clara! I must tell Clara.' Bruce's voice was broken.

'We've been trying to get her on the phone for a long time, Bruce. If you can get yourself to the hospital I will go and fetch her and bring her to you. Have you got your front door key on you?'

Bruce fumbled for his car keys and took one off from the bunch.

'Now, you get along to the hospital. Bruce, drive carefully. You're in shock. You must get there in one piece. Kitty will need you.'

'—if she's still alive' said Bruce grimly.

Oliver raced to Richmond-upon-Thames. The traffic was beginning to build up but was nothing compared to the congested roads in a couple of hours' time. Oliver prayed all the way.

'Lord. You know the secrets of our hearts. Please — *please* save Kitty.'

It was as if this phrase was stuck on a loop in his head. Then another verse of scripture came.

The Lord is my helper. I will not be afraid.

Again, the loop — all the way to Richmond-upon-Thames.

Oliver rang the bell in warning and opened the front door. He climbed the stairs two at a time and went into the double bedroom which he presumed was Bruce and Clara's. No Clara, so he went into the spare room at the back of the house. There she lay, chestnut hair splayed over the pillow, completely naked, not even a sheet over her. It was a very warm August night.

When Clara and he had been working at the same theatre, he as a chaplain and she as an actor, the two of them had had a wildly passionate encounter, just once, but neither of them had ever forgotten it, such had been the strength of the physical attraction. The affair was felt acutely by Oliver, as Clara had been a married woman. Now, as he looked at her asleep, he thought how strange it was that although he had once made love to her, he had never seen her naked. It had all been too rapid and urgent. Now, he quickly banished the thought and averted his eyes, refusing to go down that road in his mind. All his love and commitment were to Connie now, and anyway, the task in hand was both grizzly and immediate.

What Oliver did not realise that thoughts 'recollected in tranquillity' as Wordsworth put it, can come back at will to delight, disturb and lead astray.

He shook Clara, at first gently, then more firmly.

'Clara. Wake up! It's Kitty. She needs you. There's been an accident.'

No response.

'*Clara!*' he almost shouted, removing her earmuffs.

Clara woke with a start and stared at Oliver.

'What on *earth* are you doing here, Oli?'

'Clara. Listen to me.'

He told Clara the news, his heart pounding rapidly. The colour drained from her face. She leapt out of bed and dragged on T-shirt and flimsy trousers.

'Bruce. Where is he?'

'He's at the hospital. I'm here to drive you there.'

'Oh Oli, thank you,' she said, bursting into tears.

Oliver drove as fast as he could to Charing Cross Hospital. He dropped Clara off at the Casualty department.

'Please phone me as soon as you can, Clara. We'll be terribly anxious for news.'

'Will you come in too?' asked Clara softly.

'No, this is between you two, Clara.'

Suddenly Clara clung to Oliver.

'Pray for us, Oli,' she said urgently.

'Of course,' said Oliver. 'All the time, Clara, I promise,' he said, kissing the top of her head lightly. Her hair still smelt of apples, as in the old days.

Clara made her way through a host of people waiting at the desk.

'Kitty Connors? I think she's here, isn't she? I'm her mother.'

'Kitty Connors? Yes. She was on *The Grand Duchess?*' said the receptionist.

'Yes.'

'Terrible business by the sound of it. So many people trapped underneath and they say...'

Clara cut in sharply.

'Just tell me where she is please.'

'Turn left at the double doors and you should find her,' the receptionist replied brusquely, affronted at being cut off mid-sentence.

Clara found Bruce and Kitty. Bruce was sitting on a chair by Kitty's bed, holding her hand. She was never to forget this moment of finding her daughter alive. There was Kitty, looking very pale and bedraggled, head flopped back on two pillows, hair still damp, but she was *alive!* Clara rushed up to the bed.

'Kitty, oh Kitty! Thank God.'

Bruce touched Clara gently on the back and she swung around.

'Oh, Bruce! Thank God that you've found her. It must have been dreadful for you.'

Bruce smiled.

'But not any more. Our daughter's going to be all right, Clara. We're the lucky ones, aren't we? What a terrible calamity.'

'Oh yes, yes,' said Clara fervently.

'You stay there with her,' said Bruce gently. 'And I'll get you a cup of coffee from the machine.'

'Thank you, darling. You know, you're a bit of an angel, Brucie, aren't you?'

'Very heavily disguised!' said Bruce, but he went away with his heart singing. Kitty was alive, and Clara had actually paid him a compliment. What more could a man want? Bruce thanked God for both of them.

As he walked back with the drinks, his heart profoundly ached for those who had been so tragically lost that night and the devastated parents who had not found their child alive in a hospital bed.

CHAPTER 29

Hope was eight months pregnant and beginning to feel uncomfortable. Her lively baby would insist on kicking her high up in her abdomen and making the bottom of her ribs sore. The midwife at the hospital explained breezily that the baby was clearly a footballer and one who was bound to be fickle as he could not make up his mind which way round he should be in the womb. At the moment the baby did not seem to have any intention of engaging its head into the pelvis in preparation for its birth. The midwife wrote on the hospital form that this one would almost certainly be a breach presentation if it didn't turn soon.

Hope was not really phased by this, except that it would have been even better if the baby decided to come out headfirst, the right way up! Everything else was normal: blood pressure was good, iron levels good, the baby's heartbeat was strong, the estimated size was average and Hope had put on just about enough weight. She was warned, however, that if her weight did not increase more during the final month, they might think about inducing the baby.

'It will be safer in the cradle than in your womb,' the midwife explained breezily.

Far from being anxious, the thought of her baby in the cradle made everything in her leap for joy, including her boisterous little resident.

Hope, now revealed as the Connors half-sister, was welcomed by everyone in the family including the children, and their affection for her soon grew into love, just as Sadie had predicted. Connie was intrigued to have another sibling, although shocked and furious that Hope's mother had been treated so mercilessly by their father. Connie had forgiven her father shortly before he died for his abuse of her as a young child and had subsequently tended to his dying needs with compassion. This new revelation, however, chipped away at her ability to hold her father's memory with love. He really did seem to have been a man with few morals and a high degree of disregard for their sweet mother Rosa and, as she now learnt from his treatment of Hope's mother, for women in general.

Connie, Sadie and Hope talked into the night on many occasions, ruminating over their father's actions. Hope saw the sexual choices her father made as a sickness rather than blatant cruelty, but she had not been on the receiving end of their father's constant abuse, neither had she seen the bullying that went on towards their brothers. The damage wrought on them was limitless, so much so that the oldest boy James took his own life, and the other, Bruce, was severely impeded in his marriage to Clara. His impotence eventually was helped partly through the wisdom of a sexual councillor, but most particularly after his father was dead and buried, which clearly released

Bruce psychologically from the damaging grip of his childhood memories.

The three young women formed a deep bond of support and love. Oliver was a big-hearted, generous man, but he began to feel rather side-lined as the sisters spent evening after evening in the warm summer garden of the vicarage. For the first time in their marriage, Oliver found himself going to bed on his own and unable to sleep, spending hours waiting for Connie. It was often nearly two o'clock in the morning before she tucked herself in, quite electric from the conversations in the garden. Oliver knew it was entirely unworthy of him to have these thoughts, but they would rise up in his mind unbidden. He must talk to Connie about it before it became a problem. She would understand. She always did.

Hope had never known such happiness as in those early days at the vicarage. In the orphanage during her childhood, she had been relatively well cared for as far as her daily needs were concerned, but her emotional life turned inwards on herself from a lack of love and personal attention. She sought out the convent as soon as she could, deciding that her faith in God was such that she knew absolutely how much she was loved by *Him,* even if by no one else. She felt sustained and nourished by her faith, and this led her to the decision to dedicate herself to a life of prayer and service. She became a postulant and found the structure and rhythm of the convent helpful in anchoring her faith and enabling her feelings of insecurity to slowly subside.

Always, like an insistent drumbeat in Hope's head, was the fact that her mother had lost her life giving birth to her, and her father had simply disappeared. She wanted to seek him out, to see him, and most of all to give him a piece of her mind and see if it would lead to some kind of reconciliation. She aimed to forgive him as an act of will for her own peace of mind as much as for his, but she could not do that unless her father showed some remorse.

Sadie and Hope had several wonderful shopping trips in Southwark and beyond. Just browsing around the shops was a strange experience for Hope. At first, she would not linger, feeling guilty that she should be doing something "more meaningful", but gradually she relaxed and now, at eight months pregnant, enjoyed nothing more than popping out to buy another tiny garment for the baby. On the whole, she went to "Bring and Buy" sales and in order to have something to "bring" she knitted tiny vests by the dozen and bought one or two matinee jackets. She decided her new baby was going to be dressed only in white, or at a pinch, cream. What she did not know was that Sadie was filling a drawer with colourful garments — a pair of lime green booties, a little first-size bright yellow crotched jacket, a multicoloured striped blanket, a soft lilac bonnet, a tiny blue balaclava, a jade green all-in-one tiny towelling Babygro suit.

The whole operation of helping Hope to prepare for her baby was cathartic and healing for Sadie, especially as Hope reiterated how much she was relying on her to help her with it. Connie would have loved to join in but could see that this was invaluable for Sadie, so slightly wistfully left them to it. She had some pale shell pink two-ply baby wool left over from a jacket she had knitted for Rosy after she was born, so set about secretly making a first size matinee jacket "just in case" Hope's baby was a girl (for which Rosy was fervently praying!).

Meanwhile, Sadie was secretly wrestling with thoughts of Jack. She had collected a few blue and pink items when she was pregnant with him and had knitted some very tiny blue cardigans after he was born. Now, wrapped in tissue paper, they were lying in her secret drawer of memorabilia marked simply "JACK". She wanted to give them to Hope but was dubious about parting with them. She remembered the mixed feelings when he was on the way, and how hard it had been to accept that it was her own father who had made her pregnant. She had hated him with a passion but could not bring herself to have bad thoughts about the infant she was carrying.

It was a similar thought process going on in Hope. She remembered with horror and recurring nightmares the rape; how the young men, one after the other, had used her mercilessly. She tried to disassociate the baby from the men and their cruel act, not wanting to feel that her child was tainted by them. But in the dark watches of the night, she could not avoid the knowledge that one of them was the father. She would never know which one. The only ones she could remember with any clarity was the one with the slicked-back, bleached blond hair and two with Mohican-style hairstyles. The remaining two were to Hope anonymous, revolting brutes.

What Hope did not know, of course, was that the one with the slicked-back, bleached blond hair, was peacefully tucked up in Robbie's bed in the room next to hers on the top landing.

CHAPTER 30

There were two bathrooms on the top floor of the vicarage. One was for Robbie's use and the other was for Sadie, which she now shared with Hope. There was one separate toilet. If it was occupied when someone wanted it, then there was always another on the middle landing which was mainly used by the Connors family.

At seven fifteen a.m. on the morning after *The Grand Duchess* tragedy, Gary awoke with a start from a short but deep sleep. He knew he had to get out of this house quickly before the rest of the family saw him. Putting on the navy towelling robe he made for the toilet, after which his plan was to beat a hasty retreat back to the tunnel where he would make plans for his next move. He decided he must leave the vicinity, probably moving out of London, with his hair dyed dark brown.

Hope was coming out of her room, dressed in a short pink nightie (one of Connie's pregnancy ones), which stretched tightly over her pregnancy bump. She was half asleep, but the baby had been lying on her bladder with predictable consequences. She stopped abruptly in her tracks and let out a small scream as if she had seen a ghost. Had this man stepped out of her recurring nightmare? She clutched the baby inside her and steadied herself on a door handle.

'Oh, sorry love. Didn't mean to frighten you. It's a long story. I've had a bed for the night here.'

Gary did not recognize Hope but Hope certainly recognized Gary and it had sent her into a tailspin of shock. She slowly sank to the floor, trembling, and sat there dumbfounded.

'When's it due, then? Quite a size, innit.'

Hope finally found a voice. Although shocked to the core, she was determined to call this young man to account for his part in the gang rape.

'You don't recognize me, do you, Gary Johnson?'

Gary stared. There was something vaguely familiar about her face and particularly her voice, but he could not place it.

'I'm not surprised about that really,' she continued. 'You and your disgusting friends were in rather a hurry.'

Slowly Gary began to piece her small statements together. Finally, he whispered.

'You're not that Nun in the market, are you?'

'I am,' replied Hope.

Gary was silent. Then, surprisingly, he started crying.

'Oh blimey, oh bloody hell. Never thought I'd see *you* again.'

'No.'

There was silence. Hope was trembling inside but she remained resolute.

'You see, God has a way of calling us all to account.'

'You're not kidding, Sister. See, I thought I'd done something good tonight for a change, but it don't count, do it? Not likely 'cos it's *me,* innit? Bleedin' worthless.'

'What do you mean?'

'Pulled a girl out of the Thames tonight, didn't I? Robbie said I done a brave thing and the Fuzz even said I was a bit of a hero, but like I say, it don't count, does it?'

'It's not only good works that count,' Hope said coolly. 'I think it's also how we treat people along the way. Mind you,' she added, softening, hearing her judgemental and moralistic tones. 'That sounds like a very brave thing that you did.'

Gary was silent. After a minute he said.

'No good sayin' I'm sorry, I s'pose, is it? Anyway, looks like the damage is done,' he said, staring at Hope's bump. A new thought occurred to him.

'This isn't "damage", Gary,' she said, putting her hand softly on her bump. 'This is a new human being. That's how I'm thinking of it. The damage was the rape you all took part in, not this baby.'

She kept her hand on her tummy protectively.

'S'pose — you don't — you don't know whose nipper it is, then?'

'How could I? There were five of you.'

Gary had stopped crying. Surprisingly he blurted out,

'Oh, I wannit to be mine! Always wanted a kid I have. Ain't got nuffing of me own. Just me binoculars. S'pose there's no way of finding out which of us is its old man?'

Suddenly Hope felt a sharp pain that took her breath away for a few seconds. She winced. Gary saw it.

'Oh no. What can I do? It's hurting, innit? Does it hurt with a babby inside then?'

Hope composed herself once the pain had passed.

'I expect it's what they call "Practice Contractions".'

'Wot?'

The pain was worse again and suddenly Hope felt her waters breaking and gushing out of her.

Gary saw the water pool onto the floor.

'Oh no. What's that? Is your baby coming? Quick, tell me what to do.'

'Wake Sadie in the room over there. Tell her to come quickly.'

Gary banged hard on her door.

'You in there! Sadie, innit? Come out quick! It's Sister 'Ope.'

Sadie appeared in an instant wearing nothing very much. She stared in shock at Gary and ran back to reach for a dressing gown.

'What on earth?'

'Sadie, can you just come over here?' Hope called. 'Gary, fetch me a towel please.'

Gary rushed to the bathroom. Sadie sat down by the side of Hope.

'I think it's the shock, Sadie. I just met him on the landing. He's one of the five. The baby must be coming! My waters have broken.'

Sadie suddenly became super-efficient.

'Right, where is your file of notes to take to the hospital, Hope? And where will I find your bag with your hospital stay stuff in it.' Then, she gave Hope a reassuring smile and patted her hand. 'We'll need the baby's clothes for coming home in too. And what *on earth* is *he* doing here?'

218

'Do you think the baby will be all right, Sadie? It's four weeks early.'

'Right as ninepence' replied Sadie. 'They can survive at thirty weeks or even earlier and you're thirty-six weeks, aren't you?'

Hope nodded.

Gary returned with a bath towel.

'Here you are, Sister Hope. Shall I get something to do the carpet with? It's soaking. You all right? Fancy the baby coming just when I'm 'ere!' he smiled. 'That's two rounds of excitement in one night! A life saved and a life coming. Like a fairy-tale, sort of.'

Hope and Sadie exchanged glances. Even in the midst of this crisis, they both realised that Gary Johnson, for all his roughness and previous cruelty, had a bit of poetry about him. Perceiving this in him reminded Hope that the young man who was showing such care to her now was a walking tragedy, more sinned against than sinning. Over the years she had learned that awareness of being loved brought about a freedom to express kindness from a secure place inside.

In Hope's case, she had been deprived of love as a child but found it through her faith and the ministry of the nuns. Gary was not given any such opportunity. There had not been a crumb of love in his life until now. She understood that when Gary said he longed to be a father he was expressing a deeply felt and simply articulated need. In that few minutes of contemplation between her contractions, Hope's prayer was that her anger at him would gradually be transformed into a desire to see this damaged lad come good.

'Gary,' she said. 'Please drop the "Sister" bit. I'm just plain Hope now.'

'Nothing plain about you, Miss. You're gorgeous. Never knew it when you had that black stuff on.'

As soon as he had said it, Gary wished he hadn't. It would be wrongly interpreted considering his previous vile act. Fortunately, Hope smiled at him.

'You want a girl or a little lad then, *Hope,*' he said, emphasizing her name.

'Just a healthy baby,' replied Hope.

'So, where's the pains gone? Is the babby coming or not? Reckon it's a boy — seems to be causing a lot of bovver. We all do, us blokes,' he said, eyeing Hope to see her reaction.

Hope was saved from formulating an answer by a fierce contraction which took her breath away. Just as it happened, Robbie came pounding up the stairs, immediately followed by Connie and Oliver. Later, Connie was to paint a picture in oils of what she saw on the upper landing: a woman in labour wearing a pink nightie sitting on the floor in pain, a vagrant lad, blond hair dishevelled, wiping the carpet down with a sponge, and Sadie with a flimsy robe on, her body outline clear to see, with a suitcase open in front of her checking small baby clothes. It was easy to recall in her mind's eye. It was a surreal and compelling scene.

Connie decided that an ambulance should be called as Hope's contractions were now coming thick and fast.

Oliver would have driven her to hospital but neither Connie nor Sadie fancied delivering the baby in the back of the car. While they were waiting for an ambulance, Hope asked Sadie and Connie if they would both go with her to the hospital. Oliver, out of his depth, packed them up a few sandwiches and slipped them into the bag of baby clothes. The ambulance arrived quickly and Hope managed to climb its ramp, graciously declining the wheelchair offered. Soon they were whisked away to St. Thomas's Hospital for the delivery of the baby.

Oliver needed to feel useful. He put together a cooked breakfast for Gary and Robbie before the children woke, and Gary had the very best breakfast of his life: eggs, bacon, sausage, baked beans, toast, marmalade and a giant mug of tea. He sat in the kitchen and looked around. He had never had, nor was likely to have, any home like this, How could he ever get to be like these people, or have what they had? He knew it was a lost cause, and quite suddenly he rose from the table and excused himself.

'Lovely breakfast thanks, Mr Vicar and Robbie. Won't forget it.'

'You don't have to rush off, Gary.'

'I do,' said Gary. 'Things to do.'

With that, he whisked up the stairs to collect his binoculars. He couldn't resist nicking a towel, more as a keepsake than anything else, stuffed it in his tee shirt and tiptoed down the stairs and out of the front door. Thereafter, he ran back to the tunnel and sat and stared into space. The whole experience of the last five hours had left him emotionally and physically exhausted. He lay down on the hard concrete and slept for several hours.

When he finally awoke, he got to his feet quickly with one thought only running through his mind. He headed off into the town where he would move through the shoppers like quicksilver.

CHAPTER 31

Hope's labour was protracted. Although her waters had broken, her contractions stopped when she reached the hospital. Had it not been for the rupturing of the membranes, Hope could easily have regarded it now as a false alarm. However, an internal examination by the midwife on duty, together with all the usual checks, indicated that Hope had done the right thing by coming into the hospital. Her cervix was six centimetres dilated, her contractions had stopped and the baby had remained in the breech position so the delivery might be challenging.

Connie went to the hospital's cafeteria, brought three cups of tea and took them up to the ward to find Sadie tucking into the sandwiches Oliver had made them.

'Oli makes a mean sandwich,' remarked Sadie. 'Even if the new baby clothes do smell of cheese and onion!'

'He's a very nice man,' said Hope. 'And a great father,' adding rather wistfully, patting her tummy. 'He or she won't have one, so I'll have to be mother and father to it.'

'Hope, we'll be by your side all the time. He may not have a dad, but he'll have three mums!'

Hope smiled broadly.

'Lucky baby, then!'

Had Oliver heard this conversation, a warning bell would have sounded in his head, even though he would have dampened it immediately.

Suddenly, as she was sipping her tea, Hope held her abdomen with her other hand and screwed up her face. Sadie took the hot tea away quickly. Hope's labour had begun in earnest, thank goodness.

A little girl was born later that evening. The birth, despite the predictions, had been entirely straightforward and during the last three hours, the baby had obligingly turned herself the right way up. She was tiny and beautiful; just six pounds and healthy, so although she was nearly four weeks premature, there were no alarm bells ringing. With a soft feathery cap of blonde-gold hair, she was, as Connie said, 'As pretty as a picture and the image of her mum!'

Hope gazed at the baby as she lay in the crook of her arm, and thanked God for her miracle child. She kissed her gently before the midwife took her away for a routine post-birth examination with the paediatrician.

'She's perfect,' said Sadie through her tears. 'You *are* lucky, Hope,' she said as she thought of the moment she had seen poor little twisted Jack. She had loved him instantly but was full of guilt throughout his short life that she had produced a physically imperfect child who was destined to struggle in life.

Connie took Sadie's hand, knowing her sister was wrestling with memories and held it tightly. She thought about how both her sisters had suffered in their own ways.

'You are both so brave,' she said. 'You've coped with such a lot.'

'She's a gift from God, this baby,' replied Hope.

'What name have you finally decided on?' asked Connie.

'I think Lucy,' replied Hope. 'Lucy means "Light": "Lucy Grace Erin" — Grace meaning "goodness and generosity" and Erin after my mother.'

'That's lovely,' said Sadie. 'It suits her.'

'Yes, it's a beautiful name for her, Hope,' said Connie. 'She'll be the light of all our lives — especially Rosy's!'

They chatted on gently, with Hope resting her head on the pillow and relishing the quietly glowing feeling that all was well.

The paediatrician came in, followed by the nurse wheeling the baby in her see-through hospital cradle.

'Well,' he said. 'She is well, although I have to tell you that she is not quite perfect.'

Hope sat up. A myriad of possibilities rushed through her head.

'Tell me quickly please,' she said. 'What's the matter with her? She *looks* so perfect.'

'Your baby has a condition known as "Syndactyly".'

The women gasped. None of them had ever heard of it, and Sadie thought she had read every medical book ever published when looking for as much detailed information about Jack's condition as she could. She had not come across this one.

'What is it?' whispered Hope, hardly breathing.

'If you look at her toes, you will see,' replied the Paediatrician. 'Nurse, can you pick her up, please? Put her on the bed for a minute alongside Mother.'

Even though Sadie was shocked by the news, she decided that this man was far too abrupt in his delivery of bad news, and furthermore, patronising in tone to address Hope simply as "Mother". Sadie had hated being addressed like that when Jack was born.

The Paediatrician carefully loosened the cellular blanket in which the baby was cocooned, revealing her two tiny feet moving constantly.

'If you see here, and here,' he lifted her right foot to reveal the middle toe and the one next to it fused together by extra skin.

'Oh, a couple of webbed toes,' said Sadie matter-of-factly. 'Oh Hope, that's *nothing* despite its fancy name.'

'It means that her walking may be affected as the two toes fused together are classed as a disability,' said the paediatrician, giving Sadie a withering glance. 'But no, my assistant paediatrician here,' — he waved a hand dismissively at Sadie — 'is right in that it is nothing to worry about unduly. We can give her a small operation when we see whether it is affecting her walking.'

Hope leaned over her baby and kissed her tiny foot.

'What causes it, doctor?'

'It's genetic — something that probably happens in early pregnancy when the foetus is forming. Has any of your family got any webbing?' he asked in the matter-of-fact tone of a medic.

'Not that I know of,' replied Hope.

'What about the father? It can be handed down on the male or the female side. It's slightly more common in boys.'

'I don't know about the father,' replied Hope simply.

There was silence in the room as the Paediatrician flicked through the file of notes.

'Ah yes. You've had a very unfortunate time, Hope, haven't you?' He coughed, suddenly embarrassed. 'It says here that you were ra—' he stopped, suddenly lost for words. 'Well, never mind. These things happen. You have a lovely baby as a result of the — er — as a result of it.'

Sadie glared at him again and decided there and then that this warranted a letter of complaint. This time the Paediatrician averted his eyes and coughed, embarrassed. That could have been put better, thought Hope, but it was absolutely true. She had the baby. This was her child and she would spend her life looking after her needs and surrounding her with love.

The Paediatrician and the nurse left. Hope held her baby close.

'Well, Lucy Grace Erin O'Neill. In my eyes you are perfect.'

'And in God's eyes,' whispered Connie.

'Amen to that,' whispered Sadie through her softly falling tears. Her flash of anger was spent and replaced by a quiet sorrow over Jack combined with huge and honest relief that Lucy's condition was nothing much to worry about in the great scheme of things.

CHAPTER 32

Gary woke up refreshed. He'd had more nourishing food inside him than practically ever, thanks to Oliver's cooking, and he felt energized. He was amazed to see that he had slept till mid-afternoon. He thought little of having saved Kitty Connors from certain death, but a great deal about meeting the pregnant Sister Hope in the small hours of the morning. He became obsessed with the thought that the baby might be his. After all, he was first in line to help himself to Hope that day in the market. The other four came after him so his "little swimmers" must have got to their target first, he reasoned.

He knew nothing of what a woman's labour was like, or its early stages, although he'd witnessed puppies and kittens being born. He had taken great delight in drowning many of them at birth, as instructed by his scheming parents. He did not remember much about his mother and father, except that they paid him in gobstoppers and chewing gum for all sorts of savagely cruel and depraved acts with animals. His father filmed them all with relish, sold the photographs and videos on the black market and made a small fortune. He remembered that sometimes he was allowed to sleep in his mother's bed with her afterwards. That reward was far greater than any gobstopper because if it had been a particularly satisfactory session, she would cuddle him and tell him he was a good boy.

Now Gary held great bitterness in his heart towards them. Neither of them could be bothered to seek him out when they were released from prison. He couldn't understand how his mother could show him such love in her bed and then fail to find him later. He had no idea where they were now. For all he knew, they could be back in jail following more acts of bestiality with another unsuspecting child at their mercy. Worst case scenario (or was it the worst-case scenario?), one or both of them could be dead.

It was a small wonder, then, that Gary's life had become unravelled and steeped in criminal acts. He knew he had a problem with his sexual urges. They drove him constantly and no matter how many times he relieved himself one way or another, they continued to be a persistent voice urging him on and giving him an insatiable appetite in this direction. Sometimes his sexual urges threatened to drive him insane. His parents had been accused of "Corruption of a Minor and Child Molestation" and the fact of the matter, which Gary knew nothing of, was that they had reoffended within months of being released and found themselves back inside within a year. The legacy they had left Gary with was an unbearably cruel and sad one and was wrecking his life. The accusation of child molestation and corruption that they had been found guilty of was only part of it. The psychological and emotional wounds they had dealt out to their only son were deep and lasting. His behaviour had been distorted and he would bear the scars forever.

Today, though, Gary was upbeat. He had a daring plan and was intent on executing it.

He had been particularly successful in stealing not one but three wallets from the back pockets of unsuspecting men who sauntered through Southwark city centre, in Gary's eyes as though they owned the place. Gary thought "more fool them" as their wallets were barely concealed and just begging to be taken. These idiots deserved it. The wallets were particularly bountiful in £5.00 notes, which suited Gary's project, and one of them had four twenty-pound notes in it. Yes, it had certainly been a good harvest so far.

Today, Gary slipped into Borough Road Market, his favourite stamping ground, and immediately bought a large sports bag. He then toured the aisles until he came to the one stall that sold cut-price baby goods of all kinds. He bought a variety of items, ranging from disposable nappies to two soft toys, one pink and one blue, and stuffed them in the bag. He found actually paying for his purchases rather a novel experience. Usually, Borough Road was his favourite place to nick as much as he could, hide the goods under his denim jacket and then slither, snake-like, out of danger.

As he was making his way out of the market, he saw plastered over the billboard outside a newsagents, the headline:

Tragedy on Thames Pleasure Steamer Sinks.

Gary was not a particularly good reader, but because of the headline, he bought an evening paper. Immediately he reached his makeshift home in the tunnel, which consisted of a duvet and pillow, a small stove, a saucepan, and an old whistling kettle, he sat down and spread out the paper.

He flicked through the pages, skimming the sketchy details about the tragedy on the Thames. Virtually the whole of the evening newspaper had been handed over to the story of the night before. Suddenly, Gary froze. There, on page four of the paper, he read:

Anonymous Thames Hero Saves Girl.

Underneath the headline was a photograph of himself, dripping wet on the beach at Bankside. Gary stared, dumbfounded. Who on earth had taken that? He had seen no photographer, just a couple of police on the beach and after a few minutes, the paramedics. His mind raced.

Thank God, I never told them my name, he thought, appalled at the exposure. This picture would have severe ramifications with the police, he knew.

Decision made: he must move right away, maybe even out of London, but not before his mission was accomplished in Southwark. After all, the baby must have been born by now, whether a boy or a girl it really didn't matter to Gary as long as he could prove it was his.

CHAPTER 33

Hope brought the baby home after five days. Mother and child were both doing well. Sadie and Connie clucked around Hope and Lucy like a couple of mother hens and the baby was surrounded by love and adoration. Oliver was very pleased to see Hope so happy. The baby really was very sweet, and Rosy was delighted. She had constantly whined to Connie about not being allowed a baby brother or sister, so maybe the presence of Lucy Grace Erin would quieten her for a while. Both he and Connie felt that to go in for a fourth child would be rather excessive considering the way their time was taken up with parish commitments and a busy household, for all of whom Connie usually cooked. Oliver quietly performed a huge variety of practical chores and ran repairs in the rambling vicarage, squeezing them in between ministering to his flock in St. Luke's parish and trying to be a good father.

The early September weather was exceptionally warm, in fact it was categorized officially as an Indian Summer. The flat and rooms at the top of the vicarage retained the heat and Hope noticed that the temperature went up to ninety-four degrees Fahrenheit in her bedroom. The baby, now three weeks old, was tetchy in the heat, and after a few days, Hope decided to put her outside in the pram. The front garden was secluded, and well shielded by a beautiful tall golden Azalea hedge. By putting Lucy under the leafy tree in the front garden Hope would be able to look down on her frequently from the upstairs window. Rosy was forever gently rocking the pram and seemed content simply to be a kindly guard dog to the baby. She loved gently twirling the fringes of the white canopy and gazing into Lucy. Her cup of joy was overflowing. A new baby at last!

It was two o'clock in the afternoon. Lucy was safely fed and put back outside. Hope thought how lovely it was that she could put her out in the air in nothing but a nappy and a tiny white angel top — a good start in life for her. The baby had now settled since being put out in the shade and Sadie was out shopping, so Hope had the sitting room to herself. She curled herself into the armchair intending to relax for ten minutes before doing her regular check on Lucy, but, weary from the heat and what seemed like endless breastfeeding, she nodded quietly off into a light sleep.

Suddenly her peace was shattered by Rosy pounding up the stairs, followed by Connie and Oliver.

'Auntie Hope! Auntie Hope! Lucy's gone! She's gone!'

The words tumbled out of Lucy. Hope leapt up and frantically peered out of the window.

'I had my fish fingers for lunch and mummy said I could go out again for a little while with her and when — and when I looked, she was *gone!*'

Rosy began howling in dismay.

233

'Someone must have taken her! Daddy! Find her!'

They all rushed back downstairs. Hope could feel her legs had turned to jelly and she had only just saved herself from fainting when Rosy made the devastating announcement. Once they reached the empty pram, Oliver said authoritatively.

'Now. It's no good our just darting around and panicking. I'll phone the police and then we will all go in different directions and see if we can see anyone with Lucy. Chances are we'll find her if we're quick. She can't have gone very far. I guess it might be a woman.'

'Do we know of anyone in the parish who has just lost a baby, Oliver?' asked Connie.

'Auntie Hope has, stupid, silly Mummy.' Rosy stamped her feet in anguish.

'Rosy, you and I will go towards the market,' Connie said, worried sick about the terrible impact this was bound to have on her daughter in addition to the anguish of her beloved half-sister.

'Oliver, you decide with Hope which way you two will go.'

'Hope, I think it would be better if you stay here,' said Oliver.

'I can't possibly stay here, Oliver. I've got to search for my baby.' Her face was white and stricken. This was without exception the worst day of her life.

James and Peter had been to the local swimming pool as the new term had not quite started. Oliver saw them strolling down the hill towards the house, hair wet and

234

tousled, laughing companionably, swimming towels rolled up and tucked under their arms.

'Jamie, Peter, get a move on.' Oliver barked out the instruction. 'Stay indoors and if the police come tell them to wait.'

'All right, Dad, keep your hair on. What's up?' asked James.

'What's up is that Lucy has been stolen.'

'*Stolen!*' exclaimed Peter. 'Wow! Some pervert I expect.'

Even amidst the crisis, Oliver could not let his son get away with the remark.

'Or some desperately sick person,' he said to Peter.

'Oh Dad,' said James. 'Just for once call wickedness "wickedness", for goodness' sake. You can't protect the whole world you know. Stealing a baby is stealing a baby,' he said with all the superior knowledge of an adolescent boy.

Despite the frantic search, the baby was nowhere to be found. After half an hour of desperate rushing around and questioning virtually every woman in sight, Hope returned to the vicarage in a state of collapse. She sank down in the armchair in Oliver's study and put her head in her hands. She wasn't sure, and neither was anyone else, whether she was desperately praying or dying inside, or perhaps both.

The police had already arrived and were being entertained by the two boys, who decided to tell the police all they knew about the law and how crime should be dealt with in Southwark.

'Your sons really are something else, Rev. Connors' said one of them. 'I reckon he'll be head of the Met and the other — this one,' he said, pointing to Peter. 'Will be prime minister.'

Oliver had not got the energy to respond. He was proud of his sons, but they had a lot to learn. One of the worst things in Oliver's eyes was that they should grow up thinking they knew everything and had every issue tied up and sorted. Oliver couldn't abide black and white thinking, believing that most balanced decisions were made somewhere in the middle of the two. But the boys were young and very opinionated — but with promising intellects.

The police were kind to Hope, questioning her gently about the time the baby was put out in the garden, what she was wearing, if one of them had seen anyone lurking around or acting suspiciously, if there had been a troubled soul in the hospital who might have a vendetta against Hope, or whose baby had died, and so on. They then turned their attention to Rosy.

'Rosy, you've been a good girl guarding the baby, haven't you?' said one officer.

Rosy said amidst her tears, 'Yes, but I had to have my fish fingers, didn't I? Mummy called me in and I do *not* like them soggy and cold.'

'Of course,' he replied. 'I just wondered if you had seen anyone looking in the front garden, or coming up the slope or wanting to talk to you?'

'I saw the postman.'

'Yes, and did he say anything to you?'

He said, 'I've got a big pile of letters for your Mum and Dad and a recorded delivery one for Ms Sadie Connors.'

'Anything else?'

He leant over the pram and said, 'That's a nice baby. Didn't know your mum had had a baby.' 'Well, she has,' I said. 'I had forgotten it was Auntie Hope's baby.'

Connie and Oliver could not resist the smallest of smiles. Rosy just had to fulfil her dream world and a baby sister was top of the list.

The questioning of everyone continued for some time. Sadie left the room briefly.

'Do you ever pick Lottie up, Rosy?'

'Lucy! Stupid!

'Rosy,' warned Oliver.

'I'm only allowed to pick her up indoors when Auntie Hope says I can,' replied Rosy.

There was silence for a minute.

'Whoever has taken Lo -'

'*Lucy!*' shouted Rosy. 'Can't you even get her name right, Mr Policeman?'

'Lucy,' he replied, studiously ignoring Rosy. 'Will be found, Mrs um — Hope.'

'My name is Miss O'Neill, Officer.'

'Sorry *Miss* O'Neill,' he replied, quickly making a mental note in his bigoted mind that this was yet another unmarried mother to be a drain on society.

'He or she must be desperately needy to steal a newborn,' said Oliver.

The policemen said nothing — and here was yet another of these individuals who would send even the most hardened criminals away with a small kick up the backside and a packet of tea. Still, they supposed it was in his job description to forgive sinners.

'Look Miss — Um… O'Neill. These cases are usually solved — eventually — but you might have to prepare yourself for a bit of a wait.'

The police left and Hope collapsed in tears. This was the worst thing they could possibly have said to her. All she wanted was her baby back — *now*. Already she could feel the milk filling her breasts for Lucy. Sadie furtively hid the recorded letter she had just opened down her blouse and put her arms around Hope.

'Listen, everyone. I'm going to put up a reward for £10,000 for the safe return of Lucy. Don't say a word and don't argue. Never mind how I have that sort of money. Robbie, I want to draw up some posters like you do when you're advertising an event at the youth club, and Oliver, please will you display one on your notice board outside the church? We'll photocopy a few and put them around.'

Sadie spoke decisively. It would be a brave person, thought Oliver, to contradict her when she was in this sort of mood. He wasn't sure where all this sat with the police but didn't question her.

'I will explain about the money, but for now, let's just get this done.'

Hope was beyond taking all this in, but she knew she wanted to telephone the faithful nuns in the Convent in Ireland and ask them urgently to instate a prayer vigil for

Lucy. In cases of need or danger, the nuns would stay up all night and pray. Hope had always felt that intercessory prayer was the nuns' most important work and they had seen some wonderful answers. Hope had let the Abbess know when her daughter had been born, and the nuns had collectively sent her a small package of knitted and crocheted baby clothes they had made. For all their shock and misgivings about Hope's pregnancy and her decision to go to England, they had been delighted to hear of Lucy Grace Erin O'Neill's birth and celebrated the news with a glass of very special home-brewed mead made out of honey, sugar and apples, believing it to be "completely harmless and full of goodness", as the Abbess put it.

It was 20% alcohol.

The nuns spent a particularly merry evening together wetting the baby's head. Several of them overslept the following morning, missing Matins completely.

CHAPTER 34

Quick as a flash, Gary had lifted the baby from her pram and put her in the unzipped sports bag he had bought specifically for that purpose. He had been watching the house for some time. The baby didn't make a sound and remained asleep until they reached Bankside beach. There were a worrying number of people sunbathing, which made life tricky for Gary. He knew he must on no account be noticed with the baby, so his only chance of anonymity was to climb high up on the steep rocks that characterised the central London beach. Fortunately, he was fleet of foot so made it to the top easily.

He put the bag down carefully. This was some baby! Despite everything, it was still sleeping and Gary was longing for him or her to wake up. He was not going to keep it for long — just a few hours — which would be enough time for him to have something in his possession that was his and his alone for a few hours, and also prove he could care for his baby. He wanted to scrutinize the baby as he had become obsessed with trying to find out if he was its father. That would be beyond his wildest dreams. Gary Johnson had nothing in this life. Even his long-suffering black and white mongrel dog Patch, who had been his faithful friend for years, was dead. In the past,

Gary would often go without food himself to feed Patch with a sandwich kindly left.

If he could prove he was the father of the baby somehow, maybe Hope would let him into her life. These were unfamiliar feelings to Gary. This was the boy who had pulled wings off butterflies, drowned kittens and puppies with impunity and lined up slugs and crunched them one after the other with the front wheel of his old tricycle, examining their entrails with satisfaction. This was also the boy who cut live worms into little pieces, watching each piece squirm, and had joined his parents in stimulating animals to such an extent that they were in effect being tortured, and then, when finished with, his job was to tie them up and dump them onto a fast road to meet their fate with an unsuspecting lorry driver.

Here he was, to his own amazement, putting up a toy tent that he had bought to keep the sun off the baby. Not knowing what he or she had been named, he was going to call it simply Baby Hope. He picked the newborn infant up carefully from the sports bag. Baby Hope began to wake and moved her tiny hands and feet. Gary had bought a bottle of water and a teaspoon. Fortunately, she didn't seem hungry or thirsty. He spoke to the baby gently.

'Hello, Babby. This is your daddy speakin'. I'm gonna look after you, I is. You'll see. You belong to me, don't cha?'

Lucy began to cry.

'Don't you worry. We'll get you back to your ma soon enough. This is just a little visit to your daddy. You're gonna love me when you get to know me, yes you is, yes you is,' he crooned. 'Look, I've bought you a toy rabbit. Now, is it going to be pink or blue? Nice, 'ain't they?'

He jiggled both rabbits in front of the baby's eyes, then noticed that the white angel top was wringing wet from her overheated little body. Taking it off was quite a complicated manoeuvre. Suddenly, the baby seemed to have arms and legs everywhere, and he struggled to get the tiny arms out of their sleeves without hurting them. Eventually, it was done. The baby became calmer. He lay her down on the base of the toy tent and took her nappy off. He stared at her naked little front. A girl! So secret, so perfect, so beautiful!

Gary did not bring thoughts to the surface, but subconsciously something in him was wrestling with the memories of his abuse of women, and beginning to perceive what violating behaviour it had been against them. No one had better abuse his Baby Hope when she grew up. Oh no. Just let them try!

He gazed at her for some time. He had never seen anything so tiny and so utterly perfect. He stroked her arms and held her finger. She clutched it tightly, which made his spirit sing. Opening the packet of disposable nappies, he took one out and eventually worked out how to put it on. She kicked.

'Oh, I gotcha. You're gonna be a little girlie footballer for your daddy, is you? Let's have a look at those kicking feet then!'

He stroked her feet and suddenly stopped. He saw her two tiny toes joined together by extra skin, forming a web. Rapidly, hardly daring to breathe, he undid his trainer and put his right foot on a rock. There, absolutely, was evidence that he was the father of the baby! He had the same two toes as the baby's completely co-joined by flesh. His mother, he knew, had two webbed fingers which made it difficult, she said, to wear her wedding ring, (but which in actuality aided her extramarital affairs). She had always told Gary that her father had been to blame because he had handed on the gene, adding grimly, 'What did he fink we wanted to be — *Ducks?* Your kids'll be the same, Gary. Webbed, like bleedin' frogs, thanks to your granddad. It's handed down.'

Gary picked the baby up and held her close. Unquestionably this was his daughter. He would take her back to Hope, but no way was he getting out of her life. Oh no! He was staying close by her for as long as the Fuzz didn't catch up with him, and even then, he wouldn't be inside for all of her life. Gary spent a happy hour on the beach gazing at Lucy until she started crying with hunger. He poured a little of the water onto a spoon and tipped it into the baby's mouth, succeeding in causing her to splutter and choke; so much so that he began to worry that she would never get her breath back, despite his frantic thumping on her back. Finally, when she did breathe, she screamed and screamed.

The sun was just beginning to lose some of its heat and Gary was now nervous of the intense crying the baby was making. He thought that any minute someone would hear the crying and challenge him. He put Lucy into the sports bag, much to her fury, packed up the bag and climbed back down the rocks, leaving the tent behind.

Walking through the town centre, he was aware that the baby had stopped crying. Maybe that was because he had taken a chance and zipped up the bag, apart from a couple of inches. He knew he must be very watchful in case the baby suffocated. He hurried along, and then saw the huge poster outside the church, together with a box of leaflets.

Vicarage baby missing. Substantial reward for safe return

Take a leaflet for details

Hardly daring to breathe, Gary sat on a bench and unzipped the bag. The baby was extremely hot and had fallen asleep. He haltingly read the leaflet. The "substantial reward" was ten thousand pounds. Ten thousand smackers! Gary's mind was working overtime. He could ditch the nappies and toys and take the baby back to the vicarage and claim he had found her abandoned in a sports bag. What a gift!

He furtively threw away the nappies and toys, hesitating momentarily over the pink rabbit. He had chosen the blue and the pink with care for the baby — but — £10,000! Hesitation was gone at the thought of it, so he threw the rabbits into the bin and moved on. In his mind he was playing and replaying how he was going to explain everything; where he "found" the sports bag with the baby in it and — yes, please could he have his reward?

Gary's mind, however, was mulling over a crucial question. If he handed the baby back and took the reward, would he still be able to point out the webbed feet, and more importantly, would Hope allow him into the baby's life? Gary was not used to pondering questions, particularly this kind of potentially life-changing type. He generally acted on instinct. It was animal instinct that made him join in the gang rape of Hope. It was that same instinct that drove him to trap Kitty Connors into going to the market with him in order that he might rape her. It was also his instinct that made him wade into the water at Bankside and rescue the girl hanging onto the beer barrel. The Paramedics had called him a hero, but he knew there was nothing heroic about it. It was not an act of bravery that made him swim to the girl. It was simply instinct that drove him forward. It didn't take him any courage, he argued to himself because swimming was nothing to him. ('What'dya fink I've got webbed feet for?') If the girl had struggled in the water, and if it had been a case of saving himself or the girl, he knew he would have saved himself.

What Gary could not analyse, and would not accept in himself at any level, was that there was any goodness at all in him. He would not have acknowledged it had anyone pointed it out. In many ways, he was cocksure, street-wise, and superficially arrogant, but it would not have taken a behavioural psychologist long to work out that Gary had no self-esteem whatever. His parents' lack of seeking out the whereabouts of their son after their exit from prison had seen to that. The total indifference on their part was staggering. Gary was horribly deprived.

He was hurrying past Borough Road market. Fortunately for Gary, the baby was quiet. In actuality, Lucy was becoming floppy from heatstroke and in danger of severe dehydration which could lead her into unconsciousness.

Suddenly, Gary heard familiar voices shouting at him.

'Hey! Watcha Gary! Where you been? Ain't seen you lately.'

'Look at ya posh sports bag. Where d'you nick that from?'

'Saw your picture in the paper, Gaz. Hero, eh?'

'Watcha, Gang,' replied Gary, the fear rising in his throat. 'Yeh, I nicked it. Nice, innit?'

'Watcha got inside Gary mate? Pickings for all?'

With that, Mickey, the boldest of the gang, took Gary by surprise by pulling the bag swiftly out of his hands and unzipping it, thinking he'd find loot in there that they could share out. That had always been the agreement between the gang. Girls' bodies were shared, as with Sister Hope, and any stolen goods or pick-pocketed money was split five ways.

Mickey stood back aghast.

'A *babby!* Where d'ya get that from? Who'd it belong to?'

'This ain't the kid that's missing is it? Saw something outside the church up there.'

'What, the one that said 'Substantial Reward?' said the Mohican lookalike.

'Where d'ya find it, then?

'On the beach' Gary lied, 'and I'm just returning her. Give her back. I need to get her to her ma. She's too hot.'

'Oh dear me,' mocked Mickey. 'Since when did you become *Doctor* Gary then?' He swung the bag to and fro, taunting Gary.

'Right, maybe we should follow you. You claim the reward and then it's the usual deal: Split five ways, right?'

They all chimed in, 'Right!.'

'Now listen, *Doctor* Gary. I reckon we'll wait here for you here. Bit conspicuous-like if we all trundle up. We ain't going away until you're back, so don't be long,' leered Mickey.

'Give it here,' Gary said desperately. 'Tell you what,' he said, lifting the baby out of the sports bag. 'Take the bag and I'll be back for it and then we'll share the pickings.'

'Yeah, we'll take the bag,' said the other Mohican lad. 'The market's just closing. We'll have to be quick. See if we can fill the bag with stuff, fellas. They're packing up, and besides, they always drop loads of fruit and stuff.'

'We'll be right here for you,' said Mickey. 'And if you don't come back, then you know what we do to liars and cheats.'

Gary did indeed. The Gang would stop at nothing, and he realised that he was one part of the gang of five who dealt out indiscriminate violence, theft, rape and anything else that suited them. He briefly surveyed the gang, with their mocking and threatening faces, and realised in one fell swoop that something inside him wanted to change.

By removing the baby from the bag and carrying her in his arms the rest of the way to the vicarage, Gary had probably saved her little life. She was a tiny newborn, born a month early and was very near to suffering fatal heatstroke, her hair soaking wet and her skin bright pink but she was beginning to revive in the air and started whimpering.

'All right little girlie, you'll soon be at your ma's house.'

Gary knew he now had another dimension to his dilemma. If he took the reward, he would have to split it five ways, which didn't sit with him very well. If he didn't take the reward he would be answerable to the gang and he knew the punishment they would dish out. What a stroke of bad luck to meet them when he did!

He knocked at the vicarage door, still undecided how to play out this scenario. A tear-stained and bedraggled Hope answered it. Immediately she saw Gary with Lucy she pulled the baby out of his arms.

'My baby, my baby! Where did you find her, where was she?' she cried, but she didn't wait for an answer. Quick as a flash she started unbuttoning her blouse. The baby, sensing her, started screaming for her.

'There, there. Mummy's here now.' She put the baby to her exposed breast. Gary had never seen anyone breastfeeding a baby. He stared in disbelief. This Sister Hope, the virgin who had been done up in layers of long black, was baring her breast in front of him without a qualm. All that mattered to her was to feed her baby again. The baby stopped crying immediately, latched on to Hope's breast and sucked hungrily. Gary saw in one fell swoop the power of mother love.

With Lucy still at her breast, Hope walked carefully down the hallway and called Connie.

'Connie! Come quickly! She's back!'

Connie came out of the kitchen and stared incredulously.

'Thank you God, thank you God,' she said aloud.

Rosy and Oliver appeared.

'Oh goody, goody! Lucy's back. I knew she'd be safe 'cos I prayed hard to Jesus last night and he said, "It's OK Rosy, I've got her".'

Oliver smiled at his daughter. What a girl — even if she could be rude to policemen!

'Well, Rosy, we'd better thank him for his message then, hadn't we?'

Thereby the front door, in front of Gary, Oliver took Rosy's hands in his.

'Dear Father God. Thank you. Thank you for Lucy's safe return. Amen.'

'Come in, Gary,' said Oliver, grateful that he had recalled his name. 'You seem to be quite the hero. First, you rescue Kitty, then you find Hope's precious baby. Remarkable.'

At that minute, Sadie came hurrying down the stairs.

'Oh my goodness! Oh thank God! Is she OK, Hope?'

But Hope was on her way out to Connie's kitchen to continue feeding the baby. She just nodded, smiling broadly and weeping at the same; a rainbow of emotions.

Sadie looked at Gary searchingly.

'Gary, did you steal her or did you find her?'

249

Sadie was always direct, and this question took his breath away with its direct challenge.

'Gary wouldn't steal her!' said Rosy, appalled.

'Gary?' Sadie challenged again. 'Stolen or Found?'

'I found her.'

'Where?'

'On Bankside Beach.'

'There's loads of money as a reward,' chimed in Rosy. '*Ten thousand pounds!*'

'That's right,' said Oliver. 'Sadie has put up the money.'

'Right. Thanks. It'll come in handy,' said Gary, appearing nonchalant.

'*Handy?* What will you do with that amount, Gary?' asked Oliver.

'Oh, this and that,' replied Gary.

'Have you got a bank account?' Sadie knew the answer before the question had left her lips. 'If not, I'll write a cheque with a covering note and you can cash it in at the bank.'

'Any chance of cash now?' asked Gary, stopping at nothing.

'Afraid not. I don't exactly keep ten thousand pounds in cash under my mattress you know.'

'Yeah. A note with a cheque would be fine and dandy then.'

Sadie disappeared just as Robbie was swinging through the front door.

'Oh no, not you again!' said Robbie, joking. 'Rescued anyone else, then Gary?' he said flippantly.

'He has, in a manner of speaking,' said Oliver. 'Hope's baby.'

'*What!*'

Gary filled Robbie in with the story of how he had found the baby abandoned on the beach, seen the billboard, knew where the vicarage was and handed her over to be reunited with her mother. Robbie was silent. He was immediately deeply suspicious. Having been involved in a life of crime himself up until a few years ago, he knew the lengths criminals would go to secure what they wanted (usually money), and the lies they would tell along the way. He looked Gary straight in the eye and his gaze was unwavering.

'Gary. Are you *sure* that is the truth?'

'Course it is,' said Gary, feigning incredulity. Robbie continued his penetrating gaze and Gary's eyes began to shift around the room, avoiding eye contact with him.

'Would I lie to you, mate?' he said, still avoiding looking at Robbie.

'I hope not, Gary, I do hope not, because it's not worth it.'

Sadie reappeared with the cheque and the note and handed it unceremoniously over to Gary.

'There you are,' she said. I hope you get some pleasure from it. Don't spend it all at once! She laughed.

Just then, Hope reappeared, the baby still feeding from her.

'I just want to say that I don't know how to thank you, Gary. You helped me on the top landing when my labour started, and here you are again helping me by returning my precious little lamb. Thank you from the bottom of my heart. If there's anything I can do in return, please just say.'

Gary was silent. He felt a shadow of guilt pass over him briefly, but the cheque was twitching in his hand. He had to get out quickly before he ruined everything.

'OK, OK. It was nuffin'. Well, thanks all. Bye then,' he said, opening the front door. He got to the bottom of the slope and turned back.

'Can I just give Baby Hope a bit of a kiss?' he said, half embarrassed at his expression of affection. 'She's a nice little'un. Me and her are like this,' he crossed his index and middle fingers.'

'Of course, you can,' said Hope.

Gary bent over Lucy's head and gave her a gentle kiss on her forehead.

'Bye little'un. You're a sweetheart, you is.'

He walked off towards Borough Road, then stopped in the middle of the pavement, sank down and wept. It was as if he was glued to the spot. After several minutes he turned slowly and headed back up to the vicarage.

The day was not over yet.

CHAPTER 35

Gary walked back up the slope of the vicarage and hesitated in front of the door. Was he *really* doing this? What had got into him?

He knocked at the door. Robbie answered it.

'I've come to speak to Sister Hope,' he said.

'You've just seen her,' said Robbie. 'Something else was there?'

'Yeah.'

'Well, mate, she's just gone upstairs with the little'un. I'm on my way up too. I'll ask her to come down. Something up, is there?' he asked, innately suspicious.

Gary avoided Robbie's penetrating gaze and his question. There was a pause.

'Tell you what,' he said at last. 'Come up with me, but knock first. Don't just barge in,' he advised.

'Whatd'ya take me for? 'Course I'll knock.'

They went up the two flights of stairs. Gary knocked and waited, his heart in his mouth.

'Just a minute,' called Hope. 'I'm changing Lucy.'

After a minute she opened the door. Lucy was on the changing mat, kicking gently. Hope smiled broadly at Gary.

'I just want to give this back,' said Gary, waving the cheque in front of Hope.

'*What?*' said Hope incredulously. 'You want to give ten thousand pounds back when you look as though you haven't got two beans to rub together? It's your reward, Gary.'

'Yeah. Well, you see…' Gary hesitated. 'You see — I never *found* 'er. I *took* 'er.'

'You *what?*' exclaimed Hope, turning pale.

'Well, I took her. I dunno why really except I wanted to —'

Hope turned swiftly and terrifyingly into a fearsome tigress, her eyes flashing as she spat out the words.

'Get away from us, get out — how dare you? How *dare you?* Why? Why would you?' she shouted. She picked Lucy up from the changing mat and held her close.

'Do you realize what you've put me through, *us* through? How *dare* you?'

'Well, you see, I—'

'You're a liar, Gary Johnson you're not fit to be near her,' she yelled.

Hope was fast becoming out of control. The last twenty-four hours had been the worst in her life. She had never known anxiety and stress like it. In her mind, she had prepared herself to face the fact that Lucy might be dead. Something inside her now snapped in two and she hurled abuse at Gary.

'You're a filthy liar. Bloody well get out!' she yelled, and then burst into floods of tears. Lucy started crying.

Robbie and Sadie had come out of their rooms and were staring at the transformation in Hope.

'Oh, so that's all the thanks I get for bringing 'er back safe, is it and giving the money back too? You're nuffin' but a sham you are, *Sister Hope*. Dear, dear, I'm surprised at such a *holy* shitty lady using language like that!'

Gary lowered his voice menacingly.

'Well, I'll tell you somefink else,' he snarled. 'I'm her dad, and I can prove it, so put that in your pipe and smoke it, lady. You ain't seen the last of me, oh no you ain't! She's half *mine,'* he said, pointing at Lucy.

He raced down the stairs, let himself out and ran as fast as he could towards his home in the tunnel.

Sadie went to put her arm around Hope. Hope shrugged it off. She was crying furiously. In between the tears she said,

'That good-for-nothing stole my baby and put us through this agony.'

'Yes, and then had the gall to come here as if he'd found her, and take the money,' added Sadie.

Robbie spoke quietly, attempting to lower the heat in the two women.

'Yes, but he's brought the money back, hasn't he? Look at it. He stole Lucy — we don't know quite what drove him to it yet, — but he brought her back unharmed after a few hours, and now he's given the money back.'

They both stared at him.

'Look, we don't know what's been going on in his mind, do we? I know what it's like when your mum and dad couldn't care less about you. You feel totally lost inside. No real point of reference somehow.' Robbie ran his fingers through his hair, stressed at the memory. 'Well,

I guess Gary's like that. His parents abused him something shocking and then didn't even bother to find him when they came out of prison. That's hard.'

'Yes it is,' said Sadie. 'Well, we've all had some of those feelings, one way and another,' she said bitterly. 'And some of us have lost a whole lot more. But we don't all turn criminal.'

Hope was still and silent. Finally, she spoke.

'I think I'd like to be on my own, now if you don't mind,' she said quietly.

''Course you would,' said Robbie. 'It's all been dreadful for you.'

'Thank God she's back,' replied Sadie. 'I suppose at least something must have driven that Gary to bring the cheque back.'

In a whisper, Hope added.

'And my poor baby.'

Gary reached the tunnel, sank down on his duvet and buried his head in his pillow. That had all gone badly wrong and now he was up shit creek without a paddle as he later graphically described the situation. People he had just begun to trust would undoubtedly turn their backs on him. He had wrecked his chances of maintaining contact with his daughter, and now he had to face the gang knowing for certain what they would do to him when they found he had not got the money.

He began to realise that perhaps his greatest grief was that the whole family in the vicarage would now reject him and never want to see him again. He thought of the breakfast Oliver Lockwood had cooked him the morning

Hope had gone into labour. That had made him feel warm and special and wanted. He thought of Robbie's kindness, taking him in, letting him use his bath and bed. He had that same feeling of being special and wanted then. He remembered Hope's waters breaking and how he had felt useful and valued as he reached for towels for her.

Most of all, however, he remembered what he had said to Hope. The words had come out of a desire to retaliate and hurt, and for perhaps the first time in his life, Gary felt a pang of remorse. *She* didn't deserve it. She had screamed and sworn at him, but he knew *he* deserved it and more. That was the difference. She didn't, he did.

In his own way, he analysed the problem but had no idea what to do about it to make it better. He made himself a mug of tea on his rickety stove and thought perhaps Robbie might be the way forward. Robbie had seemed to understand Gary. Perhaps Gary should hang about in the morning, wait till Robbie appeared out of the vicarage and approach him.

What he did not know was that Robbie was planning to seek Gary out. Robbie had no idea whether Gary would have a conscience over what had happened but wanted to see if he was all right. Hope had been totally out of character when she had lashed out at Gary verbally. Gary had asked for it, but it was still harsh.

Neither of those things were to happen, however. The gang would see to that.

CHAPTER 36

Hope had a sleepless night, and it wasn't primarily because of Lucy's nocturnal feeds. She was shocked to the core at how she had sworn and shouted at Gary and was not sure from where all that viciousness had suddenly come. What was this maternal instinct that had driven her to dredge up from deep inside her, a violence which at that minute would have cheerfully knocked Gary senseless had she had the strength of a man? She had no idea it was even inside her.

Now she was calmer, she appraised the facts. He had stolen the baby, but as Robbie had pointed out, had returned her within a few hours. He had lied to claim the reward money, but again, as Robbie had said, he had come to give it back. What was her part in it now? She knew in the core of her being that her belief in the Christ who forgave sinners was calling her to forgive Gary. But what had He also said? 'Go and sin no more,' and again, only the person *without sin* should throw the first stone. There was no such person on earth who was qualified to throw that first stone she knew, and now she realised with sadness she had fallen very, very short of those high ideals of discipleship.

She thought hard about Gary. He was thin to the point of skeletal and his clothes were hanging off him. He had a continual pallor and despite his upbeat and cheeky manner, Hope had the insight to know that this was probably bravado, a front to help him cope with the world. Robbie had told her a little about Gary's background. It now seemed to her, with his history of bestiality crimes forced upon him by his abusing parents, that it was a miracle the baby had come back unharmed, or even at all. His request for Hope to give Lucy, or Baby Hope as he had rather endearingly called her, 'A bit of a kiss from me,' spoke volumes. She also reflected on how helpful and involved he had been when her waters had broken on the landing three weeks ago. This was a lad who may have discovered a soft side of his nature through his contact with her daughter before and after birth.

Her daughter. Was it just wishful thinking on his part, or cruel taunting, that had made him state, 'She's half mine?' Hope now had an urgent need to know what he meant. She must find him somehow. The greater driver within her, however, even more than the paternity issue, was to make peace with him, to be reconciled with him and apologise for losing her temper. Her next move was not at all clear, and as she put the baby to her breast for the early morning feed, she prayed hard for the situation. She had let God down. She knew from years ago that He had extended mercy to her and demanded holiness from her. It was she who must sin no more. She saw that clearly now. It was fundamental to everything she believed her life and her faith were about.

Hope changed the baby, talking to her softly all the while, then placed her back in her crib and put the kettle on for a cup of tea. Very shortly, Sadie came padding out of her bedroom, full of sleep still. She put her arm around Hope.

'Are you OK, Hope? I was so worried about you last night. You had reached the end of your endurance, hadn't you?'

'Yes, I suppose so,' Hope paused. She didn't feel she was ready to talk about her bad behaviour, so changed the subject.

'Sadie, I can't believe you put up all that money for a reward.'

She was longing to ask Sadie how she had managed it considering a few months ago Sadie had shared with her that she had virtually no money apart from a small rent she sometimes received from her caravan in Scotland. Knowing this, Oliver and Connie did not want any rent from her. Sadie simply covered her electricity and gas bills and bought food for the evening meal once a week for all of them.

'No, I can't believe it either,' she laughed. 'Shall I tell you about it, Hope?'

Sadie's voice became dark and soft.

'When Jack had his accident, I was in pieces. That feeling has never left me, but I can handle it a little better now — a *little* better.' She touched Hope's hand. 'You have made an enormous difference to me, Hope, and sharing your precious newborn has helped to mend me.'

Sadie looked at Hope. Hope was sitting in her kitchen with a pale blue summer dressing gown they had chosen together for her, the colour of her cornflower blue eyes.

Her golden hair was tousled and her face slim and beautiful and pale. Sadie knew absolutely now that her feelings for Hope were more than simply sisterly. She had realised that when she first saw Hope in the Convent and had got to know her a little and become aware of her beautiful spirit. Sadie was constantly having to work hard to keep a check on any out of place signs of affection she might be tempted to show her. She found Hope was so lovely, so vulnerable, yet so strong, a combination of attributes that she found irresistible. Sadie had never had a boyfriend or man-friend, her experiences of rape with her father having affected her for life. Neither had she realised it was in her to have feelings for a woman in the way that she had for Hope. She was shocked at her discovery. Actually, it rocked her to the core. Yet, she argued to herself, it felt a very pure kind of love. It was not carnal in any way, was it? The fact was that Sadie was primarily deeply attracted to Hope's gentle spirituality. She had an aura. She was like Connie only even more so.

'The wheelchair that Jack was in had a fatal fault,' Sadie continued. 'I received a letter four weeks after Jack's accident from the wheelchair company telling me the model of chair Jack was in was being recalled. His particular wheelchair, and all others of the same type, was found to have faulty brake cables. It was a catastrophe waiting to happen, and it happened to my Jack.'

Hope gasped. She had never known the full story.

'There was a form contained in the envelope which was about seeking compensation. I didn't even read it. I remember throwing it aside. The thought appalled me.

How could anyone or anything compensate for my Jack's life?'

Sadie paused and gulped. Her grief was rising to the surface and threatening to overwhelm her again.

'Unbeknown to me, Oliver and Connie filled in the compensation form for me and simply asked me to sign it. They read me the details but I was in no fit state to take it in. I signed it, and that is the last I thought about it. It was of no consequence to me.'

'Well, the day before yesterday, a letter arrived, but because Lucy was missing I was completely caught up with that, as we all were. I opened the letter later. In it was a cheque for four hundred and seventy-five thousand pounds.'

Hope gasped and stared at Sadie.

'They said that it was at the top of the scale they could pay out for a death and realised it did not compensate for a life.'

She paused and reached for a tissue.

'It doesn't, not a tiny bit, but at least I was able to offer a reward immediately for Lucy's safe return,' she said. 'And it worked. Who knows whether Gary would have returned her if he had not seen the poster we put up outside the church?'

Hope hugged Sadie and held her tightly.

'I will never be able to thank you, Sadie.'

'You don't need to, Hope. Being united with my half-sister is more than I could possibly ever have wished for. Love you, Hope.'

'And I love you, Sadie. So, so much. You and your family are the best things that have ever happened to me. I feel I belong somewhere at last.'

CHAPTER 37

Gary had slept fitfully during the night. He knew the gang would be looking for him in the morning to claim their share of the pickings. The members met daily at around noon to plan their day's events, whether it be to steal, to rape or to find some other form of criminal activity in order to dissipate their group anger against society in particular and the world in general.

On this day, they decided that they would raid a local sports warehouse and grab as many baseball bats as they could. They had done it before and knew their way around the place and the timetables of the men who worked there. Mickey also possessed the gang's secret weapon: a gun. He had stolen it from his father some weeks ago, much to the gang's huge delight. His father had illegally converted and reactivated the shotgun. Mickey knew it was loaded as his father often bragged about it. He said he kept it for self-defence purposes. Once, Mickey had challenged him.

'Dad, this ain't America. What you gonna defend yourself against then?'

'Gangs like yours, son.'

His father picked up the gun and pointed it at various objects in the room, including Mickey, who shrank back, then opened the window.

'See that bird up there, Mick? I could shoot it dead in one second flat.'

'Go on, then Dad. Stop braggin' and show me.'

But Mickey's dad didn't. He was afraid someone would hear the gunshot and he would be reported. He'd save it for the real thing.

His father was so drunk for so much of the time, that he did not even notice when Mickey walked out right in front of him with the gun.

***

Gary decided to go down to Bankside beach for a swim to cool down and clean off the day. Not long afterwards, Robbie set out to find Gary, and five minutes later Hope left a note for Sadie and wheeled Lucy in the pram down the vicarage ramp. The four gang members were also on the move, each one armed with a baseball bat, and Mickey had his prize possession in his back pocket. They were going to find their fifth member, who owed each one of them £2,000 and they were going to get it, oh yes they were.

The sea was refreshing. It was early September so it still carried the summer warmth, and the water's ambient temperature was maintained by the Indian Summer that had blessed England. London particularly held its heat, due partly to the close proximity of many buildings, the tiles and clay bricks acting as giant thermal insulators.

Gary rubbed his hair, roughly towelled down his near-naked body with the towel he had stolen from the vicarage, then climbed up the slope of the beach, refreshed. When he reached the mouth of the tunnel, he stopped in fear. There were the four members of the gang straddled across the entrance, each holding a baseball bat in aggressive attitude. Heart beating wildly, Gary adopted a nonchalant air which belied his terror inside.

'Watcha fellas. Just been for a swim. Sorry I wasn't here, mates.'

'You will be, Gary boy,' said Mickey. Where's the money? You said you'd bring it yesterday.'

'Yeh I did, but — well, the situation's changed a bit.'

'You not given the nipper back yet? Where is it then?'

'I gave her back, but the reward wasn't — available.'

'Wasn't *available*,' said one of the gang. 'What does that mean in plain bloody English?'

'It wasn't ready.'

'Don't fuckin' lie to us. You've pocketed the lot, ain't ya?' Mickey shouted.

'Yeh. That's about the score,' said another.

'OK boys, let's do it,' said Mickey.

Mickey drew out the gun.

'Back further, Gary boy.'

Gun pointing at him, Gary shrank back into the tunnel.

'Now against the wall,' said Mickey.

Gary backed, knowing exactly what was coming. He had been one of the perpetrators of this violent punishment several times before. The gang set upon him, beating him down with the baseball bats and swiping his legs viciously, making him scream out in pain. He began bleeding in several places. One of them smashed his precious binoculars to pieces with a baseball bat. Gary saw them and groaned. They were a priceless part of his life.

'OK, OK, I'll get it. I'll get it. Just give us a chance,' he said haltingly.

'OK lads,' said Mickey. 'Anuvver couple of rounds then stop.'

They resumed beating Gary — shoulders, back, arms, body, legs, feet. He had no clothes on to protect him apart from his underpants in which he had swum. He yelled loudly as they beat him into the ground. Still the gun was pointing at him.

'Stop!' shouted someone from the entrance of the tunnel. 'Just stop there!.'

The gang turned as one body. Mickey pointed the gun towards the entrance of the tunnel.

'You bloody mind your own fuckin' business,' Mickey shouted as he saw Robbie standing silhouetted against the entrance.

'This *is* my business,' yelled Robbie back. 'Put the gun down before you get yourself into real trouble, mate.'

But Mickey's blood was up. He shot the gun in the air and the sound reverberated through the tunnel. Seizing his moment, with superhuman strength Gary was up off the ground where he had sunk and limped fast towards Robbie for safety. Mickey aimed the gun and viciously shot Gary twice, once in each leg.

The gang members threw their baseball bats down and ran. Robbie knelt on the ground where Gary was bleeding profusely. Mickey's aim had been meticulous. He had managed to shoot Gary in both calf muscles, rendering it impossible for him to walk, but avoiding any vital organs and therefore a murder charge. Robbie knew without a doubt that Gary would need surgery, or at the very least, medical attention immediately in the Emergency Department of the hospital. He must find a phone box to call 999, but at the moment Gary's legs were pumping blood out fast so Robbie knew he had to do something *now*.

He tore his green and white checked shirt off and bound one of Gary's legs with it, holding it very tightly so that it acted as a tourniquet. What about the other one?

Just then, miraculously, Hope appeared in search of Gary. She had heard he lived in the tunnel. She hadn't told anyone in the vicarage where she was going, knowing that they would try to dissuade her from her task on which she was absolutely set, so quietly slipped out while they were having breakfast.

Hope stopped in astonishment at the scene. There was Gary lying on the ground groaning and striking his arms out wildly, while Robbie was kneeling by the injured legs surrounded by an increasingly large and vivid pool of blood.

'Hope!' exclaimed Robbie.

'What on earth has happened?' said Hope, parking the pram quickly by the side of the scene.

'He's been shot,' said Robbie. 'I haven't got anything else to bind around his other leg.'

Quick as a flash, Hope went to the pram and lifted the pristine white cellular blanket which was covering Lucy loosely for comfort rather than warmth.

She knelt down and spoke softly.

'Hello, Gary. It's Hope. I'm just going to bind up your leg. This is nasty for you.'

'Sister Hope,' said Gary weakly. 'Ta. Ta very much.'

Hope bound his leg with the utmost gentleness but then held it very tightly, so that Gary yelped a bit. She then reached for a clean muslin nappy which she always carried as a spare in the basket of the pram.

'Here we are, let's wipe some of this blood off.' She kept holding his leg tightly with one hand and mopped as much blood from his body as she could.

'You're going to have a very nasty bruise here, you poor thing. Who did this to you?'

Gary replied faintly.

'The gang. Same ones as got you.'

'Hope, we must get him to the hospital.' Then, in a whisper, 'He's going to bleed out. Can you stay with Gary here and I'll bring the car down? It will be quicker than waiting for an ambulance.'

'Gary. Do you think you could manage to get into the back of my car, mate?'

'I will, if it kills me. Don't call an ambulance,' said Gary weakly. 'They'll bring the Fuzz with 'em.'

'You go quickly,' said Hope.

Robbie left. He was pretty sure the gang would not be back. They were probably more than a mile away by now and planning where to hide. Gary had started trembling violently.

'Gary, you're in a bit of shock. Where are your clothes?'

'Down there,' he said, waving his arm weakly into the tunnel.

'Can you manage to put a little pressure on this leg with your hand, Gary?'

Gary did the best he could while Hope, wheeling the baby further in, found a dishevelled heap of tatty clothes and a pair of old trainers amongst the squalor of Gary's makeshift home. She took in the scene. Was this *really* where Gary lived? Her heart ached for him as she realised the lad did not stand much of a chance in life, and probably never had. She took the clothes back. Fortunately, Lucy always had a long sleep after her morning feed. Hope reached Gary.

'Here they are. Now, can I dress you, Gary? I'll be very gentle, but we must get some warmth on you quickly.'

He nodded and said weakly.

'I think you're an angel come to 'elp me.'

'I'm no angel,' she replied, smiling. 'As you very well know. I'm sorry for that, Gary.'

'I deserved it,' whispered Gary. 'Me binoculars. They smashed me binoculars,' he wept.

Hope carefully dressed Gary. First came the tee shirt with a gruesome war motif printed on it. She then had the dilemma of whether she could get his extremely tight drainpipe jeans on over his wet swimming pants. The jeans would protect the wounds once he was squeezed into them, and, more importantly, put a little more pressure on them, but it meant taking his pants off. Gary anticipated her problem.

'Just take 'em off. They're making me cold,' he shivered. 'Promise I won't try anything on,' he weakly smiled. 'Chance'd be a fine thing!'

Hope hesitated. She had never seen a naked man before. The most she had ever glimpsed of a man's genitals was on a marble statue, and even then the interesting part was usually modestly covered with a fig leaf. She certainly did not want to see Gary in all his glory. Gary was by now almost passing out. He was intensely cold, with blood seeping rapidly through the binding on his legs, and he looked as white as a sheet.

'Come on then, Gary. Gently does it.' She shut her eyes and pulled his pants off, felt for his jeans, took a quick glance at them, arranged them so that she could pull them on without looking at Gary's body, shut her eyes again and determinedly she pulled them up.

'There we are,' she said, relieved that she had been able to manoeuvre without once even glancing at Gary's private parts. 'Now it's just the trainers.'

She undid the laces, flexed the tongue of the shoes out, took one foot in her hands and with some difficulty put the trainer on. Then she picked up the other foot and stopped dead in her tracks. There in front of her was a miniature version of Lucy's foot, the same two webbed toes as clear as daylight for her to see. Her heart pounding, she put the shoe on. She was incredulous and realised why Gary was so adamant that he was Lucy's father. She looked at his legs again and saw that blood was already seeping through his thick jeans. She knew she must not get diverted by the serious matter at hand and decided to think about the

271

implications of Gary's webbed toes later. What mattered now was getting Gary warm. He was slipping fast into unconsciousness.

She glanced quickly at the baby again. Still asleep. She sat down on the ground next to Gary, put her arm around him and gathered him to her to keep him warm. She spoke softly.

'We'll soon get you mended, Gary. Don't worry. We'll all take care of you till you're better.' She shook him and spoke more firmly.

'Do *not* go to sleep, Gary. Tell me about your binoculars.'

Robbie meanwhile had run like the wind and, without explanation to anyone, had grabbed the car keys to his old Ford Escort and was now parked directly at the tunnel's entrance.

He saw Hope cradling Gary and in a flash, it reminded him of how Connie had cradled her dying father. There was that same holy tenderness in both Hope and her sister Connie. Oliver had said it was the gift of unlimited love that the sisters both gave in abundance.

He suddenly felt awed in her presence.

CHAPTER 38

Gary had his wounds attended to in Charing Cross Hospital. Robbie stayed with him throughout the day while Gary had various procedures performed including a close analysis of the bullet wounds in his calves. These were thoroughly cleaned, intravenous antibiotics were administered, and the consultant explained that with bullets that had not touched vital organs, the current practice was to leave them in rather than damage the skin further, thereby giving time for the muscles to heal. The surrounding skin, apparently, would gradually encapsulate the bullet, preventing it from dissolving and affecting the bloodstream.

The consultant commented that Gary had got off comparatively lightly, and the two tourniquets, comprising the checked shirt and the cellular blanket tied tightly round each calf, had almost certainly saved his life as he could have bled out. As it was, Gary received two pints of transfused blood, which, as Robbie and Hope agreed later, reinforced the fact that the large pool of blood on the tunnel floor had indeed told its own story and thank God they had acted fast.

The Consultant explained that they were keeping Gary in hospital for at least twenty four hours, and then would review the situation. The police picked up the gang of four as each member was weaving his way skilfully towards Hungerford Bridge. The sound of shots and sightings had been reported and the police decided the perpetrators almost certainly were the notorious gang whose capture had eluded them for many months.

This was a triumphant day for the police. This infamous gang had proved incredibly slippery to apprehend. When finally taken into custody, none of the gang let on about the shooting of Gary. On being asked where the fifth member was, each of the four looked blank and feigned complete ignorance. To give away Gary would be to disclose the fact that they themselves had shot him. It was Gary's lucky day in their eyes, sod him, unless of course he had died from his wounds.

Mickey had thrown his father's gun as far as he could off London Bridge into the fast-flowing Thames but it did not stop the forensic department from finding traces of gunpowder on his clothes. Mickey would go down for a long time.

Hope arrived back at the vicarage with large patches of Gary's blood saturating her lightweight summer dress. The slight incline back to home seemed like a very steep hill to her, and she realised by her breathing that she was probably suffering from shock. She had risen to the crisis in the tunnel and coped, but now the surge of adrenalin had stopped she felt utterly depleted of energy, added to which she had given birth just three weeks ago. She was shocked on several counts. Firstly, the sight of a human being possibly bleeding to death was appalling. She had acted quickly but the "what if's" were numerous. Without a doubt, had Robbie and Hope arrived even five minutes after they had, the outcome might have been very different. Secondly, she was horrified at the sight of Gary's hovel in the tunnel which had served him as a home for she knew not how long. She had seen poverty-stricken households in Ireland, where several small children were brought up with barely enough food to survive on by a mother who had very little in terms of material goods, but who loved her children and lived in terror of their being taken away from her. But Gary's filthy single duvet and pillow on the cold floor that served as a bed chilled Hope to the core, and the grimy billy can and rickety stove spoke to her of extreme deprivation. There were empty baked bean cans and crisp packets around, plus several empty beer cans. It was squalid and probably rat infested.

Greatest of all, however, now that she had time to acknowledge it, was the shock of seeing Gary's webbed toes on one foot. The toes affected were the same as Lucy's: the second and third toes. "Unilateral Syndactyly" the Paediatrician had called it. The Paediatrician had checked very carefully to make sure the baby had no other congenital issues that would indicate she had a serious syndrome. Thankfully, Lucy was pronounced one hundred percent fit and Hope reminded herself again that she had been told that the toe deformity was actually of little consequence.

There they were, the webbed toes — living proof that Gary was Lucy's father. Hope had no idea how to handle this discovery or its ramifications for the future. She would shelve that for a time when she was less stressed.

Sadie and Connie heard Hope's key in the lock and rushed up to her with concern. Oliver was standing at the kitchen door.

'Hope, where have you been? We've been so worried about you,' said Connie.

'It's just not like you. You could've left us a note,' said Sadie reproachfully.

Connie looked down at Hope's dress.

'Hope, what *has* happened to you? Come into the kitchen. Oliver, could you manage a cup of tea for Hope, please?'

Shocked and sorry as he was for the state Hope was clearly in, Oliver could not push a rogue thought away that it seemed to him that his major contribution to life in the vicarage nowadays seemed to be making endless cups of tea for the three women. He never complained, but a small but significant resentment set in which persuaded him that Connie's priority was no longer him and the children. She was looking worn out by it all. Her attention was being spread thinly, and the greater portion was going towards her sisters.

Reproaching himself soundly for having such infantile thoughts, he put the kettle on and vowed he must try to help Connie more.

'Snap out of it, Lockwood!' he heard the voice of one of his teachers say. 'There's no place for self-pity in this life. Self-pity is addictive.'

'Here we are. Three teas,' Oliver said, determinedly cheerful. 'Now, Hope, please could you tell me what happened, you poor thing — something very bad, clearly.'

Oliver had obeyed the inner voice of his teacher, chased away the demons and was working hard on presenting as his usual genial self.

Hope told them how she discovered Robbie with wounded Gary and how his condition was rapidly deteriorating. They were all flabbergasted to hear of her courage in the face of the emergency.

'I think I'd better go to the hospital to support Robbie,' said Oliver. He was already reaching for his car keys. 'I suppose we ought to sort out some rehabilitation for him, too.'

'He just can't go back to the tunnel,' said Hope. 'It's dreadful.'

'I'll talk to the church army about him,' said Oliver as he kissed Connie's cheek lightly on the way out.

'Love you, Con,' he said.

'Love you, Oli,' she replied.

Oliver had been a chaplain in the church army, which is where he first met Robbie. He had great respect and affection for it. It tuned in to everything he sought to do in his ministry. It was heavily committed to supporting and working with folk on the margins of society, including the homeless. He was sure that they would take Gary in, as he seemed to fit their criteria for acceptance exactly.

Connie telephoned Bruce with the news of Gary's hospitalization. He had been in touch with Connie several times lately as they all wanted to find Gary and thank him in person for rescuing Kitty the night of the tragic sinking. Kitty, particularly, wanted to see him again. He had saved her life, and whatever had happened before paled into

277

insignificance for her. Clara asked if Connie had any suggestions about what they could buy Gary as a thank you present. She had.

When Oliver arrived at the hospital, he was greeted by a watchdog of a matron who was sitting in her office by the entrance to the ward. He asked if he could see Gary. The answer was a resounding 'No,' qualified by a brusque statement that Gary had "his companion" with him, and even that was stretching the rules. The fact that Oliver was wearing his dog collar did not cut any ice with her.

Could he just pop in to give Gary's companion a message please?

'No, but if you write it down I will make sure he gets it.' She handed him a short, stubby pencil and a sheet of paper from the back of her notebook. Reading and writing were not Robbie's strong points. He had absented himself from school at fourteen. Oliver simply put,

'Phone me, Robbie,' and then scribbled his mobile telephone number down as a reminder.

'Thank you, Matron,' said Oliver as he handed paper and pencil back. She looked up but twitched only the faintest of smiles at him.

Oliver could not resist it. He began to walk out of the door and then turned.

'Matron — just remember — Jesus wants you for a sunbeam.'

CHAPTER 39

Oliver didn't want to go home immediately. Much as he loved Connie's two sisters, he was growing rather weary of the constant baby worship. Connie spent a lot of time upstairs with Hope and Sadie, and Rosy dashed up there too as soon as she was home from school. Very often, when Oliver came in from an afternoon's work in the parish, the boys were downstairs watching television when they should have been doing their homework, and his wife and daughter were nowhere to be seen. He knew he was being unreasonable and that he certainly did not think his wife should be standing there to greet him. He hated the thought that he might be turning into a male chauvinist. He remembered hearing a sermon once on marriage in which the rector had asked the women in the congregation:

'Now, wives. Do you sometimes wait at the top of the stairs naked to greet your husband and make him know how much he is wanted?'

When Oliver told Connie, she had exploded gleefully into laughter. They both did.

'Why not?' she retorted. 'I'll tell you why not! (a), I'd be cold, (b), What about the children? and (c), I would presume the rector is single and fantasizing!.'

Oliver adored his wife's laughter. He was missing her, and by that, he meant the "pre-Hope" her. He found Hope a really lovely human being and it was not personal. It was his problem, he knew.

Oliver chastised himself for being so selfish. He was always the first person to say that everyone had 'feet of clay' and therefore should be given the benefit of the doubt in challenging situations; everyone, that is, except Oliver Lockwood. He expected and worked towards perfection in himself.

That perfection, however, was soon to be challenged.

Oliver bought himself a coffee at a local pavement cafe and sat thinking. He thought about Connie. She was always up late now, catching up with chores she had shelved during the day — putting washing in the washing machine, tidying up, chatting with Sadie or, exhausted, flopping out in front of a late-night film. Oliver and she had always shared household jobs, but he wasn't going to come in from a late evening meeting at church and roll up his sleeves to wash saucepans. He'd have to get up early and do them in the morning.

Connie and he had not made love since before Hope's baby had been born. What had always been a rich and lovely part of their marriage seemed to have quietly receded. Unusually for her, Connie lately had simply had not felt like it. She was always tired and turned away whenever he made physical overtures. It wasn't really the sex per se that Oliver missed. It was the intimacy with his wife on every level. He loved her deeply. He also knew, putting it bluntly, that he was thinking like a spoilt brat. He wondered if the presence of Sister Hope and her baby had changed things for good.

Again, he heard the voice of his teacher shouting at him after he had been injured during a rugby match: *Get over it, Lockwood! Self-pity is addictive.*

Oliver took his newly acquired mobile phone out of his pocket. He sat turning it over in his hand, tossing up whether to act on a whim. Suddenly, he was tired of being noble. After a minute, he phoned Clara Connors.

Oliver and Clara had history. They had had a brief but passionate encounter when they were both at Richmond Theatre, she as a budding actor and he a pastoral chaplain. Oliver was not married then but had taken a self-imposed vow of celibacy, feeling that was what God was requiring of him. Clara was beautiful and seductive — and married — and in a moment of weakness and high passion, they had both given in to their magnetic physical attraction for each other. It was only the once, but neither had ever forgotten it, although neither ever referred to it.

'Hi, Oli. To what do I owe this pleasure?'

Her voice was warm and welcoming.

'I — I just thought I'd tell you that Gary Johnson is now recovering in hospital: Ward four, level three — in case you and Kitty wanted to visit him.'

He had chatted with Clara hundreds of times perfectly normally in the intervening years between Richmond Theatre and now, but this time his heart was pounding. He knew that his motive was not entirely pure.

'Oh thanks, Oli. How is he doing?' she purred.

'He's battered and bruised but on the up,' replied Oliver.

There was a long pause.

281

'Oli, are you OK? You sound — different.'

'No. I'm not that OK,' he suddenly confessed. 'It's a bit — a bit hard just now.'

'I'm not surprised with all that's happened. Now you have a new *baby* in the house,' she said, as if it was a distasteful experience or a bad smell under her nose. Clara had never had an abundance of maternal instinct.

'Do you want to talk, Oli? Shall we meet somewhere?'

Oliver knew this was a defining moment. He could, he *should*, say no. If he said 'yes' then he was opening the door to all sorts of forbidden fruits.

'That would be great, Clara, if you've got the time.'

'I'll make the time,' replied Clara softly. 'Any chance you could meet me pre-show?' she asked. 'Today? If you're at Charing Cross hospital it's a very short drive to here isn't it? I'll arrange a parking permit for you.'

Oliver drove recklessly. If he got there soon, he could have an hour with Clara before she had to get ready for curtain up at seven-thirty. Connie would wonder where he was, but he couldn't help that. To phone her would mean he would have to explain, and he wasn't prepared to lie to her. Anyway, he had no explanation for his impulsive behaviour.

He arrived at the theatre and there was Clara, standing outside in her black tee shirt and leggings, just as she had been dressed the first time Oliver had met her. Just as beautiful, figure as perfect, he conceded, despite the intervening years. She waved him into the staff car park and stuck a permit on the car. She opened the car door for Oliver.

'Oliver Lockwood!' she said. 'This is a nice surprise! Come into my dressing room. How's that for an invitation,' she laughed. 'I have my own now, I'm a superstar,' she said, smiling her most enchanting smile.

'How's the show going, Clara?'

'OK, I think. It's got some good reviews. Have you seen them?'

Oliver had, and he was glad. Clara had worked unfailingly hard at her art and deserved all the success she had. She also had an abundance of talent.

'Sit down, Rev,' she said smiling, using her name for him of years ago. It sent a seductive message to him that her memory of those days was still intact.

'What's up, Oli? Trouble in camp?'

She reached out and put her hand on his knee. It lingered a fraction too long. The old electric charge of years ago shot through Oliver. Clara had perfected the art of slow seduction. She leaned forward and looked straight into his eyes.

'Come on, Oli. Spill the beans. You know you can trust me. It won't go any further.'

Just then Oliver's mobile phone rang. He ignored it.

'It's nothing in particular,' he replied. 'Except — except,' he fought for words, not wanting to be disloyal to Connie, who had done nothing wrong. 'It's just that the baby is dominating everything in a strange way. She's terribly sweet,' he said, immediately qualifying his statement. 'But Connie and Sadie seem to want to spend all their time with Hope and Lucy. I understand it, but —'

'But you feel you've lost your wife. That's what Bruce's constant complaint is, but he does have a reason. You little boys must have a hundred percent of your woman's attention, diddumses both,' she said, twisting his nose playfully. 'Bruce says the same. He thinks my performances dominate everything now. Mind you,' she laughed. 'He's right, I must admit.'

'The baby dominates everything,' said Oliver softly. Clara was now running her fingers through her chestnut hair and twirling the ends into curls — an old seduction trick of hers, he knew. He wanted to know if it still smelt of orchard apples. Suddenly, Clara bent down in front of Oliver and kissed him; not a peck on the cheek but a full-blown, sexual kiss. Oliver's body responded immediately and he kissed her, and then kissed her again, and then again, more urgently each time. His hands found their way under her tee shirt.

'Oli, we've got half an hour. For old-time's sake? Just a one-off? No commitment of course,' she said, working her hands down. 'Do it, enjoy it, forget it, kind of thing? You need it, I can tell' She kissed him again.

'Oh Clara, stop, stop,' he said, everything in him screaming the opposite.

He stroked her breasts, longing to see them in the flesh. Taunted by the memory of her lying on her bed naked just before he had broken the bad news to her, he had tried to exorcise the mental image but occasionally it had come back unbidden. Now he knew what she looked like, he was desperate to see her fully again.

His mobile phone rang a second time. Quickly he drew it out of his pocket. It was Connie. She was probably wondering where he was.

'Don't take it, Oli,' said Clara huskily. 'She'll leave a message if it's urgent. Now, *this* is what I call urgent. The matter in hand'.

Hungrily he began to reach for her.

The phone rang a third time.

With a huge act of will, Oliver pulled back. Everything in him wanted to consummate the act with Clara then, but he heard Connie's voice recording on his phone. She sounded extremely distressed.

'Oli, where are you? Can you come? As quickly as you can — *please*? It's really urgent.'

Quick as a flash he drew away from Clara, untwining himself.

'Clara, I have to go. Connie needs me.'

'Connie can wait,' said Clara, clearly irritated by the interruption. Then, 'Oli,' she said softly. 'You just try resisting me now.' She pulled off her black tee shirt to reveal her breasts. She taunted him as and she stood in a model-like pose

'More, Oliver?' she said, 'Oh yes, you'd like more, wouldn't you?'

'No, Clara. Stop!' and this time he meant it. Connie's voice had brought him back to his senses, away from this aberration. What *was* he thinking of? Was he throwing everything precious away that he and Connie meant to each other?

'I'm so sorry, so, so sorry Clara. I shouldn't be here. Please forgive me.'

'Just the same as last time,' she said witheringly. 'Only last time you *did* complete things, and a fine mess that got us into!'

Oliver remembered well enough — the subsequent pregnancy and the interminable wondering if the child was his. Kitty turned out to be Bruce's miracle baby, but the whole scenario was agonising. He went to kiss Clara goodbye, but she turned her head away fiercely.

'Don't ever, ever come back, Oliver Lockwood. You've made a fool of me,' she said, folding her arms to cover her breasts, suddenly vulnerable and wanting to hide them. 'And just you remember that it was y*ou* who contacted me, and not the other way round. But don't worry, there are plenty more fish in the sea for me,' she said defiantly. 'I actually have to swim away hard to keep them at arm's length. Anyway,' she added more softly. 'Bruce and I are pretty good nowadays. Quite adventurous, in fact.'

'I'm sure you are,' replied Oliver. 'I'm so sorry, Clara. For everything.'

With that, he was gone. Clara furiously pulled on her tee shirt and viciously brushed her hair, then sat down and wept tears of humiliation and disappointment. She had never quite been able to stop loving The Reverend Oliver Lockwood, dammit, but the show must go on.

CHAPTER 40

Oliver drove home at the speed of light, sure he was going to be picked up by the police, but that was of no consequence compared to his need to reach Connie. He was chastising himself mercilessly for being such an idiot, hardly believing what had come over him a little while earlier.

He put his key in the vicarage door and was greeted by James, Peter and Rosy in their pyjamas, white-faced and distressed. Rosy burst into tears when she saw Oliver, Peter twitched, blinked and agitated his hands furiously, and James was standing like a block of ice, rigid and expressionless.

'Daddy, Mummy's been taken to hospital in an ambulance. She had *terrible* tummy ache,' wept Rosy.

'She told Auntie Sadie there was blood,' said James darkly. 'Where *were* you, Dad? Mum thought you'd be home ages ago.'

'Not to worry, not to worry, not to worry,' Peter said parrot-fashion in a sing-song voice and continued waving incessantly in stress.

Hope came running out of the kitchen when she heard the children with Oliver.

'Oh, Oliver! We've been trying to get hold of you. I'm afraid Connie was in a really bad way. She had awful pain in her pelvis. She was doubled up in agony and was nearly passing out with it. I called an ambulance. Sadie is out seeing Gary with Robbie. Poor Connie had to go off on her own because I was needed for the children. We did try to call you.'

Oliver gasped and had to sit down.

'I've been trying to reassure the children but I'm afraid they saw it all.'

'Mum was just doing the washing up. I was drying and all of a sudden she bent double over the sink and screamed. Dad, it was awful,' said James..

'Awful, it was awful, it was awful. Yes, it was, it was, it was,' Peter chanted.

Oliver pulled Peter to him and sat him on his lap, stroking his hair, holding him tightly and gently restraining his arm movements. He grew calmer.

'Is Mummy going to die, Daddy? Is she going to heaven like Jack?' Rosy asked.

'I'll go and see Mummy now, Rosy, and I'll come back and tell you how she is. I'm sure the doctor will sort her out ("please God" he added silently). Hope, can you manage to carry on looking after them?'

'For as long as it takes, Oliver. You just stay with Connie. She needs you. She was so worried about you.'

'Want to come, please, want to come, Dad? See her.'

'Next time, Peter. I'll tell you how she is when I get home.'

Oliver dared not give in to his feelings of guilt at the moment. They ran too deep. He was not there for his wife in her crisis, his children had needed him earlier. What was he doing meanwhile? Messing around with another woman. In addition, he had been negative to Clara about Hope's presence in their lives. Here was Hope now, looking after his children tenderly, angel that she was, and he knew if it took a month for him to come home from the hospital Hope's love and patience would not run out.

As he went to the door, Hope followed him.

'Oliver, I think it is serious' she said softly, out of earshot of the children. 'She was collapsing with the pain. Will you ring me as soon as you can with news? If Sadie comes back soon I'll let her know what's happened.'

Oliver kissed her lightly on the cheek and held her.

'Thank you for everything, Hope. You are an angel, a godsend,' said Oliver, and meant it.

He arrived at the hospital and was told that Connie was currently in the operating theatre, although the receptionist could not say why. How could he find out more about his wife? Which operating theatre was she in? How long would she be down? There was no one around to answer his questions, so he took the lift up to the operating suite and waited at the entrance of the corridor, panic-stricken for Connie's safety. He paced up and down, up and down, and finally found a seat. Putting his head in his hands, he knew there were no adequate words to describe how he was feeling — panic-stricken, guilty, ashamed, desperate, distressed — none of those came near it; and very, very afraid for Connie.

After about half an hour the swing doors opened from one of the operating rooms. Two porters were wheeling a female patient out with several tubes dripping various fluids into her arm: plasma, dextrose solution, intravenous antibiotics, liquid morphine. The patient was still asleep from the anaesthetic. Oliver looked closer and saw that it was his Connie, pale, delicate, beautiful in her fragility, and without a single doubt the love of his life.

'Connie, sweetheart, I'm here, I'm here,' he murmured close to her.

'Please stand back, sir. You can see her when she comes round. We'll get her settled in Intensive Care first,' said one of the nurses.

Oliver quickly pushed the swing doors back open into the operating theatre. Two surgeons were taking their gloves off and washing their hands at a sink, their masks still on. An extract from *Carmina Burana* by Carl Orff was playing loudly.

'Sorry, sir, you can't come in here. How did you get in? This is a sterile area. You must leave quickly please,' one of the surgeons called from the sink. 'We can't have any contamination in here.'

'I want to know what's happened to my wife,' said Oliver. 'I couldn't find anyone to ask.'

'You must leave, I'm afraid. You will have to go and wait outside the intensive care unit. We can't give you details now. You will have to be security checked first.'

'How critical is she? Please just tell me that.'

'She's heading for the recovery room. Now, sir,' he said walking over, dripping water on the floor from his surgical gloves. 'I really must ask you to leave.'

'OK, OK, I'm going. Sorry, but I know nothing about what's happened to my wife except that she was brought here by ambulance.'

'Go and wait outside recovery, sir. They will help you. Down one floor and second on the left,' he said more kindly. 'Talk to the sister on duty. She'll fill you in. I'm sorry you've had a shock. We've been dealing with your wife. Good job she came in when she did.'

Once downstairs, Oliver spoke to the Sister, who took his details and then explained carefully and calmly that Connie had suffered an ectopic pregnancy and her fallopian tube had ruptured.

'I'm afraid when this happens it's very serious, a medical emergency,' she explained. 'It can be a life-threatening situation, but fortunately, her sister phoned us in the nick of time. Inevitably the baby was lost, I'm afraid. The good news is that your wife will be all right.'

Oliver sat down, his head reeling.

'I'm sorry, sir. It does halve the chances of your wife becoming pregnant again as they had to remove the ruptured fallopian tube, but her remaining one is very healthy. It will just take you longer to conceive.'

'We didn't even know she was pregnant,' said Oliver in a whisper.

'That can happen,' replied the Sister. 'The monthly cycle doesn't always disappear, as is usual with a straightforward pregnancy. It just becomes scantier in some cases, or heavier in others — the unpredictability of Mother Nature, I'm afraid,' she smiled.

'When can I see her?' asked Oliver.

'She'll be kept in intensive care overnight. All being well, we'll transfer her up to the ward after that. Look,' she added kindly. 'I'll get you a cup of tea. You can wait here till she comes out of the anaesthetic and then you can pop in for a few minutes. She's been pretty poorly but she should be coming round very soon now. Sugar?'

'Oh. Um — no thanks. Thank you. That would be great.'

He sat there feeling shell-shocked. Once the tea had arrived and he had taken a few sips, he felt calmer and began to reflect. Thoughts and memories tumbled into his mind. What a traumatic year it had been so far, what with poor Jack being killed on the road, learning that his wife had a half-sister, the subsequent rape of Hope, the sinking of the stricken *Grand Duchess* vessel, with Gary rescuing his niece from the Thames, and then his arrival at the vicarage. To follow, there had been the dramatic birth of Hope's baby, the terrible knifing of Gary, and for Oliver, worst of all on a personal level in a way, his sudden deviant and impulsive behaviour with Clara. Now, God forgive him, his beloved wife Connie had been closer to death than he could bear to imagine and he was absent in her hour of need.

Stranger than fiction, he thought. You wouldn't find this in a novel. You'd say it was an implausible plot and too far-fetched. No family had all those things happen to them in less than a year.

Oliver started pacing up and down again like an agitated caged lion. He needed something to keep his mind occupied and remembered that Gary was still in the hospital, so decided to take the lift to the ward to say a brief hello before returning to be on the watch for Connie. It was nearly time for lights out, but this time the Rottweiler, as he had named the ward matron in his mind, let him in with a half-smile. Either he had simply caught her in a bad mood before or she was definitely trying hard now to be a sunbeam. He responded with a quick smile and nod of acknowledgement.

As it happened, Gary was asleep and Robbie had finally left for home, having spent most of the day with him. Oliver said a quick prayer over Gary, who looked distinctly shattered and pale, then returned to the intensive care unit where he was greeted by a nurse who said he could go in to see Connie as she was now round from the operation. Oliver donned the required plastic coat and mask tentatively crept in, and was immediately struck by the almost eerie silence of the place, only interspersed by the sounds of bleeps of machines, some rhythmical, others random, which kept accurate watch over their subjects. Nurses moved around quietly, checking drips and scrutinizing temperature and blood pressure charts.

Oliver took Connie's hand.

'Connie, my poor, poor darling.'

'Hi Oli,' she said haltingly, weakly. 'I tried to reach you but couldn't get through.'

'I'm here now. I'm so sorry for what you've been through.'

'We've lost a baby, Oli,' she said softly, a few tears escaping from her eyes.

'Did you have any idea you were pregnant, Con? You weren't keeping it from me, were you?' he asked gently.

'Course not, Oli. We share everything, don't we? I had no idea, except—' she hesitated, 'I've been feeling very "off" and tired lately.'

'How are you feeling now, Con?'

'Whoosy and drunk,' she said, smiling the smile that Oliver had fallen in love with sixteen years ago.

He kissed her forehead gently. The nurse came softly up to him.

'Small is beautiful at the moment, sir' she said to him. 'She's been through rather an ordeal. Come back tomorrow. She's in good hands.'

'I must go now, darling,' said Oli, kissing Connie tenderly on her cheek. 'I love you so.'

'Bye,' said Connie weakly. 'I love you too. Sorry for the fuss.'

'Bye, darling.' He started going.

Connie softly called him back.

'Oli, one question—'

This is it, thought Oliver — the question he had been dreading — where were you? He held his breath.

'Oli, let's have another baby if we can.'

Taken aback, he smiled and blew her a kiss.

What an extraordinary thing this maternal instinct is, he thought. She is barely conscious and yet is asking this question! He mused on the inexhaustible drive in the human race to procreate itself. He remembered that when their firstborn James was two days old, and after a particularly long and gruelling labour, Connie wanted to discuss how soon they could have another child!

One thing he knew for certain, however. He preferred this question to the one he had been dreading. The one that never came, thank God.

CHAPTER 41

Bruce, Clara and Kitty were on a shopping spree which focussed particularly on choosing a special pair of binoculars as a thank you present for Gary. The family was very aware that if Gary had not rescued Kitty from the water, she would certainly have drowned. This gave the three of them a greater awareness of the preciousness of each to the other. Clara bought some striped gift wrap paper, Sellotape and a roll of bright ribbon The binoculars were duly wrapped in the hospital car park and on their way to the hospital with the trio.

Oliver had not told Bruce about his sister's emergency. As Connie was over the worst, thank God, he decided to delay telling him. He would leave that to Connie. To be honest, he was terrified of phoning and hearing Clara's voice at the end of the line, coward that he was, he thought to himself.

***

Having reassured his anxious children as soon as he set foot in the door of the home, he answered their myriads of questions, carefully avoiding any mention of a baby (Rosy would be devastated if she knew). Oliver then talked things through with Hope and Sadie, including the dilemma of Gary, went to bed, slept for a few hours, and set off for the hospital again at the earliest opportunity. There, he was told his wife was recovering well and would soon be moved to the main ward. As she was currently having a supervised shower Oliver paid another quick visit to Gary.

This time Gary was awake. He smiled weakly at Oliver.

'Good at causing a bit of trouble, ain't I, Guv — Mr Revd?'

'You certainly like a bit of drama,' replied Oliver, smiling and gently shaking Gary's free hand in greeting.

'They're saying I can go home in a few days if I go on like this. Hope me duvet and stuff haven't been nicked from the tunnel.'

'Gary, you can't go back there. You'll need a bit of TLC when you come out.'

'TLC? What's that, Guv?'

'*Tender Loving Care.*'

'Blimey, chance'd be a fine thing. Never 'ad any of that, apart from you lot, that is.' He lay back on the pillow.

Oliver knew that he and Connie would have taken Gary in and looked after him if Connie had been well, and then made plans for a place for him at the Church Army, subject to Gary's agreement. He certainly could not go back to the tunnel. He would need recuperation time, that was for sure, and Oliver would not countenance putting Connie under any kind of strain, so something had to be sorted out for him. Robbie would probably have everything in hand. He thought briefly about what a miraculous story it had been with Robbie. Shunned by his own parents, a "workhouse kid" to use his own phrase regarding his upbringing, imprisoned twice for grievous bodily harm, Robbie found himself in a church army hostel where Oliver befriended him and later gave him a home.

It was mainly through the power of Oliver and Connie's unconditional love that Robbie slowly began to change. He became a colourful, if unconventional Christian through their example, and, combined with his own determination and the power of prayer, he was eventually employed by Oliver's church to run the youth club, with particular responsibility for reaching out to the homeless youngsters of Southwark. If circumstances were different, Oliver reflected, he and Connie would have found enough love and space in their lives to support Gary the way they had for Robbie, and help him build a new life. That way, with a huge helping of God's grace, Gary might stand a chance. Gary had no idea where his parents were, although he assumed they were in prison. He had no known siblings, no relations, no friends, so actually up to now there had been not one soul in the world to care if he lived or died.

Oliver said goodbye to Gary, who was clearly still weak and in pain and went to leave, longing to see Connie again. Walking out of the ward, he came face to face with Clara and Kitty, the latter carrying an ornately packaged and ribboned gift. They both stopped in their tracks. Clara looking shocked. Kitty looked past Oliver, saw Gary in bed and walked quickly over to him, leaving Clara and Oliver alone.

'Clara!' exclaimed Oliver with horror.

'Oli,' replied Clara coldly. 'What are you doing here? Oh, stupid,' she said, answering her own question. 'You've come to see Gary, the same as we have.'

'I have, yes. Clara,' he paused and took a deep breath. 'I'm very, very sorry about my behaviour.'

'You've already said that,' replied Clara coolly, tossing her chestnut hair back like a mane.

'Connie has nearly died,' he blurted out. 'I got my punishment, Clara. When she needed me most, I was with you.'

Clara gasped.

'Oh *no!* What's the matter with her, Oli?'

Oliver explained about the ectopic pregnancy and was going into the details when Bruce joined them, jangling his keys.

'Sodding hospital car parks,' he grumbled. 'Always the same, and then they charge you an arm and a leg for the pleasure. Hi, Oliver,' he added, his furrowed face softening into a smile.

'Connie's been very ill, Bruce,' said Clara quickly.

Oliver explained again.

Bruce was concerned and angry, in about equal measure.

'Look, she's my sister. Why has no one told me? Oliver?' he asked darkly.

'It all happened so fast,' said Oliver. 'The first I knew was when I got home. Connie had been trying to reach me but I was with…'

He stopped in his tracks. What *was* he saying?

'Oh well, as long as she's OK, that's the main thing I suppose.'

'Sorry, Bruce. I really am. We were all caught up in the situation, and Clara,' he looked knowingly at her. 'I'm really sorry.'

Seeing his acute distress, Clara softened.

'It's OK, Oli. It's all OK.'

Bruce looked puzzled for a second and then saw Gary, with Kitty sitting by him holding his hand.

'Aye, aye. We'll have to watch this,' he said. 'The rescue will give that Gary carte blanche with my daughter.'

'Bye Bruce. I'd better keep my eye on this little scenario,' he repeated, with which he shook Oliver's hand briefly. 'Now, *please* keep me posted about Connie,' he said and walked briskly up to Gary's bed.

Suddenly he called back.

'I'll come and see her. Give her my love, will you?'

Clara took both of Oliver's hands in hers for a split second.

'Oliver, I'm truly sorry about Connie,' she paused. 'You know, I'll always have a place in my heart for you. I think you know that, but,' her eyes bored into him. '*Never ever* do that again, unless of course —' and now she flashed her eyes seductively. '— unless you intend to complete the task in hand,' she whispered in his ear briefly. Tossing her hair seductively she walked off, leaving that familiar smell of orchard apples behind her.

Kitty had helped hoist Gary up on his pillow. He was opening his present by the time Clara reached his bed and exclaiming joyfully.

'Bloody hell. I don't believe it! Never 'ad a present before. Wow! Look at the paper! Blimey!' He drew the binoculars out of their secure wrapping. 'These are epic! Epic!' He looked through them, training the binoculars on the other patients in the ward one after the other.

'Bloody hell,' he repeated. 'These are amazing. Thanks guys.' He flopped back on his pillow, exhausted by the sudden rush of energy expended.

'It's a pleasure,' said Clara. 'You saved Kitty's life.'

'It was nuffink. Enjoyed the swim,' he said.

'The binoculars are top of the range, Gary. Nothing but the best for my personal life saver!' she said, suddenly kissing his forehead twice.

'OK, Kitty. That's enough,' warned Bruce quietly, trying to sound light-hearted despite the red warning lights flashing in his head.

'Bruce!' said Clara. 'She's just grateful. Don't be a killjoy.'

'Come on, *Dad*! She owes me,' Gary said, winking at Bruce.

Yes, and that's exactly what I'm afraid of thought Bruce. He hadn't forgotten the sight of Gary with his hand up his daughter's skirt, pinning her against the wall, even if everyone else had. Bruce knew he was on the point of raping her and the image haunted him.

CHAPTER 42

Connie's traumatic condition had focussed Sadie's mind sharply. Determined to find something practical that would support Connie when she came home from the hospital, she bought the largest dishwasher she could find, and a replacement for Connie's old tumble drier, which always cranked and spluttered ominously each time before it finally heaved itself into life.

Sadie needed to talk about money with Hope. The huge amount of financial compensation for Jack's accident she had received weighed heavily on her. She was determined to do something worthwhile with it and needed Hope's wisdom on the subject. Hope was the most non-materialistic person in the world, Sadie had decided, and could be relied upon to have a thoughtful and cautious approach when it came to money. What's more, Hope was bound to spend a lot of time in prayer over the matter, and although Sadie was not a believer, she respected Hope's deep faith and knew that if anyone could get through to God, Hope could.

Sadie continued to work hard at keeping her feelings for Hope under tight control, justifying her increasing feelings of love for her by saying to herself, 'She's my sister. It's allowed.' Having the baby around had helped Sadie enormously in terms of her ability to find outward expression of the love that should have been for Jack. Everything about Jack tore at her heartstrings, leaving a hole she knew would never be filled. The most she could hope was that in time life would heal *around* the gaping wound, carving out a different kind of future for her. There was no doubt that Hope was a major part of that re-growth, and any thoughts that Sadie had about moving back to her caravan in Scotland had gone. Her attraction to Hope, mentally, emotionally, spiritually and maybe yes, she had to admit it, even physically, precluded that. She really needed to talk seriously to Hope.

Sadie was also worried about Connie. She had seen her sister looking exhausted. Early pregnancy might have accounted for some of that, but when Sadie took a step back from the situation at home she saw that the full vicarage with all its demands, extra meals, lack of privacy and so on might have a bearing on it too. Connie was far too kind ever to complain about things, but now that Hope and the baby lived there, and she and Robbie were permanent features on the top floor, things may have become a bit much for her.

Then there was Peter. Peter was a dear boy, everyone saw that, but his autism meant that Connie was ever watchful about upsetting him and sending him tail spinning into one of his ferocious temper tantrums. He needed careful handling and understanding. It was tiring and ongoing for Connie and Oliver, much as they adored him. He was a constant cause of concern for them.

Then there was Gary. Robbie had intimated that he would like to bring him back to the vicarage to recuperate until he could take up a place at the church army shelter. Another body in the house, however, meant more strain on Connie, although she would fiercely deny it. Sadie had noticed recently that Oliver had gone out more and more as Connie became increasingly involved with Hope and Lucy. Heaven forbid that anything came between that marriage, which had always seemed so strong and steady. Sadie concluded that action needed to be taken, and she was the one to take it.

Firstly, there was her caravan up in Scotland. Her aunt had been the only one to know of Sadie's pregnancy and had given her enough money to buy a new, spacious two-berth caravan which she rented out when she could. Should it be brought down here and parked in the huge vicarage back garden? The first part of the garden was laid to lawn, with an abundance of flowers and shrubs, which more or less survived depending on whether it was the football season, which James and Peter honoured not wisely but too well. The rear part of the garden, which was at least eighty feet in length, was a raggedy, higgledy-piggledy kind of "wild" area, which was intended to be ecologically sound, but suffered, as Oliver and Connie both agreed, from neglect and was little short of a wilderness. The parish coffers could not afford a gardener and neither could Oliver and Connie. A caravan would fit perfectly down there. For Robbie? For Gary? For her and — and... which brought her to the crucial point...

A good conversation between Sadie and Hope had taken place before Lucy was born about Sadie's role in the new baby's life. Sadie was now wondering whether Hope would join her if she moved into a manageable house or ground floor flat nearby? The money would more than cover its purchase, and there would be plenty left over for a very special project which Sadie was formulating in her mind. She had looked up house prices. The average price for what she might be able to find in central London was around seventy-five thousand pounds, From 1986 to 1988 the prices had moved upwards by twenty thousand pounds, so if she was going to buy one, she had better do it now. Prices were predicted to rocket.

Then there was her project, her dream. She had seen how marvellous ex-prisoner Robbie had been from his very first meeting with Jack. He had a natural rapport with the boy and related to him without a hint of condescension. Jack adored him. Robbie was also a natural when it came to relating to Peter and again, there was mutual respect, love and ease between them. Sadie had marvelled, too, when she had heard hardened criminal Gary asking Hope if he could give the baby a kiss, and Sadie had witnessed a tangible tenderness in him towards the tiny infant. Could she do something with some of the money to set up a project which might include "dropouts" working with children with disabilities of some kind? It seemed to her like a pipe dream and furthermore she had no idea how to set about it but could research what was available in this kind of area. She was sure that Oliver and Robbie would welcome the idea. They were often talking about ways of reaching the various groups of people who were shamefully described by both citizens and politicians as "outsiders of society" and much of the thrust of Oliver's time in the Southwark diocese was focussed on teaching and fostering attitudes of inclusively across the various groups within the city. If Sadie's money could provide some kind of well-furnished and attractive meeting place, where participants would feel welcomed and wanted, then that would be a start.

Two days later at the hospital, Gary and Robbie were talking seriously together about Gary's immediate future. Gary was adamant that he would go back to sleeping on the streets, but would like to keep in contact with Robbie. He was soon to be discharged, but to whom and to where? Robbie knew he must do everything in his power to protect Gary from his own abusive lifestyle, and was determined to find decent shelter for him. He regarded Gary as a personal project. He was rescued years ago so why not try and do the same for Gary?

Three floors up in the hospital, Connie and Oliver were having a conversation along the same lines. Connie was making a good recovery although had required a transfusion of three pints of blood to restore a decent blood count for her. Her abdominal wound was healing well and she would be allowed out in two or three days' time as long as she promised to rest. Connie had Gary on her mind. Robbie had approached them before Connie's crisis to ask if Gary could stay for a few days to rehabilitate. Oliver was wary now because of Connie's fragile condition but Connie was insistent that she would ask their son, Jamie, to move in with Peter for a few nights so that Gary could have a bed for a period of convalescence.

Oliver flirted with the idea of asking Bruce and Clara if they could help out. They had one child and two spare bedrooms, but he almost as quickly realised that an arrangement like this that would not work. He had seen how Bruce had reacted when Kitty and Gary seemed to be, in his eyes, too close for comfort during the hospital visit. In addition, Oliver doubted if Clara would want the inconvenience of having to think of someone else, even if that someone had saved her daughter's life. He knew that Connie had never quite come to terms with what she saw as an extremely selfish streak in Clara, but had opened her arms wide to her nevertheless, even though was always greeted with a lukewarm response.

They all agreed that for Gary to go back on the streets was not an option. The conversations continued with his future well-being at the heart of their thoughts. They all wanted to rescue the young man if they possibly could.

CHAPTER 43

Sadie waited till Lucy had taken her fill of her six o'clock feed before she asked Hope if they could have a chat. Lucy was progressing well and was an exceptionally easy baby. Barely one month old, she was already sleeping until five a.m. after her ten o'clock feed. Hope loved her profoundly and constantly marvelled at how such a terrible event in her life could possibly have produced this amazing blessing. She knew from Lucy's webbed toes, which looked identical to Gary's, that Gary was the father. She didn't need to have any investigation or paternity testing to prove that as it was blindingly obvious.

While Hope was rightly wary of Gary, she reminded herself that his action over the theft of the baby was connected with a desire to prove something. Whilst not knowing what the law would say regarding his rights to Lucy, Hope knew he had made an emotional connection with her. She had seen a tenderness in him towards her, and try as she would to dismiss him from her thoughts, the way he had been stabbed haunted her. She had helped save his life, had bound up his leg, soothed the wound on his head and talked comfortingly to him. She had seen him stripped bare of his bravado, his fake manliness, instead finding a fragile, needy vulnerable person who had never had a chance in life. She had an urge to help Gary, but her maternal instinct to protect Lucy overrode every other consideration.

She prayed over Lucy's crib as she did every night, softly sang a nursery rhyme, kissed her forehead and went for the coffee Sadie had promised her. She would never be able to repay Sadie's kindness, she knew that. She had grown to love and admire the grit in Sadie's character which demonstrated a bravery of spirit in her loss of Jack and she loved watching her as she took on a different persona cradling Lucy in her arms.

'Is she asleep, Hope?' asked Sadie.

'Almost,' replied Hope.

'Because I don't want you to be distracted when I talk to you,' Sadie said.

'Goodness! This sounds a bit serious.'

'It is,' replied Sadie.

Sadie looked across the table at Hope. How was it that Hope always looked serene, unruffled? Mind you, Sadie surmised, she had seen her the opposite when the baby was missing. Sadie knew she wanted to spend the rest of her life with Hope. She felt she had found something incredibly special in this woman.

'I've been doing a lot of thinking,' said Sadie, taking Hope's hands briefly in hers before launching in.

'Hope,' Sadie hesitated. How far should she go? She didn't want to scare Hope off by being too direct. However, within a second or two she decided it was best simply to launch in.

'Hope, you've changed my life, you know. From the moment I first met you in Ireland, I felt you were special, even before I knew you were my half-sister. I don't want a life without you now.'

Sadie paused. Already too much? Hope was now looking down and had ceased to make eye contact with her.

'I wondered if you would contemplate sharing a home with me? I've got this money, you see — enough to buy us a home in this locality. Don't feel you…'

Hope interrupted her. She cupped both of Sadie's hands in hers across the table.

'Sadie, I feel the same about you. I want to stay with you. I know my feelings for you are pure. We should have no worry about our love for each other. I have to tell you that two of the nuns in the convent formed what I suspect was— a particularly close alliance — too close for comfort. They had to leave in the end. I won't spell out why, but you can guess. But love has to go somewhere, doesn't it? The love I have been given for you feels like a gift you know, but it is not the same as their kind of loving.'

'Yes — no, I mean I agree,' replied Sadie softly, her emotions in turmoil.

'Sadie, I would love to share your home, wherever it is. It's a beautiful thing you have asked me. Do you know that verse from the book of Ruth in the Bible?'

Entreat me not to leave you, or to turn back from following after you; for wherever you lodge, I will lodge, your people shall be my people, and your God my God.

'That's how I feel, Sadie. I want to play a central part of your life — please.'

'And I yours,' replied Sadie, a few tears falling down her cheeks. 'And Hope, you must tell me in plain words about your God some time, and exactly what He means to *you.*'

'I will,' replied Hope, and went round to Sadie and held her tightly. 'And Lucy will be the most blessed baby in the world because she will have two mothers to love her and turn to.'

'No,' said Sadie. 'Correction. *I* am the most blessed in the world, because in spite losing my precious, precious Jack, I have gained a soul mate and a daughter.'

They held each other for a long minute.

'Now,' said Sadie, straightening herself. 'I've been to the estate agent, and I think we need to see a few properties. Will you come with me, Hope.'

Hope's eyes shone.

'What do you think?' she replied.

Connie returned home, much to the joy of all the children. James and Rosy expressed their relief and happiness in a 'mainstream' kind of way. Peter, however, said nothing much but kept coming up to Connie's bedroom with various items: a particularly delicious pastry that a parishioner had made, a magazine for her that he had spent his pocket money on and a bunch of freesias that he knew were Connie's favourite flowers. Peter had always touched Connie's heart with the restrained gestures and well-chosen words that only he could express so uniquely and she saw in him unusual traits and gifts that she felt sure would blossom as he grew up, and transform him into a very special kind of person.

Connie was adamant that Gary should come back to the vicarage for a week or two before transferring to the Church Army, presuming they could find a place for him. She knew that Sadie, Hope, Robbie and Oliver, when he was free, would between them see to meals, and she suggested they might buy fish and chips and the occasional takeaway curry or Chinese meal to help feed everyone. Sadie had that in hand, anyhow. Peter and James were reasonable about sharing a room, with a proviso that it would be for ten days maximum. James extracted a promise from Oliver to this effect and Peter wrote a contract:

This is to certify that Gary Johnson may stay in my bedroom for a maximum of ten days. Penalty of overstaying: Peter Connors will be forced to find another dwelling. In addition, Gary Johnson must swear on oath never to touch my stones.

Signed: _____ Oliver Lockwood
_____ Constance Lockwood

Oliver and Connie smiled at each other and signed the contract, realising that it was very important not to place too much stress on their special son. He just might be serious. You never quite knew with Peter.

Oliver's next move was to sound out the Church Army hostel. Having been a Chaplain to the hostel near Wandsworth Prison some years ago he knew the protocol for accepting "Outcasts and Criminals", the terminology used in the church army's original statement in 1882 when it was set up. The hostels were fairly rough and ready places run by kind and caring no-nonsense men and women and served by many volunteers in addition. A hot meal was provided every day, which was certainly more than Gary would have ever had on the streets, plus a reasonable bed.

Oliver joined a small queue of needy folk, some certainly the worst for wear, but others, he knew, were perfectly decent, law-abiding citizens who had been unlucky in life and fallen on hard times. Had Oliver worn his dog collar he knew he would have been ushered to the front of the queue by one of the staff, but his faith required him to take on an attitude of humility. Oliver had always shunned any kind of privilege the role might bring. There was just one exception, however. He could not resist the offer of a free seat in the Players' Pavilion at Lord's Cricket Ground to watch England VS Australia in the Ashes tournament!

'Everybody has their breaking point,' Oliver sometimes quipped.

In front of him in the queue at the church army was a young man who swayed and staggered and reeked of alcohol. His clothes hung off him and Oliver noticed that there was the distinctive smell of cocaine about his person. There was a very long journey ahead of him if he was to kick either addiction. Oliver knew for certain that alcohol was disallowed in all church army hostels. The young man might be let in after being searched, but within a day or two would almost certainly be back on the streets begging for money or surreptitiously stealing a bottle of the hard stuff, often whisky, and continuing to feed his addiction by any means possible. The road out of self-destruction would be dubious for him unless he was very carefully monitored, mentored and cared for with tough love.

A woman joined the queue behind him. Wearing bright red lipstick and old-style rouge dabs on her cheeks, she returned Oliver's smile, revealing a random assortment of blackish teeth and toothless gums. With her bright orange hair revealing several inches of grey at its roots, a brown fur coat which was threadbare in patches, and wearing emerald green stiletto-heeled broken-down shoes, Oliver had to resist the internal voice that shouted at him to scoop her up, take her home and try to give her some kind of a start on her road to rehabilitation. What was her story? — an unsavoury one, Oliver surmised, and undoubtedly a sad one — perhaps, to use a euphemism, she was a worn-out Lady of the Night? She was carrying two bulging carrier bags which reminded Oliver of Ralph Mctell's lyrics of "Streets of London", which pulled at his heartstrings every time he heard it when describing the woman on the streets who was "carrying her home in two carrier bags".

Oliver eventually reached the church army officer who was making notes, and told him about Gary Johnson, giving the vicarage name and address and the date Gary needed a placement. The officer was rather hard of hearing, as well as being seated behind an unhelpful glass screen, so Oliver was required to speak up. The captain smiled in recognition of him and assured Oliver he would secure Gary a place, no problem. The man ahead of him and the woman behind him may not be so lucky. They were not represented by anyone, let alone a man of the cloth. Oliver knew it was no use trying to be incognito as the local vicar. Along with the role came both the privileges and the pain of recognition, whether he liked it or not and on this occasion he was very grateful for the promise of a placement for Gary.

Oliver went straight to the hospital and up to Gary's ward. Gary was out of bed, dressed and sitting in his bedside chair looking distinctly better.

'Watcha Guv,' he called to Oliver. 'How's your Connie?'

'She's doing OK,' answered Oliver as he walked up the ward towards him. 'Thanks for asking.'

'She's nice, she is, and so's her sister, the mother of my kid,' said Gary with a smile.

Gary could be charming, but Oliver had to remember that Gary had viciously raped Hope without a thought for her well-being. Oliver would never forget the sight of her the day it happened as she emerged from her hiding place under the bedclothes to reveal her tragic, shocked, alabaster-white face. Gary had also attempted to rape his special niece Kitty and was stopped in time by Bruce and Robbie. Oliver reminded himself that Gary had brandished a knife that day and without a second thought had stabbed Robbie viciously and could have killed him. These were the actions of the young man who was sitting up in a chair, cleanly shaved and looking as though butter wouldn't melt in his mouth. Oliver's memory served as a timely reminder to act at all times towards this boy with extreme caution as well as compassion. There was a darkness and violence in him.

Oliver told Gary of the plan he had put together regarding accommodation to see if Gary would approve.

'Thanks, Guv, Rev. Really nice of yer. I like the first bit, but not the second. No way am I going to a church set up. Couldn't stand the thought of all them do-gooders praying the devil out of me. Had that before. Never again. I'll find another tunnel that no one will know about.'

'Except your gang would, Gary and the police are bound to catch up with you.'

'No, they won't. I saved Kitty-Kat 'erself from drowning, didn't I? More likely I'd get a medal.'

'You only need one of your gang to give you away, Gary, and you'll be locked up. Besides,' Oliver took a deep breath. 'There would be no praying the devil away at the Church Army — just a group of people doing their best for you. Listen, Gary. I know it's hard to take in, but God loves you.'

'Oh yeh?' Gary had found his sneering face and voice. 'Oh yeh? — well, why did he let my mum and dad make me do all those things with the animals then? And then get banged up and when they came out never looked me up or tried to find me? Where was the love in that, Rev? There was no one lookin' out for me when I was a kid, and that's the truth.'

Oliver heard him. His stomach lurched. What he was saying was absolutely true. Gary had been damaged not only by what he had been made to do but more than that, by lack of love. Without knowing it, Gary had touched on two universal problems that Oliver was expected to give convincing answers to several times a week as a Christian minister: "Why Suffering?" and "Why Forgiveness?" Whatever vocabulary and phraseology Gary had used, his questions were universal questions and had their roots in the mystery of faith. Oliver's challenge was to answer Gary in a way that might satisfy him a little whilst not watering down his faith.

'Think of anyone in your life that has loved you just a little, Gary. There must be someone. Maybe a teacher? In that person, you might possibly have seen the love of God in action.'

Gary was quiet for a long time. Eventually, he spoke.

'Never been loved, Rev. No one when I was a kid. No-one now. No girl. Nuffink,' he paused. Everything was quiet in the ward apart from a few monitors bleeping intermittently.

'Nuffink, that is, until now. I think Hope cares about me a little bit, and Robbie, and your missus, and—' he paused. 'And you, Rev?'

'Yes,' said Oliver. 'I care about you.'

'That's God comin' out of you then, innit, mate? I can feel it y'know. You got it in bucket-loads, Rev.''

Oliver felt a rush of warmth run through him and gave Gary a hug.

'I'll pick you up in two days when you're discharged. And you're coming back to the vicarage and we'll work from there about the future. OK?'

'OK,' replied Gary. 'Nice one.'

Oliver took a few steps towards the door and then turned back. He realised Gary was beginning to cry.

'Thanks, Rev. Never 'ad a proper home. You got me there,' he said, blowing his nose on the pristine white bed sheet.

Oliver went back to Gary's bed and gave him another hug, left the ward, wiped his eyes, blew his nose hard and headed back to the warmth of his family.

CHAPTER 44

When Connie came home she stayed resting on her bed for a couple of days, after which she felt strong enough to come downstairs and slowly begin to pick up the threads of vicarage family life again. She felt weak but no longer ill or in much pain. Sadie had been on the lookout for the time when she felt Connie was able to discuss the plans she had been hatching with Hope.

Sadie cooked a roast lamb supper for them all on the second evening Connie was home, and the subject of Gary's immediate future arose naturally out of the convivial atmosphere. Connie was adamant that Gary should have Peter's room on a temporary basis, but if Robbie was agreeable, he should take on his supervision until he took up his place at the Church Army hostel in a couple of weeks' time. Sadie was emphatic that Connie and Oliver should not be placed under any further strain following Connie's emergency operation, but Connie could occasionally put her foot down resolutely, and this was one of those occasions. She would not hear of any alternative plan for Gary until he was completely well. The plan was therefore agreed upon, although inwardly Hope had some reservations on a personal level.

She wanted to see Gary cared for properly, and would certainly take her fair share in this. She was anxious, however, that Gary might form too close a bond with Lucy and find it hard to move on. She pondered long and hard on the rights he should have in Lucy's upbringing and decided he should have very few, if any at all. The baby was the result of a rape, Hope being the victim, and by law, Gary should have been charged with sexual assault rather than being allowed to live with the very person he had victimised. Hope was the last person on God's earth to be vindictive or withhold forgiveness where it was due, but Gary's presence perturbed and distressed her considerably more than she indicated to the family. She decided she would ration the time Gary could see Lucy and would breathe a sigh of relief when the two-week sojourn was up.

Sadie took a deep breath, trying to work out why she was finding it difficult to broach the subject of the house she hoped to buy for Hope and herself. Was it because in her secret heart she knew her feelings for Hope ran deep in her and that living together was a way of keeping Hope close to her, both physically and in her heart. She knew the move would be open to misinterpretation.

'Connie, you and Oliver are kindness itself,' she began. 'No one could have wished for a lovelier home, and Jack and I were as happy as we could ever be. He loved being with your family, and so have I. But…' Sadie paused and found herself welling up.

'Sadie, what is it?' Connie asked, stroking her hand.

'I think it's time to move on, and Hope has agreed to come with me.'

There was a very long pause.

'Why do you think it's time to move on?' asked Oliver eventually, wanting to fill the tense silence.

Sadie outlined all the reasons, including her anxiety about putting too much pressure on the household.

'We'll look for a ground floor flat or small house around here. I've priced them, and I can afford it.'

Hope was silent. Oliver had an uneasy stirring in his stomach. This was, in effect, two sisters opting to live together, which was entirely reasonable. He had noticed, however, that Sadie was clearly incredibly fond of Hope, and unusually tactile with her for someone who was generally cautious about outward expressions of feelings. He could barely formulate at present the thoughts that were making his stomach churn. Who was he, anyway, to question the right of two people to love each other? They were siblings, weren't they? — half-siblings at any rate. Did it matter that Sadie's love might be more than simply that of one sibling to another? Neither was married, and neither had a partner. Sadie had never had a partner to his knowledge. Her abusive father had made sure that she was repelled by most men and she had said again and again that she never wanted a relationship of any kind. Jack with his disabilities and needs had taken up all her energy and all her love, she had told Oliver one day in a moment of an intimate conversation between the two of them.

Oliver had always found the teachings of the church in this area difficult. He had seen many homosexual and gay relationships flourish, often displaying a quality of love to which many heterosexual relationships could not aspire. As a man of the cloth, however, he was required to

321

represent the church's teaching on these issues. He knew he was wildly jumping to conclusions about Sadie and Hope. He would talk to Connie in bed about it tonight. He relied on her balance and wisdom when his were going awry.

'I think that sounds an exciting plan,' he finally replied, quashing his thoughts with an effort. 'But we will miss you both so much, won't we, Con?'

Connie could not answer. She felt she was losing two sisters. She swallowed hard, determined to fight back the tears that were welling up. Jack, Sadie, Hope, Lucy, and in addition an unknown but precious premature baby, all gone. Such losses, such pain! So many unravellings in such a short space of time were hard to bear.

'And I have another plan for the rest of the money,' Sadie said quickly, sensing the pain in Connie and the questioning in Oliver. She was not ready to face either. First, she reminded them about *Chicken Shed*, an imaginative creation in North London comprising inclusive theatre and music workshops during which disabled and able-bodied young people worked together towards performance. Sadie outlined her deep desire to build something that would accommodate small groups of youngsters with disabilities together with disadvantaged youths of the city who could work with them, possibly through the arts. She had the money — at least a comfortable amount towards it, and she had the vision but needed a team of people to thrash out details and costings and see if it was credible and workable. She emphasized that at this stage it was simply a vision, but, to coin a proverb "Great oaks from little acorns grow".

She called it, "Jack's Project".

Oliver and Robbie were suddenly very interested, in fact, it was clear within a few minutes discussion that if *they* had anything to do with it, Sadie's vision would become a reality, however many twists and turns had to be negotiated. "Jack's Project" was inspirational, but Oliver and Robbie realised from the outset that setting it up would take more than simply money and good intentions. It was a vast scheme. There would be committees to negotiate, planning permission to be sought, and a great deal of hard graft to follow. But Sadie knew that for them to be caught alight by the idea and share her passion would be beyond her wildest dream, and somehow Jack's short life would be honoured through it and the financial compensation put to good use. She could not have known that subsequently both men stayed up into the small hours of the morning discussing over a bottle of wine the project and working through initial practicalities. They were both teaming with ideas, and decided they would start a marathon fund-raising effort in the parish and the diocese, once it had been passed by the Parochial Church Council and put to the Diocesan Bishop. This would ensure that Sadie's substantial contribution would be built upon to make a purpose-built, practical sanctuary for the two groups of equally deserving youngsters.

The discussion about Sadie and Hope and their relationship could wait. Oliver at last had a big project on his mind which filled his vision. It came at a time when he most needed to take his mind off other things, particularly at what he now regarded as his delusional behaviour with Clara.

Gary arrived at the vicarage three days later, courtesy of Robbie and his trusty car. Whilst he had seemed to be full of energy around in the hospital ward on his penultimate day, he realised as soon as he walked up the slope of the vicarage just how weak he was still. Robbie saw it and decided a firm hand was needed to make sure Gary respected the voice of his body as it continued to build on the good work of the hospital team.

All went well for a few days. At Gary's request, Hope carried Lucy briefly into his bedroom and once more she noticed the softness that came over him as he talked gently to the baby. He was intrigued by her efforts to smile and loved the way she gripped his finger so tightly.

'She knows me, don't she, Hope? Look at her little hand.'

'It's lovely the way she grips, isn't it?' said Hope.

'She's so pretty, ain't she? Just like her mum,' he said, and then added. 'And I reckon she's got the looks of her dad as well.'

Hope looked at Lucy. She had a fine coating of golden-blonde hair, a sweet petite face and rosebud-shaped lips. Hope could not honestly see traces of Gary in her except when she changed her nappy or bathed her and then she would scrutinize her toes once more, which she had to admit were very unusual.

Gary thrived on home cooking and the care he received. He realised it was the second time this special household had scooped him up and rescued him. He didn't want to live at the church army, but at least it was fairly close to his daughter. For the first time in his life he realised what it felt like to be loved.

CHAPTER 45

It was now mid-October and the autumn mists were beginning to swirl around London. Gary was relieved he was no longer living in the tunnel. He remembered with a shiver last winter when the night temperature in mid-January had plummeted to minus six degrees. Someone had given him a cellular blanket to add to his thin duvet and virtually threadbare tartan blanket. The trouble was, as Gary remarked ungratefully, that it had "flippin" holes in it. He hunkered down now in Peter's room under the warm and generous duvet and thanked his lucky stars he was indoors.

Some weren't so lucky. Oliver was standing at the bay window frontage of the vicarage looking out at the descending mist, which was rapidly turning into a low-visibility fog. With a shiver, he returned to Connie and the family who were in their family room next door. The television was on and the open fire logs blazed warm reds and golds. Connie was looking much better and life was beginning to return to normal.

Had Oliver stayed gazing out of the window for a couple more minutes, he would have seen the figure of a woman slowly emerging through the mist, picking her way over the uneven paving stones on the slight incline of the hill towards the vicarage. She was looking around her, checking her hand, and looking again, trying to find a certain address, impeded by the thickening mist, the unfamiliar territory and her stiletto heels.

Oliver poked the fire, as he always did whether or not it needed it, put another log on it and sat down on the old brown squishy sofa next to Connie, putting his arm around her. He didn't care what was on the television. It was just nice to have his wife back home, his children nearby, and a roaring fire in front of which to relax. He leaned his head back and closed his eyes gratefully. This was happiness. Peace at last.

A ring at the doorbell broke the calm. Inevitably, thought Oliver. Didn't it always? They all looked at each other, James's body language saying, 'Not me, Dad. Just *don't* ask me!' Oliver kissed Connie on the cheek, saying, 'I won't be a second. My family's coming first today, whoever it is.'

'Makes a change, Dad. Stick to that,' muttered James under his breath, but loud enough for Oliver to hear. Connie knew that some aspects of vicarage life put a strain on the children, but there were rewards, often in the shape of Easter Eggs, Christmas presents, money for holidays and a great deal of affection from kindly parishioners. It all balanced out.

'That's enough, Jamie, please,' said Connie. 'No more.'

Oliver opened the front door and gasped briefly in surprise.

'Hello, your Grace,' said a woman with bright red hair and a voice as jarring as metal on metal.

Oliver couldn't resist putting her right.

'Not 'Your Grace,' my friend. 'That's reserved for bishops, and I'm no bishop!' he laughed. 'I'm Oliver Lockwood. It's a nasty night. Can I help?'

'I think so, Oliver,' she replied, switching from "Your Grace" to his Christian name immediately with tones of over-familiarity. 'See, I'm looking for my son,' she said, her voice harsh and grating.

'Why here?'

'I was stood behind you in the queue at the hostel. I heard you asking for a place for a, Gary Johnson. Took down this address when you gave it in at the desk — wrote it on my hand, see?' She thrust a hand towards him, the fingernails of which were chipped with red nail varnish.

'I'm his mother.'

Oliver gasped out loud. Oliver was usually so welcoming, but his instinct now told him to keep this woman on the doorstep and at arm's length.

'He's here, in't he?' she continued. 'What's he doing here, then?'

Oliver was on his guard. The stories of Gary's parents' bestiality, their subsequent imprisonment and complete abandonment of their son had shocked him profoundly. He had heard stories and witnessed much deviant behaviour in his life one way and another, but bestiality was one particular form of perversion he had not encountered.

'Gary has been in hospital with a knife wound,' Oliver said. 'He's taking up a place in the church army as soon as he is better.'

'Where is he? Upstairs?' she said, peering around Oliver's shoulders into the hall.

'He's resting.'

'He's my boy, in't he? I want to see him.'

'Mrs Johnson, Gary said he has not seen you for years.'

'Yeh, well, all the more reason for him to see I'm here now. And call me Pearl,' she replied.

'Just a minute,' he said. Oliver felt he needed backup on this one, so he went to the bottom of the stairs and called Robbie; but the woman was immediately in, looking around her.

'Any chance of a cuppa, Oliver? It's a long walk from the hostel.'

Just then, Robbie came bounding down the stairs, two at a time as usual.

'Robbie, this is Mrs Johnson. She's…'

'Just call me Pearl, love. Pearl by name and pure as a pearl by nature.' She laughed coarsely, mirthlessly.

Robbie looked perplexed.

'This is Gary's mother,' said Oliver. 'Mrs Johnson, I must talk to Gary about this and we'll arrange a time for you to meet him, if that's what he wants.'

'That's what he wants? That's what he *wants*?' she shouted, her chin thrusting out angrily. 'Course he'll want it. I'm his long-lost mother, in't I?'

Oliver and Robbie exchanged glances. Just then, as if on cue, Gary came gingerly down the stairs, mindful of the stitches in his legs.

'OK, if I…?' He stopped.

'Gary — my boy!' exclaimed Pearl. 'I in't seen you for so long.'

Gary turned ashen pale. Eventually, he spoke.

'Mum?' he said incredulously.

'Yeh, it's your mum all right. Your dad's dead. Died inside. Good riddance, I say. I've come to collect you, my boy.'

She went to stroke his head, but Gary recoiled immediately.

'I think you'd better all come in here,' said Oliver, opening the door of his study.

'Oh my poor feet!' she exclaimed as she sat down, looking as though she owned the place. 'Mind if I take me shoes off? It's a long walk from there to here.'

She kicked off her broken-down green stilettos to reveal two very dirty feet, the toes covered in the same chipped garish red nail varnish as Oliver had noticed on her fingernails. Gary looked down at them. There, sure enough, was the familial webbed joining of two of her toes. Gary remembered in a flash from all those years ago that, yes, her toes were webbed as well as two of her fingers. Double proof that she was Lucy's maternal grandmother!

'Now, Gary my boy,' she rattled on, her voice rough and harsh. 'I know I didn't come and get yer when we was let out. Fact is, we got involved again in our — "business" as we had clients lining up for things, but we was only out a matter of months before we was banged up again. Your old man died then. This time me lock up was for longer.

Five years. But the fuzz don't learn nothing. You see it's in the blood and…'

'Mrs Johnson, are you saying you will never change?'

'Why should I? The money's good. There are a lot of dirty buggers out there, so as long as they pay, who am I to ask questions? OK, I gets banged up from time to time but it's worth it. Warm inside, any rate,' she added.

Oliver was shocked and quietly despairing. What happened to the influence of the rehabilitation and desensitization programmes the pair would have undergone? Was it all to no avail; taxpayers' money down the drain? Were they so deeply into depravity that they simply brushed help and psychotherapy away like water off a duck's back? It seemed the answer might be yes.

Gary remained looking at the floor. Oliver wasn't sure if he was ashamed of his mother or simply speechless from the shock of her sudden return.

'Anyway, now I've found you, I'll be on my way, 'cos I know you're booked into where I am in two weeks' time, Gary boy. Won't that be nice? And they gave me back me camera too.' She gave him a sideways glance.

Just as she was getting up to leave and the three of them were sighing a corporate sigh of relief, Hope knocked at the door, carrying Lucy in a sling as she often did around the rambling house. She put her head around.

'Excuse me, everyone, Oliver, but I'm making a pot of tea for Connie and wondered if you'd all like one? It's such a dreadful night out.'

Hope glanced around the room and saw Pearl Johnson sitting with her shoes off, looking like a broken-down duchess with stretched-out bare feet. She was quite at home. Looking down, Hope's eyes became riveted on the webbing between Pearl's toes. She stared, stunned, and then, not waiting for an answer, beat a hasty retreat, and went to shut the door.

Gary was on his feet.

'Hey, 'Ope, come and introduce Lucy to her grandma!' he said, finding a voice. He tugged Hope back into the room by the sleeve and over to Pearl.

'Look Ma, this is Lucy. She's half mine.'

'Oh you clever boy, so that makes 'er a quarter mine!' exclaimed Pearl. Without finesse, she moved over to Hope and pulled the sling away from Lucy's face, stroking the baby's cheek with a chipped, talon-like red fingernail. 'Oh, she's a nice one! Pretty as a picture, like her grandma. We like little girls, don't we Gary?' she said, nudging him and giving him another sidelong glance.

Gary felt nauseous at his mother's depraved innuendo and opened the door wide to make sure Hope could leave the room. She too felt sick as she climbed the stairs, holding her baby close. Once in her room, she took off the sling and soaked it in a strong solution of disinfectant, feeling somehow it was now tainted.

Downstairs, Oliver said brusquely, 'I think you should go now, Pearl. I have things to do.'

'OK, OK, me darlin' but I never did get that tea, did I? Thought a vicar was paid to be kind, but I've always said you can't trust a man of the cloth. They're the worst. I could tell you a story or two, oh yes I could! How long 'ave you got?' she leered.

Oliver, with Robbie not far behind him, practically pushed her out of the door.

'Bye, Gary, my son. See you soon. I'll look forward to it, my boy. There's business out there for us, y'know. Aren't you glad your old mother's come to find you?'

With that, she tottered down the steps in her bright green shoes and into the dense fog which had enveloped the city.

CHAPTER 46

Sadie and Hope collected shiny pamphlets from estate agents giving details of properties for sale in the locality together with prices. They wanted to live near Southwark centre but were prepared to look at houses and flats within a ten-mile radius. Prices were increasing almost as they looked at them, but Sadie had the money. She earmarked £250,000 for *Jack's Project*. Oliver set the wheels in motion with the diocese and the Parish Church Council, and after a fair degree of wranglings and negotiations requiring considerable patience on Oliver's part, all concerned finally sanctioned the project. Some cautious folk of the parish ("die-hards" was Sadie's phrase for them), worried about wheelchairs blocking the pavements, high levels of noise, the encouragement of crime in the locality, car parking implications and so on, while others were inspired by the whole project and determined to do all they could to support it and find practical ways to solve the problems that were flagged up.

In two weeks Connie had virtually returned to full strength physically, but was pining for the baby she never knew about and never met. It felt like an empty cavern inside, even though she had not known she was pregnant. Oliver agreed that when the time was right, they would try for another baby, feeling it was the least he could do for his wife and it would soften the blow for Rosy when adored little Lucy left the household.

Oliver pondered long and hard over his "near miss" with Clara. He knew that in itself it was not a rare thing for a man or a woman to grow restless in a relationship and have "a fling" — a phrase he hated. Goodness, he had counselled enough couples who had damaged the precious commodity of trust in each other in this way. Some had recovered, others not. It felt for Oliver a distinct falling short of what was expected of him. His vow of chastity when he became ordained was one that he tried to keep, feeling he was offering God everything he was. That was until he met Clara. He knew, if he was entirely honest with himself, that she would always be something of a temptress to him and she herself seemed to have no qualms about cheating on Bruce. Her brief, suggestive conversation with him in the ward had confirmed that.

Connie, his beloved wife, was Oliver's love and she and his family were his life. It would stay that way and he would in future make sure he was never with Clara on her own. To anyone else, in 1988, to hold these views might seem archaic. To Oliver, they were a necessity for himself, for Connie, for his family, and most of all for his Christian ministry. He regarded his marriage as a sacrament and infinitely precious, not to be thrown away in moments of temptation.

In a spirit of optimism, Sadie visited a highly sought-after wood carver and artist in Richmond upon Thames. Three weeks later she collected the ordered item and quietly wept over it as soon as she got back into the privacy of her car. It was for the outside of the building she was mainly financing. It was in the design of a rainbow, the symbol of hope, and interwoven with the painted colours were the words:

This is the house that Jack built.

Whilst fully acknowledging that nothing would ever replace her beautiful boy and she could not expect (or even want), the hole in her heart to mend, Sadie nevertheless realised that the amazing blessing to come out of all this was that she had her precious sister and soul mate with whom to share her life. She could now glimpse the joys of the future interweaving with the sorrows of the past. It seemed that the God she was beginning to acknowledge and believe in was holding her in the palm of his hand.

Gary became fit and healthy under the roof of the vicarage and he dreaded moving on. The warmth and love of the occupants of that house, in particular emanating from Connie and Oliver, were slowly healing his wounds; not simply those of the flesh but the deep and penetrating emotional lacerations inflicted on him by his disturbed parents. Their legacy was one of horror and of consequences.

The damaging twisted, knotted threads of past events seemed largely to have unravelled and were beginning to weave a brighter pattern with new threads of healing and hope for the future. Sadie, Hope, Connie, Oliver and Robbie had all, in their own way, taken arms against a sea of personal suffering, and emerged stronger from it, bearing now the hallmarks of love and courage, combined with a growing strength of spirit.

336

CODA

Gary moved into the church army hostel knowing that he would have to face his mother. It was as if, on seeing her, his childhood memories had come flooding back. He had found up until the present it was as if they had been completely blocked, clogged, in some way. He simply could not access them and was glad of that. Now, however, the images stirred up in his brain haunted him. He remembered the poor animals which were treated as commodities, caged for hours, scratching and whining until they were put to use. Having seen the Connors with their dog Toby and the way they all loved him, with the children stroking his ears and playing joyfully with him, made Gary feel sick at heart. He remembered his father in his ramshackle photographic 'studio' setting up his camera on a stand, hanging a dirty white muslin as a backdrop and putting the huge black umbrella and iridescent light in place. The rest Gary could not even contemplate.

Now, in the hostel, he was forced to communicate with the mother he loathed. He knew that Oliver Lockwood would probably say that Gary should work on forgiving her, but to Gary that was out of the question. It was quite simply asking too much. The worst thing was that she was now fawning over him, treating him like a god or a hero, but gradually he realised to his horror that there was a ghastly motive to all this.

One evening, Pearl broached the subject of his daughter Lucy. The conversation turned to the money that was to be made between Gary and Pearl if they went back into "business". She had the camera, he had the little girl. They could build up from there.

Gary returned to his room and was physically sick. He could not deal with this level of depravity even though his own life had been full of violence and ugly actions. In the light of his mother's excitement, as she presented her proposition to Gary, he saw how terrible and terrifying his own behaviour had been in the past, and top of the list was his rape of innocent Sister Hope, now the mother of his child. He was deeply and wholly ashamed and vowed that when his plan had been executed he would make amends with Hope by handing himself over to the police and taking whatever punishment was dished out to him. By redeeming himself in this way maybe Hope would see that he could be a worthy father to his daughter and prove that the sins of the father in this case were certainly not handed down to the son — or daughter.

It was in that moment of revelation and shame that Gary hatched the plan in his head. He worked it out in minute detail, checking every point over the next two weeks and gathering together what he needed for its execution.

That November was characterised by unusually heavy mists and fog, which hung over London on a daily basis like a sinister shroud. This suited Gary's plan and matched his dark and impenetrable mood. The next Sunday evening he approached his mother.

338

'Ma, you ain't had a drink since you've been here 'ave yer? I've seen you tearing your hair out.'

'Oh yes, I has. I've found the cupboard in the kitchen where the cook keeps his secret supply of cooking sherry,' she replied. 'But I ain't had much and I'm dying of it. Why? You ain't got some 'ave you?' Her eyes brightened.

'I got lots for yer, Ma, but we got to drink it off the premises. If we're seen, we'll both get chucked out.'

Pearl grinned greedily.

'You're a good boy, Gary. And have you thought any more about the plan?'

'Oh yes, Ma, I has,' Gary replied, knowing full well that she meant about his daughter. 'But we'll talk about this later. Get yer coat. We're going out to drink gin and whisky until morning. Like that, Ma?'

Yes, of course, he had thought non-stop about "the plan", but it was *his* plan, not hers.

Pearl tottered down the street holding her son's arm. Gary collected a carrier bag of two bottles of whiskey and two of gin from a hiding place. He had taken a couple of days to steal the bottles and had found a disused shed in which to hide them. Pearl's eyes filled with lust for the drink.

The weather was certainly in Gary Johnson's favour. It was very cold and murky, with hardly a soul around.

'This is a regular pea-souper,' exclaimed Pearl. 'Can't see a bleedin' thing.'

'Hang on tight, Ma. I know just the place where we can drink this.'

She tottered nearly two miles in her green high-heeled shoes, not minding about her throbbing feet or the blinding fog. She was with her boy and he was taking her out to drink until morning, oh yes he was!

Eventually, they reached Bankside beach. Gary led Pearl up to a space in the rocks where previously he had taken his tiny daughter. He opened the whisky and handed a bottle to his mother. Then he opened the gin and gave her that as well. She greedily drank first from one and then from the other. Eventually, she handed the gin to Gary.

'Come on boy. You're way behind me,' she drawled.

Good. She had already drunk nearly half a bottle of each and very soon she would be insensible, in a state of comatose. He pretended to take a swig but knew he must resist the temptation as he needed to keep a clear head. His plan was proceeding to perfection. The trickiest part was to follow: the denouement.

His mother had yet more to drink. Gary heaved her up and virtually dragged her down the rocks. She was swaying and drooling, but still, she kept swigging the whisky. Gary led her up to the end of the pier on what continued to be a perfect night for him to execute this part of his plan.

'Where we goin' boy?' she drawled.

'You'll see, Ma, you'll see. It's party time. Have another swig.'

They reached the end of the pier and stepped down onto the jetty, with Pearl staggering and swaying and Gary holding her up. A sturdy rowing boat was tethered in the water which Gary had hired earlier,* having arranged its mooring place at the end of the landing stage.

'Come on, Ma, we're going on an adventure. You ever been on the river in a fog? It's magic,' he whispered.

She did not answer but had to be lifted down onto the boat. One of her green shoes flipped off her foot and fell into the water. By now she was asleep or unconscious, Gary didn't know which — not that the distinction mattered. She was unaware of anything now. That was good. He put the oars in the rowlocks, and began to row into the centre of the river. It was calm and the tide was right for his purpose. Gary had checked on that previously. He had good knowledge from his days living in the tunnel and watching the tides day and night.

His mother was draped across the two seats of the rowing boat, the bottles swaying perilously. Gary reached the spot where he had swum out to rescue Kitty as she clung onto the floating barrel on that fateful night. He stopped. Everything was silent. The fog hung like a dark grey shroud over the river, draping it in mystery. There was no one out that night, and anyway, visibility was down to just a few yards. He took in the atmosphere, locking it in his mind's eye. Finally, he sat his mother up, propping her on the inner edge of the boat.

'Thanks for nothing, Ma,' he said darkly. 'You deserve this.'

He heaved his drunk and depraved mother up onto the side of the boat, took hold of her legs and with one heave pushed her over the edge and into the blackness below. She hardly made a sound as she reached the cold, cold water.

He watched her sink. Her head bobbed up once, her eyes wide open in shock, and then she sank without a trace.

Gary waited for a minute to make sure she did not re-surface, then rowed away hard, speeding onwards into the night.

He did not look back.